Readers love
RHYS FORD

Down and Dirty

"Definitely a must read for fans of the author and the series, or anyone that is looking for a strong read with lots of passion and story."

—MM Good Book Reviews

"*Down and Dirty* was a wonderful detour in the Cole McGinnis series and I look forward to seeing more of them in future books…"

—It's About the Book

Duck Duck Ghost

"…yes… I wear my Rhys Ford "fan girl" banner proudly. And if you're not already a fan, you'll be one too, after reading *Duck Duck Ghost*!"

—Prism Book Alliance

"With her chillingly descriptive writing and the heartfelt representation of the relationships in this book, it was a total win-win for me."

—The Novel Approach

Creature Feature 2 (with Poppy Dennison)

"…both of these tales were fabulous. They're filled with action, suspense and a ton of entertaining and 'edge of your seat' moments."

—The Blogger Girls

"Thank you to both authors for the epilogue and my happy ever afters… Excellent book!"

—Rainbow Book Reviews

D1601039

By RHYS FORD

Clockwork Tangerine
With Poppy Dennison Creature Feature 2
Grand Adventures (Dreamspinner Anthology)
Murder and Mayhem

HELLSINGER
Fish and Ghosts
Duck Duck Ghost

COLE MCGINNIS MYSTERIES
Dirty Kiss
Dirty Secret
Dirty Laundry
Dirty Deeds
Down and Dirty

SINNERS SERIES
Sinner's Gin
Whiskey and Wry
The Devil's Brew
Tequila Mockingbird

Published by DREAMSPINNER PRESS
http://www.dreamspinnerpress.com

MURDER AND MAYHEM

RHYS FORD

Published by
DREAMSPINNER PRESS

5032 Capital Circle SW, Suite 2, PMB# 279, Tallahassee, FL 32305-7886 USA
http://www.dreamspinnerpress.com/

Murder and Mayhem
© 2015 Rhys Ford.

Cover Art
© 2015 Reece Notley.
reece@vitaenoir.com
Cover content is for illustrative purposes only and any person depicted on the cover is a model.

ISBN: 978-1-63476-222-9
Digital ISBN: 978-1-63476-223-6
Library of Congress Control Number: 2015905067
First Edition June 2015

Printed in the United States of America
∞
This paper meets the requirements of
ANSI/NISO Z39.48-1992 (Permanence of Paper).

This book would not have been possible without the diligence and graceful patience of Karla Yenelie Muñoz, Armandina Muñoz, Felix Duarte, and the gorgeous Jacob Flores. Thank you all. God I love you.

Also to any of my readers who know the struggles of choosing between Doctors, still cry over Wash and Ianto, who's Pavlovian response to hearing the word werewolf is to immediately say "There, wolf. There, castle" or knows better than to eat that one thin mint—this one is for you.

Acknowledgments

As always, any book with my name on it goes to the Five; Jenn, Penn, Lea, and Tamm—as well as my beloved younger sisters, Ree, Ren, and Lisa. Couldn't have gotten here from there without you.

To Elizabeth North and the Dreamspinner staff, a huge thank you. So many to name… Grace and my long-suffering editing team, lyric whom I torture, Hayley and everyone else I torment on a daily basis. Thank you.

A shout out to the San Diego Crewe who listen to me ramble. And once more with feeling a huge hug to my Beta readers and the Dirty Ford Guinea Pigs.

This book was mostly written to AC/DC, VAST, Black Rebel Motorcycle Club, and Tool with sporadic sprinklings of Celtic Music and my terrier howling along to the sirens of passing ambulances.

One

ALL ROOK could smell was blood.

Hot. Metallic. Dirty. Blood.

It stung his senses, an angry hornets' nest of odors he couldn't outrun—even as he pounded down one of Hollywood's tight back alleys. Rook could hear shouting, piercing rushes of sound caught in the maze of brick, glass, and cement behind him.

A sun-faded aluminum can crinkled when he stepped on it. Folding up over the edge of his high-top, it clung to his foot for a stride before gravity dislodged it. Nearly tripping over his own feet, Rook stumbled, then caught himself with a grab at a rolling trash can, tipping the enormous black receptacle to the ground. Garbage poured out of the heavy bin, foul, sticky liquids gushing out from its depths, and as Rook jigged around the stream, he was very aware of the sounds of footsteps closing in on him.

He'd be damned if he let them catch him.

The river of garbage he could outrun. The blood was something else. It coated his hands and then his pants when he tried to wipe them clean. The bottom of his shoes were probably clotted thick with it from walking through the dark pool he'd found on his store's main floor, driving the drying, viscous fluid deep into the grooves of his faded black Chucks.

A groaning drew him deeper into the store then. He wasn't sure where it'd come from, but Rook would swear on a pack of Bibles signed by God himself, he heard it. It was a rattling sigh that made him pause and look again. His curiosity would be the death of him, Hawkins once told him.

Which was absolutely, ridiculously true, because when he came around the corner of the display case filled with horror flick memorabilia, he stepped directly on a dead woman's hand.

And his curiosity laughed its fool head off as it dumped him into another mess of trouble.

He didn't need any more light than the faint glow of emergency LEDs built into the bottom of the cases to see she was dead. It was as obvious as the life-sized Chewbacca statue standing a few feet away from where she lay splayed out. No one could survive what he'd seen. There'd been nothing left of her stomach and chest. Washed over silver from the curacao blue LEDs, her flesh lay in chunks across the floor, a profane slaughter of skin and meat leaving her insides spilling out in ribbons of dank meat and ichor.

There was a flicker of recognition in the small part of Rook's brain that still worked, a sensory overload hot enough to crackle his nerves. He *knew* the woman—had argued with her, bitched about how she'd cheated him and, worse, cursed her to hell when she'd run off with one of the largest takes he'd ever brought in.

Dani Anderson.

Her doll-like face was cracked open and bruised, the enormous cornflower-blue eyes she used to gull easy marks flat and blank, staring up at the store's high ceiling. She lay on her side, her arms awkwardly thrust out in front of her. Her legs were spread apart and bent at the knee, forcing her tight skirt up nearly to her hips. He'd reached out to tug at her skirt hem, not thinking about anything other than giving her some dignity in death, and drew his hand back when he felt a wetness spread over his palm. Something in her torn-apart corpse must have collapsed, because Dani's body tumbled forward, and Rook made a grab for her, as if catching Dani would save her from further pain.

That was how he was found, arms full of dead woman and skin painted with her still warm blood.

A hot, burning glow flooded the store, and Rook pulled back, startled enough to drop Dani to the floor with a wet splat. He didn't have time to take a breath before the front windows exploded and silhouettes poured in, too many to count in the blur of panic and fright.

He did see the guns, though. And felt the whisper of a bullet shear past his exposed cheek.

The collectibles shop was a warren of display cases and back rooms, as familiar to Rook as the back of his hand or the tumbling sound of an old safe's lock giving way to his skilled fingers. Potter's Field's back-room labyrinth was too dark. There should have been more lights—blinking LEDs from a high-end R2-D2 and an array of old bulb signage he'd scored from a movie set auction. If anything, he should have been able to see enough of the room from the soft glowing cold boxes bought to keep delicate collectibles in. Instead of the slightly pink suit worn in an old Charlie Chan movie or the sequined dress flashing bright colors and spangles from their sealed tight cases, Rook was met with a bank of black with only a thin orangey thread of light to see by.

He didn't need a lot of light to lead him to the sliding metal door at the side of the building, but he certainly was going to have a good talk with Charlene, his assistant, about leaving the padlock off the inside latch when she snuck out to have a quick smoke.

If he survived getting shot at.

Hell, if he survived running through Los Angeles covered in blood while a pack of gunmen hunted him, Char was probably going to get a raise for being so bubbleheaded, because he hit the automatic release bar on the door and was outside before another bullet tried to make its way into his head.

His legs were burning. Years of sliding through tight spaces kept him limber, and he'd worked to keep flexible. Which, Rook discovered as a cramp bloomed across his ribs, did shit for stamina. He'd been stupid—complacent, really. Stupid to think he'd gone straight so could give up old ingrained habits like intimately knowing his surroundings and moving about.

It was costing him dearly now.

Hollywood was built building upon building, tight, cramped spaces behind broad fronts facing the street, a set design for the masses, constructed on a grand scale. Pockets of asphalt parking lots were scattered about, giving Rook a clear path to sprint through if he wanted.

He knew better. Wide-open spaces were the easiest way to get caught. Subterfuge and shadows were his only hope in the never-quite-darkness of a late Hollywood evening. The sky shimmered with yellow splashes of light caught in the low cloud cover of an early fall. The alleys were dodgy, twists and turns speckled with debris, both garbage and throwaway people clinging to back doorways hoping their fragile shelter would hold up against the occasional sparse drizzle.

A dash of Chinese spice in the air gave Rook some idea of where he'd gotten to. Only a block and a half from where he'd started. The city's grime was thick in its bowels, stains of dirt and fallen smog leaving behind long mottled streaks nearly impervious to Los Angeles's drifting rains. In some cases, the buildings themselves were nestled in too tight to allow even a hint of fresh breeze between them, and Rook choked on a pocket of stagnant air trapped behind a run-down side street head shop, a cloud of patchouli and stale pot smoke drifting in the heat of a never-ending coil.

Behind Hollywood's streets, a different city thrived, a far cry from the glamour and glitz. Not the one sold on television and movies as a glistening, golden-bodied beauty with suntan-oiled skin and orange-kissed breath. The tightly packed town nestled into Beverly Hills's armpit had absolutely nothing in common with *that* Hollywood. If anything, that golden image was simply his town's too thickly spackled on makeup, weathered and cracked from the heat, and if anyone looked too closely, they could see the aging has-been beneath the pancake foundation and sparkling fake eyelashes.

After years spent on the carnival circuit, he'd always loved returning to Hollywood's streets under the hills, packed with expensive apartments with their wide-open windows and the frivolous wealth of every flash-in-the-pan wannabe whose face sparked up a screen for a brief instant, then faded back into the chorus along with the rest of the trash.

He'd fought hard to rise above being trash. If he hadn't been running for his life, Rook would have laughed at how easy it was to fall from grace in a split second—especially when covered in the blood of a woman he'd wished dead for years.

Twisting to the left, he nearly toppled over a grizzled old black man pulling mannequin parts out of a battered shopping cart. Reeling from the hit, Rook sidestepped the gnarled fingers reaching for him, the man's face mottled dark with anger.

"Watch where yer goin', boy," he spat at Rook, a wave of foul breath washing over him, strong enough to briefly drown the stench of blood and offal out of Rook's nostrils.

"Sorry," Rook muttered, squeezing past him. He didn't get more than a step when he felt the old man grab at his head, twisting his fingers into Rook's shaggy hair. The pain was sudden, sharp, and hard. He lurched back, surprised at the skinny man's strength. "Let go… I've got to—"

"That blood I smell?" The man's voice boomed, a grenade of sound echoing through the zigzag of crossing alleys. "You kill someone? Shit! Police!"

Rook spun about, tilting sideways when the man tightened his grip. The shouts were getting louder, indistinct cries directing the men to their prey. Panic seized Rook's belly, and he struck out, slamming his knee up into the hollow between the old man's legs. An instant later, Rook was free and he was off, determined to shake the shadows off his trail. He broke from the maze, grabbing at fresh air and a straight run to safety.

Then one of the shadows lunged out from the darkness pooled at the edges of a cluttered sidewalk and took Rook out.

The shape grew large and came too fast for Rook to avoid. He got a glimpse of jeans, a white shirt, and a suit jacket, flashes of color across his vision before the massive block of muscle and sinew hit him hard enough to pull both of them down to the gritty broken sidewalk. Rook tucked in on himself, rolling into the blow to protect his chest and belly. Years of hardscrabble fighting and honed instincts took over, and he lashed out, shoving stiff fingers into his attacker's throat. Rook heard a gagging sound—loud enough to give him hope the man would let him go, but the sidewalk had other plans.

A break in the concrete caught Rook's shoulder, and it broke his momentum, jerking him to a stop. His sneakers squeaked against a wall plastered with placards and graffiti, but he couldn't get enough traction to get to his feet. Caught with his back to his attacker, Rook scrambled to get a hold on the sidewalk as he untangled his legs, but the man was on him, pressing Rook down with a fierce shove. His head snapped forward, and Rook saw stars when his skull made contact with the ground under him. As he blinked away the sharp crack of pain, Rook's stomach sank down deep into his trembling guts.

It wasn't the man's gun that gave him pause. Nor the gold badge he wore at his belt. A gun and badge clearly exposed as the dark-haired giant's jacket pulled up when he reached for a pair of zip ties from a leather pouch near his back pocket.

"Fuck, a cop," Rook swore through the wavy sparkles flickering across his eyes. "Oh… shit."

He knew the Hispanic cop straddling him. He'd felt those large strong arms on him before, and even as he heard the click of a plastic zip tie being looped shut around his wrist, he recalled the last time he'd seen the handsome, stone-faced man, and his cock grew hard with the memory. Dark, changeable light brown eyes with almost ridiculously long lashes scanned Rook's face, and Rook caught the exact moment when the cop recognized him, just seconds after Rook realized who'd pinned him spread eagle to the ground.

This wasn't just any cop.

But the one cop in Los Angeles who wanted him dead.

And the one and only cop he'd ever let touch him.

"FUCKING ROOK Stevens," Detective Dante Montoya growled at the one-way glass looking into a small gray interrogation room off of the station's bullpen.

His hands smarted, rubbed raw from the scrapes he'd taken when taking Stevens down, and his throat ached where the supposedly former thief'd jabbed his fingers into Dante's Adam's apple, but the minor discomforts were just that—minor. He'd finally gotten a hold of fucking Rook Stevens, and from the looks of things, Stevens wasn't going to be able to wiggle his way free like he'd done in the past.

The man was a boneless sprawl of insouciance in one of the interview room's hard metal and vinyl chairs, his long legs stretched out in front of him and one arm looped over the chair's back. From Stevens's casual demeanor, no one would believe he was facing a murder charge, but small things betrayed him. His mismatched stare glanced at the door every few seconds before settling back to stare at the mirrored wall, and there was a slight tightening around Stevens's full mouth every time a shadow passed under the door.

Problem was, Rook Stevens was still as handsome as fucking hell, and Dante longed to smack the man's smugness off his face with a well-aimed fist.

If anything, the police-issued set of gray scrubs should have taken away a bit of his attractiveness, but the drab fabric only drew out the paleness of his skin and the startling blue and green-hazel oddity of his eyes. The room's bright overhead lights highlighted Stevens's high cheekbones and strong jaw, his nearly elfish features hiding the cunning intelligence Dante knew lurked behind his seemingly wide-eyed expression. Stevens's caramel-brown hair was longer than the last time Dante'd seen him, certainly longer than the recon photos from the disastrous case that ended his prior partner's career and set Dante's more than a few steps back.

Almost five years. Five long years since Dante was forced to close the case file he'd built up on Stevens and the other members of the carnie crew suspected of running a burglary ring up and down the West Coast. His old partner, Vince, had taken the case harder, more personally than Dante, and that'd been his downfall. By the time their two-year investigation went down in flames, Vince was tired of being a cop, tired of chasing criminals, and certainly sick to death of banging his head against the solid wall of lies and subterfuge spun by Rook Stevens and his partners.

"I'm too old for this shit," Vince had muttered when they'd gotten word Stevens walked free of all charges they'd brought against him. "I'm spending my life trying to nail some damned uneducated smartass who hawks sideshow games for a fucking living. Asshole *knew* we had him dead to rights, and all we had to do was find out where he fenced that damned last haul of his."

They hadn't found Stevens's fence or anyone who'd even admit to doing business with Stevens to launder the high-end goods from the mansions he'd hit when the carnival wintered in Los Angeles. None of the carnies would spill a single word from their close-lipped mouths whenever Vince and Dante came around, and if anything, the victims themselves wanted the cases swept under the rug when the detectives began to poke a little too deeply for their comfort.

Then Vince did the unthinkable. He'd crossed the line between good and bad, planting evidence so flimsy it unraveled before the accusations against Stevens could even take hold, and Vince'd almost brought Dante down with him.

He'd liked Vince. The older detective'd taken a slightly angry, gay, Cuban-Mexican baby detective under his wing and poured everything he knew about catching criminals into Dante's eager brain. In the end, Vince's career ended in a sour mess, and Dante skirted the edge of demotion when they'd been accused of taking bribes to let the crew slip out from between their fingers. Vince tried to talk Dante out of telling their captain about Dante's encounter with Stevens in a dark Hollywood club, and even then, Dante kept the details sketchy, admitting he only realized he'd almost fucked Stevens when someone accidentally turned on the bathhouse's floodlights and bleached the back rooms in a harsh white glow.

It was the last time Dante went to a club to get his needs met. It was also the first time he'd seen Stevens's sexy, nearly apologetic smile.

The asshole still got the tickle going in Dante's belly, and damned if he didn't want to dig his hands into Stevens's hair, strip him down, and fuck him until he couldn't breathe.

"So you finally got your white whale, huh, Moby?" Hank Camden, his partner of three years, wandered into the side room, a bone-white tangle of clumsy limbs topped off with a shock of red hair bright enough to set off a fire sprinkler.

"Moby Dick *was* the whale, *puto*," Dante replied, picking up the paper cup of sour cop house coffee he'd poured himself before coming into the viewing cubby. "And we haven't harpooned him yet. What's the lab say? Anything come back yet?"

"No, nothing. But shit, he was practically coated from head to toe. If there's no gunpowder residue it's because he washed it off in her damned blood." Hank saluted Dante with his own cup, a tea bag tag dangling from a string over its rim. "Huh, he doesn't look old enough to be a nemesis."

"He's old enough." Dante grunted. "Pisses me off I can't be in there. I've waited a hell of a long time to take Stevens down. Who's taking the case? O'Byrne? She's the only one I can think of who could go toe-to-toe with him."

"Just because you made the collar doesn't mean it's our case. 'Sides, Captain knows you've got a history with the guy. You and me are on door-knocking and story-taking duty until he says—"

"Montoya. Camden." The man in question, a thick-chested walrus of a cop, thrust his head into the cubby. Captain Book, a veteran of LA's long, tenuous relationship with the law, pointed at the interrogation room and LAPD's latest acquisition. "Everyone's caseload is backed up to hell and gone. You're all I've got open, so get in there and crack him. Do it clean. Do it fast. Shut him down quick."

"Yes, sir." Dante suppressed a grin as he tossed his cup into the trash. "Thanks, Captain."

"Don't fuck this up, Montoya. Get in. Get what we need, and keep it professional." Book stabbed at the air near Dante's chest with a thick finger, his severe frown thick with warning. "Camden, you watch your step. Don't give the DA any damned wiggle room to let this bastard out. Son of a bitch lawyer is rubber-stamping shit left and right. Make something stick here."

Dante waited until the captain was gone before he let his smile slip free. Jerking his head toward the mirror, he patted Hank on the shoulder and grinned widely. "Come on, man, let's go see what Stevens has to say about all that blood."

Two

THE TWO detectives entered the room as if it were a rancor pit and they were the predators coming to feed on Rook's helpless body. He barely glanced at the flaming matchstick of a man lurking behind Montoya. The Hispanic detective had all of Rook's attention, especially when he caught a flare of something hot in Montoya's gaze when he stared Rook down.

It'd been a long time since he'd seen Montoya. Rook couldn't remember which police station it'd been in. Hell, he could have even been sitting in the same damned room they'd used to try to tear him apart that last time he'd been brought up on charges. There'd been anger in Montoya's body language then, and a sense of defeat hung heavy on the cop's shoulders. His partner'd been an older man, his eyes puffy with age and drink. If anything, he'd worried the senior detective wasn't going to make it out of the police station that afternoon. Rook'd caught Montoya sliding a hand under the old man's arm when he'd fumbled a step leaving the booking area. Back then, the rage in the older detective's eyes promised Rook would come to a very unhappy end if he had anything to say about it.

If he were honest, Rook was kind of surprised it took the cops more than four years to try to nail him for something he didn't even do. He wouldn't have credited the old man for that kind of patience. Hell, when he thought about the senior detective's gray pallor and racking cough, he'd be kind of surprised if the old man was still alive.

Showing panic would send them at him like sharks on chum, so Rook forced himself to a calm he didn't feel. His belly twisted up, and his nerves keyed in to the aggressive body language of badges strolling into the room knowing they were holding all the cards. His protests about being innocent fell on deaf ears, and if possible, those ears got even deafer when Rook claimed not a single cop identified themselves when coming through Potter's Field's front windows.

Instead he'd been stripped, scraped, then raked over by a team of grim-faced forensics lab rats before being hosed down while standing on a plastic mesh evidence trap. When a hatchet-jawed man snapped on a pair of latex gloves and told Rook to spread his legs and lean forward, Rook knew he was in deeper shit than he'd ever been in before.

As if he'd even had time to shove something up his ass between the moment he'd been shot at until Montoya face-planted him into one of Hollywood's dirty sidewalks. He didn't know what the cops thought he'd have up there, but a few stinging pokes, and the Dick Tracy wannabe seemed satisfied Rook didn't have anything hidden up his butt.

His rim stung a little, but he wasn't going to give the detectives the satisfaction of seeing his discomfort. Instead Rook focused on taking a read on the men as they worked the room, settling into their roles to mind-fuck information out of him.

There wasn't a damned thing anyone could teach Rook about mind-fucking and social engineering. It was his tool of trade, something he'd learned before he ever crawled into houses to find treasures hidden in freezers and safes behind badly painted landscapes and since perfected as he wheedled people into handing over rare collectibles for a price he could turn into a huge profit.

As far as he knew, the cops had nothing on him about his past, and Rook knew as sure as shit they had nothing on him about Dani's murder. But that didn't mean they weren't going to try to stick it on him.

"Hello, Mr. Stevens."

The matchstick spoke up first, a singsong, gravelly voice Rook supposed he used to lull cranky babies to sleep.

"I'm Detective Camden. This is Detective Montoya."

Rook had to admit Montoya looked damned good. A bit leaner in his face but packed with more muscle everywhere else. He'd changed his jacket and shirt, probably because tangling with Rook smeared dirt and dried blood over the others. The latte-brown suede and corduroy jacket was tailored to fit Montoya's broad shoulders and trim waist, and the weathered gray T-shirt he wore under the corduroy was nearly thin enough to see through, its soft cotton weave sticking to Montoya's chest and flat belly. The jeans were the same, Rook noted, scuffed and speckled with a bit of grit Montoya hadn't bothered to brush off. His thighs were thick with muscle, and his 501s clung and tugged in spots, drawing attention to a creased bulge slung down Montoya's left leg.

As delectable as the man's body was, it was Montoya's face Rook enjoyed the most. Chiseled cheekbones and a full mouth softened his nearly too harsh features. Montoya's light brown eyes, wide and doe-like, made Rook smile someplace deep inside himself. Even as the man stared down at him with nothing on his face but a cold professionalism, those liquid hot amber eyes tickled away some of Rook's wariness.

Not enough for Rook to let his guard drop, but still, hot enough to send tingles up and down Rook's spine.

"Hey, Montoya. Long time, no arrest." Rook held up his hands, teasing the detective. "Look, normal number of fingers. Didn't kill your father. Or Dani either."

"What are you talking about, Stevens?" the man growled, a deep, resonant thrum accented with a rolling Cuban lilt, far different from the staccato chop of the SoCal Mexican Rook grew up with. "Do we need to get a doctor in here, or is this just another one of your games?"

"Do you think Stevens here is playing games with us, Montoya?" Camden cocked his head and studied Rook as if he were an odd bug he'd found in his food. "To what end? Get out of a few questions? It's not like he has anything to hide, right?"

"Neither one of you have heard about Inigo Montoya?" Rook looked from one cop to the other, sighing when he was met with blank stares. "Shit, what's this world coming to? And no, I've got nothing to hide there, Detective."

"You've already been read your rights. Do you need us to go over them again?" This time the redhead shot his partner an odd look when Montoya said something in Spanish beneath his breath, the whisper too low for Rook to hear. "Do you understand your rights as they've been read to you?"

Rook leaned back into the stiff-backed chair they'd given him to sit in. Its metal braces dug into his shoulders, and its thick square legs made it nearly impossible for Rook to rock it back, but he gave it his best effort, scraping the steel ends on the room's linoleum tiles. He felt something give a bit under him, and Rook grinned, a little satisfied he'd be leaving a mark on the cop house floor.

"Yeah, I understand my rights. Go ahead, Weasley. Question away." Keeping his eyes on Montoya's face, he purred, "Like I said, I've got nothing to hide. Well…." He gave Montoya a sly wink. "Mostly nothing, anyway. I try not to dredge up the past too much."

From the startled look on Montoya's face, the detective caught the flirtation Rook tossed his way, and the amber flicker in his gaze flared briefly in response. Montoya shut it down as quick as it came up but not before Rook saw it. After pulling out one of the two chairs across the table from Rook, Montoya sat down and began to flip through the portfolio he'd brought in with him. Matchstick Camden paced the length of the room before coming back to roost his hip on a corner of the table, angling his body slightly to face Rook.

Of the two detectives, Rook would have chosen Montoya to loom instead of the redheaded scarecrow trying to intimidate him by leaning into Rook's space. The skinny man barely cast a broad shadow over Rook's arm, much less psychologically pushing him into talking. Keeping one eye on Montoya, Rook let a tiny smile creep over his mouth as he stared up at Camden.

Camden continued to rattle off the particulars of recording their session and asked Rook to state his name and personal information for the record.

Shrugging, Rook replied, "Rook Martin Stevens, birthday April first... maybe twenty-six or seven years go."

"You don't know the year you were born?"

"Mom did a lot of drugs," Rook shot back. "I'm happy she got the gender part right."

The cop rolled his eyes, then continued, "Birthplace unknown. Father unknown. Mother, Beatrice Martin, location currently unknown."

"And where do you work, and what is your current residence, Stevens?" Montoya interjected.

Rook rattled off his store's address twice, painting a pleasant expression on his face when the cops asked him to clarify. "I live above my shop, Potter's Field. Used to be a dance studio, so it had a shower, and I got it renovated. Made sense at the time. Now, not so sure."

"Let's talk a little bit about your past. We'd like to go over a few things. You've got quite an arrest record here, Stevens. Even as a juvie." Camden rattled a piece of paper in the air. "Fifteen counts of breaking and entering, burglary and fraud, to name a few. Lot of charges here and not far off of a step to murder, really."

The room's florescent lights were bright enough to turn the white page transparent, and Rook quickly read a bit of a transposed menu from an Indian restaurant on Sixth. For an arrest record, it was rather sparse. It did, however, inform Rook of their five bucks all-you-can-eat luncheon buffet.

Playing along with the cop, Rook inclined his head slightly. "Yet no convictions. What does that tell you?"

"That you're slippery." Montoya's rumble ran dark beneath Camden's nearly bright pennywhistle voice. "But not that smart."

"Or you guys are shitty at your job."

That scored a direct hit on Montoya. The man was proud of being a cop, and his eyes went flat as he peered at Rook over the red file folder.

Pushing a little bit further, Rook slid in, "Or maybe just the ones who come after me."

One of the first things Rook learned while growing up barefoot and loose among the carnies was to poke the bear when he was cornered. People—especially cops—usually wore their egos close to the surface, and a few judicious jabs at their tender spots tended to make them lose control. While a dangerous thing to do to a cop out on the street, it was the perfect line of attack when sitting in an interrogation room. Loss of control could do marvelous things for someone caught in a sticky situation.

This time it was Camden who bristled up and flushed red with anger. Montoya, if anything, got colder, and Rook slid a quick look over to the redhead sitting a few feet away from him before gifting Montoya with a broad smile.

"Let's talk about Dani Anderson, shall we?" Montoya headed Camden off before the man could dig into Rook. The partners were definitely on more equal footing than the old man Rook'd seen Montoya with before. "Why'd you kill her?"

"I already told the last five people who accused me...." Rook tried to keep his voice steady, but the strain of being held was growing, especially since he couldn't seem to get the smell of Dani's death out of his nostrils, despite the Silkwood shower he'd taken in the police evidence pen. "Dani was... she was like that when I found her."

"One of the officers states they saw something in your hand when you bolted," Montoya read off a report. Unlike what Camden held in his hand for a prop, Rook was pretty certain Montoya wasn't pulling *that* particular accusation out of his ass. "Any idea where you put that thing?"

"I didn't have anything in my hands... except Dani. And that's only because she rolled over and I caught her." Rook leaned forward. "Like I told you guys before."

"That's when you say you got her blood on you." Camden's sneer was small, barely a twist of his upper lip. "Care to explain how you got so much of it on you if you only *caught* her as she rolled over? Assuming a dead woman *would* roll over. What do you think, Montoya? How likely is that to happen?"

"Gravity happens," Rook cut in before Montoya could speak. "She was on her side. I was crouching over her, and she toppled over—"

"Any reason you did that? Crouch over her, I mean. Allegedly, of course," the redhead said smugly. "Instead of maybe calling the cops because there was a dead woman on your shop floor? And don't tell me you didn't know she was dead. You blasted a hole through her abdomen."

"With what? An elephant gun? Blow darts? The Klingon disrupter I had in the front case? Did you find a weapon? Because I sure as shit didn't have one." Rook twisted in his chair to look at Montoya. The cop's shoulders were squared off and firm, but his face was unreadable. Rook hated the slight pleading waver in his voice, but he was getting desperate. "Look, Montoya, you *know* me. I wouldn't kill anyone—"

"And how would I know that?" Montoya's softly accented voice ruffled Rook's nerves.

"Because you've hounded my ass for years." He shoved down a wince at the unintentional double entendre. "I might have done some things—things I'm not going to apologize for—but I don't do murder. Especially now that I've gone—" He almost crossed a line, confessing he was out of the con and thieving business, something the cops never had proof of, and Rook realized he wasn't the only one playing at breaking another man's self-control.

Montoya was affecting him more than he liked. The whole damned thing was getting under his skin, and for the first time since he'd been brought in, Rook was scared—scared he'd found the *one* time he couldn't talk his way out of something, and it wasn't even something he'd done. "I didn't kill her."

Camden shifted his stance, rocking the table. "So you say. Thing is, Stevens, we don't believe you."

"Then I'll say it again." Taking a deep breath, Rook centered himself before speaking calmly and slowly. "I didn't kill Dani Anderson. I don't even know why she was there in my shop. Shit, I haven't seen Dani since... hell, I don't remember the last time I saw her. She screwed me over on something, and I walked away."

14

"But you definitely knew her?" Camden pressed. "And had problems with her. How about we talk about why she might have come over to your place?"

"No idea," Rook replied smoothly, keeping his attention on the redhead. "I don't even know how she got in. Charlene, my assistant, closes up on Sundays at five. Knowing Char, it was probably closer to three. Hell, it could have been noon. Dani must have gotten in after that, because even as bubbleheaded as Char is, she'd have noticed a dead woman in the middle of the store."

"We've yet to locate your assistant to find out when she closed down." The redheaded detective put his menu facedown on the table. "Any idea on where *she* is?"

"Try a street corner. Sometimes she hands out flyers and condoms to hookers," Rook snarked. "Char's what you call a free spirit. If she shows up for work, I call it a good day."

"And she's the only one who works there?" Montoya slid in.

"No. Well, yes. For now," he replied. "Look, there's a couple of part-timers that worked the store sometimes, but they moved to Oregon together. I haven't gotten around to hiring new ones."

Montoya cut in, "You told the officer who took your statement that you don't have an alibi for the afternoon. The last person who can verify your presence is a Mrs. Viola Cranson. She said you bought a few items from her estate sale and then went back to negotiate the purchase of a decoder ring, is that right?"

"Yeah. I knew her husband. He passed away, and she was selling off some of his things," Rook agreed slowly. He'd paid way too much for the ring, but Viola was old-school stubborn. Handing her a check would have gotten it thrown back in his face. "What about it?"

"Five thousand dollars. For a piece of plastic in a bag?" Montoya leaned back, meeting Rook's glance. "Do they normally run that much?"

"No," he ground out. "The lady's broke. Her husband just died. He used to work the lots and scored me a lot of deals over the years. I thought I'd do her a solid. It's worth about twenty-five bucks, tops."

"And you gave her five grand for it?" Camden whistled. "Some solid. Kind of looks like you were buying an alibi."

"Like I said, her husband did me a lot of favors, especially when I was first starting out." Rook shrugged. "I'm not the only one who gave her money. A couple of collectors were there too doing the same thing. Mark, her husband, was a good guy. A lot of people liked him."

"It's less than an hour's drive from Cranson's house to your shop. You left there at four. Where'd you go in between four and eight?" Montoya asked. The ping-pong of questions was meant to frustrate Rook. It was a move he'd used himself when sharping someone for information. Hell, he and Dani'd been great at it until she screwed him over. She'd been the last straw, the final betrayal. "You burned four hours doing what?"

"Driving, mostly." He shrugged. "I don't get days off a lot. I wanted some space, so I went to Potter's warehouse in West Hollywood, checked on a few things, then drove a bit up the coast." Rook tilted his head. "I'd have said the store's cameras would have a record of me coming in, but the cop told me the power was shut off."

"Dead cameras also are good at not showing someone being murdered," Camden pointed out. "The lines were cut at the box outside. You've got keys to that box, right? With the power out, you could have done a lot of things in that shop without anyone really knowing what you were up to."

"The whole damned block has keys to that box," Rook protested lightly, spreading his hands on the table. "Shit, it's not like it's Fort Knox. They probably use the same key for all the line boxes in Los Angeles. And those are the same fucking dead cameras that would have recorded the cops coming through the front without IDing themselves, so yeah, I'd say taking the power out fucked me over something royal, but I didn't do that either. Costs a lot of money to get an electrician out to fix that kind of thing."

"Yet you paid an old woman five K for a piece of plastic," the Hispanic detective pointed out.

"She's worth the five grand," he retorted. "Killing Dani Anderson isn't."

"No, but the fifty-carat diamond found in her pocket would be worth a hell of a lot more than the five grand you paid Cranson for her story." Montoya drew out an evidence photo showing a large, sparkling pear-shaped gem positioned against an L-shaped ruler to show its width and height. "Strangely enough, it matches a diamond you were suspected of taking six years ago. One we never recovered… until just now."

"And guess what, Stevens?" Camden slid closer, something in his pocket scratching the table with a loud screech. "It's got your fingerprints *all* over it. Now I'd call that something worth killing Dani Anderson over."

Rook dropped his gaze, confused and alarmed. He'd flipped that diamond years ago, nearly hours after he'd taken it from a Beverly Hills mansion. There'd been no connection to Dani on that job. Hell, he hadn't told *anyone* about the take from that night, not even Char, who'd been his lookout on more than one occasion. Shifting in his chair, Rook looked up and damned himself with the one word he'd wanted to avoid but now couldn't.

"What do you have to say to that, Stevens?" Montoya asked softly.

"Lawyer," Rook growled at the two cops sitting across of him. "I want my lawyer."

Three

THERE WAS a gaggle of drag queens in Dante's house.

A gaggle—if that was the right word—getting drunk off their asses and chattering loud enough to wake the dead.

To be fair, Dante reminded himself, one of them *did* live there, but no man needed to come home to find a man the size and hirsuteness of a water buffalo dressed only in a gold lame thong bending over his leather couch.

Dante avoided a pinch from a four-foot-tall Asian man slinging margaritas from the dining table, then liberated a couple of sodas from a Styrofoam cooler near the kitchen door. Another hop, skip, and dodge, then he was free, closing the screen door behind him before joining his partner on the front porch. Handing Hank a root beer, Dante winced as the questionable party inside the house erupted with bursts of high-pitched screams, giggles, and spiced profanities. He checked the cushions of one of the rattan chairs for any of the neighborhood cats, then sat down to open his drink.

"Thanks for the soda." Hank looked over his shoulder when another auditory assault hit. "Do I even want to know what's going on in there, Montoya? They need help or something?"

"Waxing," Dante muttered. "Trust me. You do *not* want to go in there."

They'd come back to Dante's house, worn down to the bone, tired, and thirsty. A brief stop at a fish taco shop on the way up Wiltshire was enough to ease their hunger, but a street party near the park stalled traffic to a standstill, cooking the detectives in Los Angeles's muggy evening stew. By the time Dante pulled up in front of the two-story bungalow he shared with his uncle, Manuel, he and Hank were drenched to the skin and more than a little bit tired of being in a car.

East Hollywood was quiet—with the exception of the burlesque and body maintenance cabaret going on behind them. Old-school Mexican music whispered out of a tiny pink adobe bungalow across the street, and a few houses down, a young woman in a yellow bathrobe stood next to a shivering tiny dog on a leash, encouraging the oversized rat to piss so she could go back inside. The sidewalks lined both sides of the street, slightly broken in spots where an old tree trunk lifted the cement or a quake rattled a panel too hard. The yards ran small, sometimes even to tiny squares of gravel or concrete painted green or terra-cotta, and nearly all of the houses boasted low chain-link or white-post fencing, mainly to keep dogs and children from wandering out into the broad street.

Gentrification was slow to move into the area. The houses were legacies passed on from one generation to the next, and Dante considered himself damned lucky to score his house from a property-seized auction nearly three months after he'd moved to Los Angeles. Neglected to the point of almost being uninhabitable, he'd installed his uncle in the mother-in-law cottage at the back of the property and spent most of his spare time breaking down walls and tearing up piss-stained carpet.

Now the back cottage was a beauty salon for Manny's occasional clients, and Dante concentrated on the smaller projects he'd put aside— like tearing out the ugly concrete water fountain languishing in his sunburned front lawn.

"Want me to run you up home?" Dante asked, sipping at his soda.

"Nah, the Red will take me right to my doorstep," Hank refused with a shake of his head. "And don't take this wrong, but the last thing I want to do is crawl into that POS speck you drove us in."

"Not my piece of shit, remember? The truck's in the shop. Just be thankful Manny loaned us his car. It was either the Z/28 or your wife's minivan."

"God no, not the Cheerio-mobile. The dog puked into the AC vent last week. I think we're going to have it exorcized or something. I can't even get into it without wanting to vomit." Hank slurped on his can, then rolled the cold aluminum across his face. "Hey, how is Manny doing? Better?"

"Yeah, doing good. *Tío* got the all clear from his oncologist last week. Cancer free, five years running. He's just happy his hair's back, but I know he was scared." Dante caught himself crossing his fingers over his chest and shot Hank a sheepish look. "I don't know what's worse, not being able to shake off old habits or just being too stupid to learn new ones."

19

Their phones buzzed and sang at the same time, and Dante frowned, dragging his cell out of his back pocket while Hank hunted his down. Scrolling through a long text message, Dante resisted the urge to fling his phone across the yard and possibly take out a piece of the damned fountain while he was at it.

Stevens was out of jail and, most likely, in the wind.

"How the fuck did he get out?" Hank gritted his teeth. "Motherfucking shit and hell. He's up for fucking murder! And they just let him walk?"

"Released on his own recognizance. You saw those lawyers marching in. You think that wasn't money they were wearing? Some of those damned suits probably cost more than my mortgage payment," Dante murmured, rereading the text from their captain. His partner stood up, and Dante watched Hank pace up and down the porch. "Surprised it took them this long to get him out. He can't go back to his place. That's locked up tighter than the rosary beads Manny got from the Pope. Where can he hide? 'Cause if we lose track of him, we're screwed."

"Next of kin was listed in his records," his partner pointed out. "Archibald Martin. Address is up in the Hills. Maybe an uncle or something? No, grandfather. The guy was listed as his grandpa."

"Living up in the Hills?" Dante snorted. "How much money do you think Stevens is making fleecing people with those plastic rings and stuffed monsters? And he's got a relative living up there?"

"Could be a gardener or an ass-licker. People up there are so rich, they pay people to live in their houses and suck up to them. Stevens looked like he could suck up really good if he wanted to. Shit, this uncle-cousin probably conned his way into some old lady's bed and is waiting for her to die so he can spend the rest of his life taking care of her poodles." Hank grimaced when Dante gave him a reproachful look. "What? Like you weren't thinking it."

"I wasn't. Mostly because it didn't dawn on me. Listen, Stevens can't go back to his place. The shop and apartment are still a crime scene, so he's got to go someplace else." Dante shrugged. He tapped at his cell's screen to look up Archibald Martin of Beverly Hills. What came up made him blink. "Holy shit."

"See if we can run a profile—" Hank stopped short as Dante held up his phone for his partner to see his search results. "What the fuck? Stevens is loaded."

"Or his family is. Something's off here, because I can tell you this relative was nowhere to be found when Vince and I were hunting him down. Now all of a sudden he's got some guy with a nice address? Something's fishy. But if Stevens is even still in LA, he's with this guy or that assistant we couldn't find."

"What was her name? Charlotte? No, Charlene? We don't have any other known associates tagged on his file. Shit, we barely *have* a file." Hank sighed. "Shit, you worked for Toss-It Harry then. I heard that asshole tossed files out like they were three-week-old Chinese food."

"Yeah, he did. He ordered us to get rid of what we'd gathered up because word came down the DA wasn't even interested in looking at Stevens—and never would. I think *that* was the final straw for Vince."

"Surprised we didn't get more lawsuits out of what he did." The redhead crumpled his empty soda can. "We're going to have to go digging through microfiche and hope Records scanned everything."

Dante thought on the boxes he'd stashed away years ago on the day Vince tossed his badge across their captain's desk and stalked off, leaving Dante behind to clean up the mess he'd made of their lives. Clearing his throat, Dante said, "Yeah, about that. Vince and I, we made copies. *Mierda*, I've got tons of files. They're upstairs... in one of the walk-in closets."

Hank blinked. "You're shitting me."

"Nope. I've still got everything Vince and I dug up on him, which wasn't a lot, but at least I have it. Names of people we thought he was pulling jobs with or for. All the way back to when he was a teen. Stevens wasn't marked as a big player in the ring until later on. He was a kid. Vince and I figured he was a runner for the fence. It's not a hell of a lot of personal stuff on him but might give us something."

"Dude, that's... against department policy. I mean, even if that asshole Vince broke every damn rule in the book tampering with evidence, you don't take shit home." Hank whistled softly. "Wow. The captain's going to have a field day with it."

"I know. I should have... turned everything over or something after Vince was forced out, but it seemed pointless. DA still wasn't going to reopen any case we had. It just... pissed me off to throw everything out because shit happens, you know? Stuff comes back up, but—"

"No, no! Montoya, don't get me wrong. I've never been more fucking proud of you in my life." Hank slapped Dante on the shoulder.

"Shit, you don't even let me jaywalk, and here you go, squirreling up a mother lode of confidential files. It's almost like you're… human."

"There is a living room full of men in there who'd love to get a hold of you," Dante pointed out. "I've got a Taser. Manny's been wanting to fix your hair for a long time. You'd be sporting a pompadour before you even hit the floor twitching, *asere*."

"Don't be a hater, Montoya. It was a compliment." Hank ran a hand over his gingery hair. "And the way I see it, we're going to need all the help we can get on this. Stevens still looks good for the murder, and there's a big damned rock sitting in evidence with one of his sticky fingerprints. We can totally make a case that Anderson broke into the store, lifted the gem from where Stevens was hiding it, and was caught when he came in."

"Lab's still got to get to the diamond. We're not even one hundred percent sure it's real or even if it's his fingerprint. We also don't have a murder weapon, and the lab wasn't sounding all too sure there was gunshot residue on him," Dante grumbled. "That break and run of his contaminated everything on him."

"You pounding him into the dirt didn't help." Hank grinned when his partner snorted. "That's what we get for responding to a call. Should have kept driving and hit up that ramen place on Second."

"I'd rather nail Stevens to the wall." Dante's cheeks flushed when he heard himself. "For the murder."

"Connecting him to the diamond is fucking genius. Shit, we need that to pan out," Hank said. "Think about it, if we can line him up with all the shit he did back when you and Vince were chasing him around, it'll be more than a simple nail-to-the-wall, it'd be a slam dunk. So, we hunt down Archibald Martin tomorrow?"

"Like his name is Daffy and it's duck season," Dante agreed. "The sooner we get our hands on Stevens, the better. I think we rattled him during the interview, but he was right. Murder's not his thing, but something happened there. Maybe killing Dani was an accident. I don't know, but if he did it, I want to be the one to shut that jail door in his face."

"If those burglary charges are still inside limitations, that would be like icing on the cake." His partner's grin nearly ate up his face, Hank's freckled cheeks pulled up into plump rosy balls on either side of his long nose. "Kind of like a last victory for Vince, eh? Even if he went sour in the end, he was a pretty decent guy to you. Better than Dawson was to me."

"A hell of a lot better." Dante nodded. "Yeah, let's nail this bastard for everything we can get to stick. We just have to do it right. I don't want him walking away, Hank. Not this time. Not again."

MANNY'S FRIENDS poured out of the house as Hank was walking down the steps. A ruffle of words, protests, and laughter, then Dante found himself waving good-bye to his partner as the evening's bartender and designated driver folded Hank into his SUV to head off to West Hollywood. Carrying in their empty soda cans, Dante turned off the porch light, then locked the front door behind him.

He found his uncle in the kitchen, puttering about in a pair of violent pink and yellow floral pajamas and house slippers that'd seen better days. Manuel Ortega stood on a low step to wash the dishes someone'd left in the sink, his sleeves rolled up nearly to his elbows to keep from dragging in the soapy water. Dante's uncle barely came up to Dante's bicep, his shortness accentuated when standing next to his six-foot-tall nephew.

Manny's pleasant, good-natured face was creased with smile lines and crow's-feet, and his wavy black hair was shot with fine silver, much more than he'd had before he'd gotten breast cancer. They'd laughed when one of Manny's friends shaved his head before he lost it all, and they'd held a funeral for his then shoulder-length curls, flushing the locks down the toilet like a dead goldfish. Having survived the rigors of treatment, Manny'd bounced back, his squat, plump body and smiling face nearly a mirror image of his older sister, Dante's mother.

And much like the days when his uncle and mother slept on the living room floor of their childhood home, they shared the same taste in clothes too.

"*Tío*, you're going to burn somebody's eyes out with those pj's," Dante teased in Spanish, picking up a cloth to dry a serving platter Manny placed in the drainer. "I'm going to have to start wearing sunglasses inside the house soon."

"Hah, you're the one who gave them to me," his uncle scoffed. "Last Christmas."

"I'd still have burns on my hands if I'd touched those in the store." Dante eyed his uncle's clothes. "I gave you a Vespa and gift cards for the mall."

"And this is what I bought with them."

Manny reached for a glass a few feet away, and Dante noticed his hand shaking slightly before his fingers closed around it. Catching his nephew's suspicious look, Manny frowned.

"Don't give me that look. I can be a walking stereotype if I want to. So I like loud colors. So what?"

"And loud people. My ears hurt from tonight." Dante nudged his uncle with his elbow. "And the pajamas are fine. At least I don't have to worry about you sneaking up on me in the dark. You and Mama, both of you dress loud enough a blind man can feel you coming."

"Ah, your mother."

His uncle tried to put on a casual face, but Dante caught the edge of need in his eyes.

"How is she? Has she called you since last week?"

"No." He started on the stacks of clean butter containers Manny used to store food in, carefully drying the lids one by one. "It's harder for her to sneak a call to me right now. Papa's business is down, I think. She's not talking about it, but I can tell."

"Still, she should call you. You're her son. Your father being an asshole, well—he likes being that hard-nosed macho stereotype. I'm glad you take after our side of the family."

It was a familiar argument. One they'd had ever since Dante moved to Los Angeles and bullied his sick uncle into living with him. Thrown out by his own Mexican family, Manny hated seeing history repeat itself in Dante. Every chance he got, Manny pushed Dante to reach out to his parents—the same parents who'd shown him the door when he confessed to being gay.

Maricón was the least offensive thing he'd been called that night.

He sported a scar on his jaw from the beating his Cuban father'd given him before physically tossing him out. A beating he'd not fought because, back then, Dante felt like he'd somehow deserved it. His uncle'd felt the same way once and welcomed Dante with open arms, glad for a companion in his exile. Manny wore his own scars, and they'd cried over their family's betrayal one night, piss drunk from whiskey shots and brandy-filled chocolates. But the person Manny missed the most was his sister, Dante's mother, the woman who said nothing as her husband beat their eldest son nearly to death.

Dante still couldn't drink whiskey without tasting tears and blood.

"The case you have, it's a bad one?" Manny handed Dante the last of the dishes, a mug he'd gotten from a Korean gentleman's club in Garden Grove.

"They're all bad, *tío*. This one is... complicated." He stood fast against Manny's assessing gaze. "We arrested someone I'd tried to bring down before. With Vince. It was our last case. Don't know if you remember that one. You had a lot going on then."

"I was sick, *mijo*. Not unconscious." His uncle turned around to lean against the counter. "That's the one Vince... he gave up, no? *Dios*, what was he thinking risking you with his stupidity?"

Trust Manny to scrape away Dante's scabs with a quick, precise cut of his tongue.

"I hated this guy got away the last time," Dante sighed. "But now I'm wondering if I *can* be fair. I can't fuck this up, *tío*. It's like a second chance I've got to fix what I fucked up the last time."

He couldn't tell his uncle he wanted Rook Stevens in his bed—nearly as badly as he wanted Stevens behind bars.

"You can't blame yourself for Vince messing up or him dying, honey. *He* made the choice not to be honest, not to get treatment." Manny began to fit lids to the empty butter containers, making sure they matched up. "He was sick, *mijo*. He could have gotten help, but he didn't. That is not your fault."

"He gave up, *tío*. Because I fucked up our case. I let Stevens get into my head. After the club. It all went to shit after that."

Dante hated he could still feel the silken smoothness of Stevens's skin on his hands and the velvet brush of the former thief's mouth on his. Especially since he was having a hard time remembering what Vince looked like when he'd been alive. The strongest memory he had of the man who'd taught him how to be a detective was a sliver of waxy yellow skin and bones, coughing himself to death in a hospital bed.

"Everybody fucks up, Dante."

"I'm a cop, *tío*. People depend upon me to be objective. I want Stevens to pay for what he's done, but it's got to be done right—by the book." Dante scrubbed at his face with his bare hand, rasping his palm over his stubble-rough jaw. "I just need to be fair, you know?"

"Of course you can be, Dante." His uncle patted his arm. "You're the fairest man I know. But what you need to be more is honest with yourself. If you have that, everything else can take care of itself. Now, help an old queen get to bed and turn the lights off after me. You know I hate to walk through a dark house."

"Ah no, not with these on." Dante tugged at the sleeve of his uncle's outrageous pajamas. He bent over, kissing his uncle on the cheek. "As long as you have these, you'll never have to be scared of the dark ever again."

Four

THE FUNNIEST thing about fear, Rook discovered, was the feeling of his gums peeling back from his teeth and the flutter of sharp cuts running up and down his lungs and chest when the terror of his life finally hit him.

It hadn't taken him a lot of effort to sneak into his place. Once his grandfather's lawyers got him cut loose, he bolted for his place to wait out the crime lab team swarming through the building. Someone at LAPD boarded up the front of his shop and wreathed the devastation in *do-not-cross* stickers, and for some reason, the cops thought a realtor lock on the back door was somehow going to keep people out. Or maybe they were thinking it would keep out the general shambling hordes of thieves and opportunists running around in Hollywood, but the truth was, a three-year-old with a plastic hammer could break apart a lock box in a matter of minutes.

It'd taken him about a second and a twist of his wrist, but Rook wasn't one to brag.

Or at least not when he had fear choking his throat as firmly as Montoya's fingers had been around his neck.

"That wasn't your neck Montoya had his hand around, fuckwad," Rook scolded himself as he mounted the stairs to his apartment. "It was your goddamned dick. Okay, almost your dick. Through your jeans, but still, dick."

He'd tried not to look at the store itself, but there was no avoiding it when he walked past a windowed wall to get to the stairwell leading up to his apartment. Avoiding the elevator itself was key. *That* particular horror was smack-dab behind the main showroom, and there was no way he could get to it without doing a full waltz across the ground floor.

Still, the police tape—the cursed yellow plastic shreds left behind in the rubble of Rook's life—was fucking everywhere, and there wasn't a damned thing he could do about it.

Including ignore it.

His legs were wobbly from his waning adrenaline rush by the time he walked onto the slick wood of his living room floor. At the time, he'd thought leaving the former dance studio's polished planks intact was a good idea, especially after he'd removed a wall of mirrors and practice rails. Now he was worried if the noise of his squeaking new sneakers would carry out of the open windows facing the street and down to the uniforms squatting in a cop car in front of the building.

It was a stark place, despite the warmth of its aged golden brick walls. He'd left most of the space unfurnished, mostly because he had no idea what to do with it. A long wall of ten-foot-tall black lacquer bookcases cordoned off the back third of the loft and hid the one piece of furniture he *had* purchased, a king-sized bed soft enough for him to bury himself in and not care if he slept the day away.

He'd miss that bed, but he didn't love it enough to risk jail for it.

Enormous mullioned crank-levered windows dotted the loft's three walls, allowing a fair amount of light into the space. Certainly enough light for him to scrape together a meal or two out of the kitchen he'd had installed against the space's one solid wall, and blackout curtains took care of the sun and nightlife when he wanted to sleep. Left open, the windows pulled in the noise of living on the boulevard, and he'd fought many a losing battle with Hollywood's erratic temperatures and breezes, usually giving up and shutting the windows to turn on the air-conditioning.

Much like he'd done when he'd planned to be away for a whole day. So Rook was slightly alarmed to find all of the drapes pulled back, leaving the windows bare—and Rook vulnerable.

He knew he didn't leave the drapes open. Hell, he could barely remember his name at the moment, but he was pretty certain he'd closed every single swinging pane, locked them down, and pulled the blackout curtains before he'd gone gallivanting up and down the California coast.

"Cops?" Rook sniffed, nearly tasting the scent of authority muddling the air. "Why the drapes? Unless they were looking for something else."

There was cop spooge everywhere. A stack of papers lay on the kitchen counter and, at the top of the pile, a boldly marked warrant authorizing access to Rook's life and property. If he read the fine print, he was pretty sure there was a disclaimer the LAPD could shove a hand up his ass and use him to teach the alphabet to drooling children if he looked hard enough.

His wall safe was definitely pushing up daisies. Torn apart and nearly ripped clean out of its brick hidey-hole. Bits and pieces of it lay strewn on the floor with the faux crayon brain splatter painting he'd placed over it leaning brokenly against the wall. The lock box was stone-cold empty, missing the few thousand dollars and a couple of rare action figures he'd stashed there for good measure. He hadn't expected any different, and Rook didn't know what offended him more—the cops ripping him off or the thug smash-and-grab they'd pulled on him to do it.

"Well, fuck. They killed the safe. Hope they at least documented what they took. Fuckers." The damage was pretty extensive, and if he'd given a shit Rook would take pictures and call in lawyers. But he was past giving a shit. He'd moved on to running until he found a place the LAPD couldn't find or reach him. Taking a fast look at the safe, he toed the bent door. "Guess fucked-by-cops isn't going to be covered by the warranty."

The safe wasn't Rook's only hidey-hole. Not by a long shot. He'd put it in plain sight to seed the belief it was all he had on him, but there were larger, more secretive stashes around the apartment, and he'd come to clean himself out. He just had to grab what he could get his hands on and get out before LAPD's forensics and burglary department came back around for a second look. Come dawn, his place would be swarming with cops again, and he wanted to be a speck on the horizon before *that* hell rained down on him.

A burbling tidbit of a song wafted out of the back of the loft, and he slowed his pace, stealthily creeping up on his intruder. It couldn't be a cop. Not with lights off. No, it was someone using Hollywood's neon glut and sparkling signs to provide them with enough light to see by—which explained the open drapes.

But not who opened them.

Rook had his answer when he stole around the screens and found a buxom, platinum bleach blonde opening the door to one of his walk-in closets, her generous hourglass figure nearly tilted off balance by the red six-inch heels she daintily balanced on as she robbed him blind. The heels made her almost as tall as he was, bringing her up to nearly six feet. Which was good for Rook, since it made it easier to grab her.

Rook slid up behind his assistant, then clamped his hand over her mouth. "Hello, Charlene."

Her scream would have been terrific. She'd once made her living from screaming at the top of her lungs while jiggling her generous assets.

Built like a sexpot voluptuous enough to star in a movie about Amazonians on the moon, Charlene knew how to work her audience. No one did wide-eyed innocence like Charlene Canada, especially while celluloid monsters were ripping her clothing. But then no one could also con a mark like Char either. It was just a pity she didn't have the brains to hold on to a con for the time it took to catch.

She'd spent most of her time on the circuit like he had, but unlike Rook's stint as a rigger, Char worked the show, usually tied to spinning wheels while heavy daggers were thrown dangerously close to her body, then skipping out when her sleazy agent scraped up yet another B-movie role for her to die in.

When Rook decided it was time to go legit, she'd tagged along for the ride, hoping her proximity to Hollywood would help her lackluster career. He hadn't the heart to tell her she'd gone the Norma Desmond route, a bit too old and dried up to compete with the newer crops of plastic dolls and pouting lips. Char still had fight in her, and he got a full dose of it when her teeth sunk into his fingers. She'd bite down hard enough to draw blood and then scream blue bloody murder when he let go, leaving him mostly deaf and nursing a migraine. He'd been around Charlene long enough to learn *that* lesson the hard way.

He also knew Charlene well enough to dodge one of those killer heels when she brought a stiletto tip up to pierce his balls, hoping he'd let go.

"Char, it's me."

She mumbled through his fingers, and he sighed. Charlene was a soft, round warmth in his arms, but he wasn't stupid. Where the stiletto might have missed, the steel-hard fake nails she sported could blind him just as quickly if she was given half the chance.

"Which me? Rook. The guy who pretty much pays your bills. I'm going to take my hand away now. Do. Not. Scream."

He lifted his hand a few centimeters away from her mouth, his palm and fingers sticky with the bright red lipstick Charlene called her signature look.

"How do I know it's you?" she accused in a hot whisper. "You could be anyone just saying you're Rook."

"Char, if you knew how much to shit and hell my life has gone to right now, you'd know *no one* would want to be me." He gently pulled away from Char, tugging the hem of her nearly too tight T-shirt back down over her butt. "How the hell did you get inside? The back door still had a lock box on it."

"Oh, someone left the loading bay door unlocked. I came in through there." She smiled prettily. "I was going to lock up when I left. I just came by for a few things and saw the cops in front, so I went out back, and, woot for me, it was open."

If it hadn't been open, Char probably would have jiggled her way past the cops and somehow conned them to let her in. She was good at that. Cold air hit his face, chilled to a temperature meant to maintain the costumes stored inside. Frowning, he was about to close the door when Charlene clamped her hand around its edge.

He eyed her. "And what are you doing in the chill-closet? The costumes in here aren't to borrow. It's inventory."

"I… um… kind of was going to borrow something to wear to a party. I found these awesome lilac shoes and some stuff to wear." Her words ran together, a sugary stream of excuses threaded together in a practiced cutesy voice she could no longer shake. "It's really important, Rook. Like producers being there and stuff. I have to look good—"

"You always look good." He began to pull her fingers off the door. "You don't need anything to—"

"It's one of those steampunk parties. I don't have anything like that." Char stepped back, studying Rook in the pale light coming from the windows. "Come on. I could really use something nice. It's very, very important. There's this part—"

"It's always important, Char." Rook was about to shut the door, then stopped. He was going to bail. What did it matter if Charlene emptied out the whole fucking chill box? Hell, he didn't even have anyone to leave the shit to. Stepping back, he threw the door open for her. "You know what, help yourself. Hell, clean the place out. And if the cops didn't get to it, there should be a tackle box in the shoe sections. Inside one of the embroidered silk slippers, there should be a couple of burner credit cards with ten grand on them. Skip town. Go under for a while, because God knows, I'm going to."

"Don't you… need it?" Charlene glanced over her shoulder to the closet, obviously torn.

"Nah, I've got my own. I'm just staying long enough to grab a few things. Like that old Bowie knife I won from Perkins. I promised him I'd give it back to him."

He stalked off, heading to the screens. Charlene made confused noises behind him, but Rook was more intent on finding the knife he'd stashed in an apothecary cabinet. Staring at the nearly twenty-five drawers, Rook wondered what the hell he had been thinking when he'd hidden the knife.

"What kind of fucking idiot hides a weapon someplace in this?" Rook focused on the cabinet, ignoring the increasingly louder tap of Charlene's stilettos on the floor. "Probably five from the bottom. That's something I'd do."

It was the wrong drawer, but from the amount of condoms he'd stashed there, he'd obviously been planning an orgy to rival Caligula.

"What do you mean do a runner? You can't run. What are you running from?"

Charlene's fingers on his shoulder were gentle, and he sighed, refusing to turn and look into her bright blue eyes. They'd be watery, brimming with tears and spiking the heavy black fake eyelashes she liked to wear. And unlike every other time he'd seen her turn on the waterworks, she'd be sincere and concerned.

Rook didn't know if he could take that worry at the moment. It would burn more than a knife to the ribs, but not answering would... *hurt* her, and he'd be damned if he sliced off another bit of Charlene's tender heart just because he wasn't man enough to look at her.

"Did you see downstairs, Char?" Rook twisted slightly and slid his arm around her tiny waist. "Did you see the blood on the floor?"

"There's blood downstairs?" Her eyes popped open and her throat fluttered with shock. If she'd been wearing pearls, Char would have clutched them in full dramatics, unable to separate the woman she was from the caricature she'd created. "I just thought someone broke in or something. How... blood? Really?"

"Do you remember Dani Anderson?"

Charlene's baby-doll face went full Chucky at the mention of the woman who'd nearly gotten Rook killed.

"Someone murdered her. Here. Downstairs. In the shop. And the cops think I did it."

"Well, who would blame you?" Charlene let out a lingering hiss. "I'd have killed her too."

"I didn't, though. Kill her. From what I can tell, they did a full Rasputin on her. Knife. Everything." Rook tilted his head back, slightly shocked at Char's blasé acceptance. "You think I'd kill her?"

"Like I said…." She shrugged. "Who'd blame you?"

"Well… I didn't. Kill her." Rook let her go so he could find Perkins's knife. "There's a suitcase in the other closet—well, a couple of them—if you want to pack up some of the stuff to take with you—"

"I can't believe you're running. You didn't *kill* her." Charlene sat down on his bed, wrinkling its dark red duvet. "You weren't even here."

"Yeah, well, I walked in, and then the bitch fell on me. It was like her final fuck-you-Rook. Damned cops stripped me naked because I had blood all over me." Rook pointed to the T-shirt and jeans the lawyer brought him to change into. "Do you really think I'd buy a pair of four-hundred-dollar jeans?"

"They're nice. You've got a really good ass." Charlene barely blinked when he shot her a dirty look. Waving away his disgust, she pouted. "Besides, you can't run. You've got to fight this. You can't let them take away everything you've done. It's just not fair."

"Done? What have I done?" The knife was elusive, but he did find a few vintage Chinese finger puzzles from a mail-in-box-top campaign from the fifties. "Shouldn't you be packing shit up instead of talking to me here? Wonder if the cops found the damned knife and took it to match up to Dani's wounds. That would be fucked-up."

"Are you really going to let them take away your normal?"

Charlene's words chilled his spine, and he stopped pulling out drawers to look at her. This time there were no tears in her big baby blues, just pity and sadness.

"Think about it, Rook honey. Here… this place… downstairs, it's the first place you could call home. It's your home, and I know you haven't gotten around to accepting that because, I mean, look around you. It's not like you've put down roots, but you could. If you tried. If you wanted to."

"I—"

"Are you going to let Dani take *this* from you too?" she asked in her whispery, sugarcoated voice. "Don't you want to have someplace where you live and everyone knows you? Like the coffee shop guy who flirts with you while he makes your order? Or the Chinese food delivery guy who knows you like wooden chopsticks instead of a plastic fork? Aren't you sick of running, Rook? Of living out of trailers and suitcases because that's all you think you're worth? Because that's what she's taking from you, baby. *Your* normal."

He wanted to protest, wanted to say something witty or even to tell Char to fuck off, but Rook found his throat closing in on his words, muffling his fear and anger. The loft was bare, boasting only a bed and a few plastic lawn chairs he'd gotten at a drug store down the street. His dishes were mostly Melmac pieces he'd found in estate lots he'd blind purchased at auctions. Hell, even his coffee machine had been one of those free-when-you-order deals online.

It was all disposable.

Just like he was.

Like he'd been.

Rook stood in front of what felt like a hundred open drawers and laid bare by Charlene's words. His stomach did a final turn before settling into a lump in his guts. Honesty was never something he'd believed in. It got in the way of too many things he needed to do, grew too many morals and ethics if allowed to nest in his life, and the last thing Rook Stevens ever wanted in the past was to be burdened by an overabundance of right and wrong.

Except now when he *hadn't* done the unthinkable—when he *hadn't* crossed the one line he'd stood firm on in the past—taking another person's life.

And he'd be damned if he was going to run for something he *hadn't* done.

Not and lose everything he'd gained by turning his back on the life he'd had before. He'd worked past the itchy feeling of owning a building, of creating a life that wasn't made out of smoke and mirrors, and even choked down the sick coming up from his stomach when he'd filled out paperwork to start a legitimate business and paid an aging starlet a decent wage so she could audition for parts she had no chance at.

Charlene was right. He'd earned his fucking *normal*, and neither Dani Anderson nor Los Angeles's finest were going to take it from him.

He closed the drawers one by one, setting them back into place, then turned around to lean against the cabinet, nodding slowly at the woman on his bed.

"Yeah, you're right. Screw running." Even saying it out loud made his nerves tingle and curl up into themselves. "I'm going to fight this out. I'm worth that much, right?"

"And more, baby." Charlene clapped, her voice hitting a high note sharp enough to pierce his eardrums. "Um, just one thing—hope you don't mind if I take the cards and the costume anyway. I mean, I love you and everything, Rook, but I ain't *that* stupid."

THE TAXI cab driver pulled up in front of the looming castle the Martins called home, and Rook silently bore the hushed whistle from the driver when he caught sight of the brick monstrosity his great-great-grandfather paid to lug over from the British Isles. The place was a Pick-Up Stix game of brick and windows, laced with creeping ivy and set in a polished setting of formal gardens, house-sized fountains, and barricaded behind bristling wrought-iron fences.

Rook liked to think of it as *Barad-dûr* because if any place deserved to be called The Dark Tower, it was his grandfather's looming mansion.

Rook'd been surprised when the taxi was waved through the fortified community gates once the security guard got his name, and he caught an even bigger surprise when the guard carded the driver's till, paying for Rook's ride with a flash of black plastic.

He was too tired to argue with the driver over a tip, pressing a twenty into the man's hand and waving him off. Rook barely heard the cab pull away, and, suddenly confronted by the enormity of what he was doing, he wondered bleakly if it was too late to simply throw himself into the gigantic pool of geysers and statues someone'd thoughtfully left in the middle of the castle's driveway.

But he wasn't so tired that it didn't shock the shit out of him when his grandfather opened the front door a second after he rang the bell.

Archibald Martin was everything Rook was not. A chiseled-from-stone despotic patriarch of a wealthy family, Archibald grew up with privilege, money, and a firm philosophy the world owed him its obedience and worship. Sporting a shock of thick white hair and a beaked nose built to intimidate, the man probably once would have towered over Rook, but time crimped his shoulders downward, and he used a cane to support an iffy back and hip. Still, Rook's mismatched eyes looked back at him from under Archie's wooly caterpillar eyebrows, hardened by resolve and age without a hint of tenderness for the young man standing on his doorstep.

"So you've come home, then?" Archibald barked, stepping slightly aside to let Rook in, a black velvet dressing gown swishing around his pajama-clad legs. "Not taking off to the wilds like your mother."

"Nah, thought I'd spit in their fucking eye for once," he commented softly, hefting a duffel of clothes and toiletries onto his shoulder. Rook still hadn't crossed the threshold, held back by the pressing finality of it all. It was one thing to let a pack of lawyers chew him out of jail, but to tuck himself up under Archibald's wing stuck something hard and sharp in his throat. Instead he stood still, silently weighing his actions.

"In or out, boy. Worse than a goddamned cat, you are," Archibald grumbled. "I don't have all night to stand here. I'm old. I need my sleep. You probably do too since those damned cops kept you for so damned long. Ought to fire those fucking lawyers if they couldn't get you out before midnight. What's the use of paying those vultures if they take that long to pick a corpse clean to the bone. Get in before I change my mind and shut the door in your face."

That brought Rook up, and he cocked his head, staring at his grandfather. Something in Rook's expression must have tickled the last remaining shred of decency in the old man's soul, because his hard face softened, and Archibald shook his head with regret.

"I shouldn't have said that. You don't deserve that kind of shit from me. Bad enough you got it from your mother. I'm just—"

"A fucking asshole?" Rook supplied smoothly, shifting the pack's strap until it lay more comfortably across his shoulder.

"I was going to say old, but fucking asshole works too," his grandfather huffed. "Come in. We'll find a place for you. You stay here and fight. I'll have your back, boy."

"Name's Rook, old man," he muttered, finally stepping across the threshold, and his grandfather sighed while closing the door.

"Yeah, I know, kid. It's already bad enough you look and sound like me," the old man muttered. "But did she have to name you after me too?"

Five

"FUCKER." ROOK ran his hand under the ice-water spigot set into the fridge, cooling off the scald he'd gotten from the complicated torture device masquerading as a coffee machine at the end of the counter.

So far that morning he'd lost a fight with the shower door, burned toast, and failed spectacularly at making a simple cup of java. A press of a button—the wrong button—and the squat metallic demon shot out a stiff tentacle and steamed his hand as if it were wrinkled cotton.

It wasn't just the coffee machine that made him nervous. The whole damned castle was a trapdoor spider waiting to pounce on him every time he turned around. The Martins called it a house. Anything with three turret towers and too many fireplaces to count was a fucking castle in his book.

Once his mother threw her family into his face, he'd studiously avoided the place every time the carnie crew hit Hollywood, despite the riches lurking in the house's depths. The edifice had been renovated numerous times, mostly patchwork rooms here and there, and apparently whomever had a hair up their ass changed the paint on only some of the walls in a failed attempt at interior design.

As a result, the place was like walking through time portals every time he moved from one room to the next. Thankfully, one of his aunts favored clean lines and strong furniture, because he'd found a bedroom he could sleep in, one without deer heads or rococo embellishments heavy enough to kill him if something toppled over. It was weird. Sleeping in the middle of things museums would beggar themselves to own. Even weirder was him not stuffing a lot of it into rolling suitcases and making a break for it.

Mostly he felt like a piece of dog shit hiding among chocolate cakes, but damned if Rook was going to tell anyone that.

Luckily, the kitchen was modern, a gleaming triumph of impractical appliances that did everything but what they were supposed to do. Rook was pretty certain the refrigerator was large enough to hold a mammoth, and he couldn't really see the need for two walk-in freezers, but someone apparently disagreed with that assessment. The first time he'd wandered into the kitchen to get something to eat, it took him nearly fifteen minutes before he found where the food was kept.

Silverware shouldn't have its own cabinet, he'd grumbled, and then scolded his fingers when they itched to open up the locked hutch just to see what was stashed inside. The temptation was still there—especially now that he was up for a murder he didn't even commit.

Not that he hadn't wanted to kill Dani Anderson, but if he was going to be pinned for it, Rook would've wanted to earn her blood on his hands.

But not as much as he longed for coffee at that moment.

Eyeing the door to the pantry room, Rook pondered, "Wonder if they have instant in this crypt?"

"The day instant coffee is served in this house will be on the day of my funeral," a rough old voice boomed from the kitchen threshold. "And that's because someone snuck it in."

Rook could see traces of himself in the old man. Mostly it was in the face, but sometimes, when the man spoke, Rook could swear he heard himself in his cranky grandfather's words. Archibald Martin's blue and green eyes were like Rook's, and they were about the same height—or had been before age stooped the man over. Their hair parted in the same way, straight down and into their faces, but the Martin patriarch's full head of silver was ruthlessly cut back away from his forehead and slicked down with what smelled like VO5. Today he wielded an ebony cane for support, but from what Rook could see, the only thing weak about his aging grandfather were his outdated opinions.

His grandfather hated Rook's homosexuality. Two gays in the family—Rook and his cousin Alex—was two too much for Archibald Martin, and hardly a day went by without his opinions being expressed loudly and clearly. Rook, on the other hand, loathed Archibald's closed-mindedness with more passion than he probably should have given the old man, but while he didn't mind being looked down on for being trash, Rook drew the line at being damned for who he fucked. They'd fought often and hard, usually resulting in one or the other throwing their hands up in disgust and quitting the field.

So while they'd reached a détente of sorts between them, Rook still had been shocked as shit to discover a team of expensively dressed lawyers popping into the interview room nearly as soon as he'd opted for legal counsel. For once, the old man's manipulative and intrusive puppet mastering did Rook some good.

He was just left wondering what it was going to cost him.

Because Archibald Rook Martin did *nothing* without exacting payment of one kind or another.

"Hey, Archie." Rook nodded at his grandfather, then turned around to the coffee machine again. "Don't suppose you know how to work this stupid thing."

"Considering this is the first damned time I've stepped foot in this kitchen in my entire life, I should say not." The old man sniffed imperiously as he ambled over to Rook's side. Eyeing the appliance, he grumbled. "Where's Rosa? She'll make your coffee for you. That's what we pay her for."

"Who's Rosa?" Rook opened a small hatch he'd not noticed before and found a tiny white booklet inside. "Ah-hah, instructions. Or a warranty. And it's in French. Fuck me sideways. Anyway, Rosa? Who's that? Wait, let me guess, you've got your own household troubleshooter who comes in to wipe your butts when you need it."

"Don't be an ass, boy. Rosa's our... cook. She should be making you coffee." Archibald snatched the booklet from Rook's fingers. "Here, let me see that. I want to throttle your mother every time I discover your ignorance in the most basic of things. Who doesn't know French?"

"Probably Rosa. Whoever she is." Rook crossed his arms over his chest, moving aside when his grandfather shoved him away from the machine. "Your cook's name isn't Rosa. She's not even a she."

"What? No, you're wrong. All right, maybe not the cook but...." A thick, furry eyebrow popped up over Archibald's green eye. "*Someone's* named Rosa."

"Nobody here." He shrugged. "You going to take a crack at that thing, or do you want to give me another try? Because I need some coffee."

"I've been calling that woman—the one who brings me everything—damn it, what is her name? She's Rosa!" Archibald's cane thumped once on the travertine floor. "Latina. Late thirties maybe. Skinny too. Needs some meat on her bones. Her name's Rosa!"

"That's the housekeeper. And no, her name's not Rosa either. And to be fair, she needs a better title than housekeeper. She fucking runs this place." Rook pulled his grandfather back just as the machine's steaming tentacle made another appearance. It shot out a burst of hot, wet air, barely missing the old man's liver-spotted hand. "Yeah, I tried that. There's beans in there, and a hot water line, but fuck if I know how to get the damned thing to combine the two."

"Mr. Martin, sir, two men are here to speak to you." A placid-faced middle-aged woman padded into the kitchen on crepe-soled shoes, brushing down the dark blue full apron she wore over her white button-up shirt and black pants. A small frown appeared on her forehead as she spied them in front of the coffee machine, but she continued as if she found Archibald Martin in the castle's kitchen every day. "They say they are detectives. Hanson has called in to the police to run their badge numbers and photos. He said everything checks out. Would you like to speak to them?"

"This is certainly about you, boy." Archibald stabbed a bony finger into Rook's chest.

"Probably," Rook admitted. "Cops and shit coming to the door usually are."

"Better go see what they want. Get yourself some of... well, whatever you need and come join us. I won't say anything in front of them that I won't say in front of you." The old man grumbled when his housekeeper slid one hand under his arm to guide him out of the kitchen. "Let go. I'll be fine. Help the boy with that thing. And for God's sake, get something in here that just makes coffee. That damned thing practically peeled my hand off."

"Yes, sir." She inclined her head slightly and smiled. "I'll order a percolator."

"Or you know, a coffee machine. The kind you dump beans and water in, then press a button," Rook suggested.

"I don't care. Just... get it," Archibald ordered. "And hurry up, boy. I don't intend to spend my day entertaining Los Angeles's finest when I could be doing more interesting things, like watching paint dry. You are more trouble than you're worth."

They both watched Archibald stride out, his cane thumping a furious beat on the floors. Shaking her head, the housekeeper gave Rook a slight smile. "He doesn't mean it, sir."

"Oh, he means it, Rosa," Rook corrected softly. "But he likes me anyway. Now, since you're here, can you show me how to make a cup of coffee? I think this thing's trying to kill me."

"HOLY FUCKING shit." Hank's voice dropped to a whisper. "Take a look at that house."

"That's not a house. That's an asylum." Dante blew out a low whistle. "*Mierda*, bad enough we'd thought this guy was a gardener. He's got to live in a castle?"

They'd done a fair amount of research on Archibald Martin before heading up to the Hills. Rook's Beverly Hills connection went from being a possible employee to a man who'd built an empire on a firm dynastic wealth. Dante'd lost the threads of Martin's holdings minutes after starting a title search, and he'd been left to wonder why Rook Stevens turned to a life of crime when he had every single silver spoon available to put into his mouth since he drew his first breath.

Further investigation uncovered Rook Stevens's indigent and reckless mother was the Martin family's wild child, who'd fled her luxurious nest to tramp around the countryside with a carnie and sideshow troupe. Rook was an afterthought from what Dante could figure out, and the Martins appeared to have only recently discovered Rook's existence.

Regardless of how long Archibald had known of his errant grandson or what he thought about Stevens, Dante had to admit that the old man had certainly moved heaven and earth to get their murder suspect out of jail.

Now Dante and Hank could only hope they hadn't lost Rook in the process.

"Guy probably doesn't even know he has gardeners. Probably thinks everything grows that way because he wants it to." His partner echoed Dante's whistle as they pulled into a circular driveway in front of the mansion. "Holy crap. Look at this place."

Like Dante could do anything *but* look at the place.

There was a gardener, an older Hispanic man who gave him the hairy eyeball when he climbed out of the unmarked land shark LAPD's motor pool gave them that morning. Dante tried to ignore the prickling uneasiness crawling out of his spine as he took in the lush landscaped lawns and gardens around him. The Martin place cast a long shadow—and not just one from its four-story turret. He'd spent many a summer working for people who believed anyone darker than a grocery store's paper bag should use the back door when coming into their homes—if Dante was even allowed into their homes. The groundskeeper gave him that same vibe, as if Dante were still a scrawny Cuban-Mexican kid from Laredo delivering furniture from his uncle's store.

Quirking a smile, he ran a finger over the badge hanging from his belt, feeling the familiar ridges and dips in the warmed metal. The skinny kid was nearly eighty pounds of muscle and had years of schooling behind him, but he was there, lurking in the shadows, still a whisper of awe at the gray stone monstrosity rising up from the hill's rippling canyon cleft.

The Martin place was literally a castle. It could have used a moat and possibly a lake monster to cruise through its murky waters in search of a meal made from hapless intruders, but Dante figured the enormous fountain set in the middle of the circle driveway was as close as the Martin family was going to get. Climbing ivy covered the castle's gray stone walls, edging close to its enormous arched windows. Stained glass broke up the green and slate, sparkling colors dotting the walls and glistening prisms where the sun struck the panes. The castle loomed up over them, a dark shape high and thick enough to cast long shadows that chilled the air when Dante walked over the driveway to reach the front door.

"I don't think there's a doorbell."

Hank bent over to study the door's frame. Dante stepped up onto the entrance's stone slab.

"Do we just shout? Or use that large knocking thing here?"

"It's called a door knocker for a reason." Dante lifted the heavy oblong ring. Before he could rap the knocker down, the door swung inward, jerking the ring out from between his fingertips. Staring down at the tiny Hispanic woman frowning at him, Dante pulled his jacket back and flashed his badge. "Hello, I'm Detective Montoya. This is Detective Camden. We're here to see Mister Archibald…."

"Is this about Mr. Martin's grandson?" Her accent rolled through Dante's memory, a strong hint of Southern Texas Spanish layered over her English. Dante nodded, and the woman's frown slipped off her brow. "Come this way, please. Let me make you comfortable in the library, and then I'll tell him you are here."

They fell into step behind her, the house's cool air folding around them as the detectives were led deeper into the castle's interior. Unlike the outside, the inside of the castle was a patchwork of styles and proportions. Even as unfamiliar as he was with interior design, Dante knew the furniture, carpets, and wall colors he passed were out of sync and in some cases even overwhelming. A few feet down the hall, a stuffed vulture battled a two-headed snake on an overembellished cabinet set next to a table bristling with a field of miniature ceramic deer around a stone monkey.

The housekeeper paused outside of an open door, motioning for the men to go in. She seemed oblivious to the monkey, deer, vulture, and snake, although Dante noticed she took a quick glance into the room before asking them if they wanted coffee.

"Coffee would be great if you've the time." Dante smiled, purposely thickening his accent. "And if you think Mr. Martin is willing to spend enough time with us to share a cup."

"You'll probably be done with your coffee before he finishes complaining about his family," the woman huffed. "Please, get comfortable. I will ask him to join you and bring some cream and sugar."

Hank's whistling went low and deep as they walked into a bookcase-filled room large enough to swallow nearly all of Dante's house. The ceiling stretched up nearly twenty feet above them, topped with a skylight-paned dome crenulated with gold and malachite insets. A wide dark wood stairway led up to a half-moon floor above them, an elaborate railing and baluster of curlicues and fleur-de-lis running around the level's edge. The upper floor held more books and trinkets, a march of glass-fronted barrister cases set against the room's pale blue walls.

"Jesus H. Christ," Hank muttered at Dante as the housekeeper left the room. "This guy's probably got *him* stashed in here too."

"Probably not, but I'm sure there's a handwritten bible someplace in here," Dante murmured, glancing about him. "Might even be a first edition."

"Shit—can I even say shit in here?" His partner turned, catching Dante's attention with a nod. "Take a look at that. Think that's the guy we're here to see?"

An oil painting dominated the space, stretching up over a broad stone fireplace. The portrait spared no courtesy to its subject, a pale, hook-nosed man with mismatched eyes and combed-back white hair. The background was indeterminate, mostly a suggestion of brushed leather and burgundy curtains, allowing the man to fill the canvas with the sheer power of his arrogant stare and pulled-in sneer. Dante studied the portrait, looking for a plaque or inscription, but its heavy wooden frame bore nothing other than a curious orange paint smear on its bottom right corner.

"Maybe." He pondered, tilting his head. "The eyes are the same as Stevens's. Curious about the damage to the frame. Looks new."

"That's what happens when I'm served tea when I've asked for coffee." A cranky-voiced old man hobbled into the library, his gnarled left hand curled down over the head of an ebony cane. The years since he'd sat for the painting hadn't been good ones. Age spots dotted his cheekbones, and deep grooved lines cut into the soft, waxy-looking skin on his face. If his mouth had seen a smile in the past decade, Dante would have laid a bet it was at someone else's expense or pain. And from the chill in the old man's hard gaze, it would be a long time until the next grin ghosted over his pale pink lips.

"Archibald Martin?" Hank spoke up, using an authoritative voice Dante secretly believed he practiced on his wife's Pekingese. "I'm Detective Henry Camden, and this is—"

"I know who you are," the old man grumbled at them, stamping the cane's rubber tip into the library's polished floor as he walked toward a set of wing chairs near the fireplace. "The question is, what do you think you're here for? Rosa—well, whatever her name is—she's bringing coffee for you freeloaders to drink while you grill me. Sit down, because I'm not going to strain my neck. I'm old. I'm not as tall as I used to be."

"We're actually here to talk to your grandson, Rook. If you know where he is," Dante said as he eased into one of the chairs. His elbow struck a ceramic vase, and he caught its lip, bobbling it a few times before setting it back down. "Excuse me."

"If you hit it again, let it break. There's too much shit in this place anyway." Archibald moved his cane out of Hank's way as the redheaded detective made his way past a side table. "Get your ass settled down, and we can talk."

"Mostly we want to know where he is, Mr. Martin." Dante cleared his throat. "As you probably know, your grandson is a suspect in a murder case—"

"Let me tell you about my grandson, Detective." Martin leaned forward in his chair and stabbed at the air in front of Dante's face. "Actually, let me tell you about all of my kids and *their* damned kids. I've got thirteen grandkids, and only two of them are worth anything, and they're both queer. The rest of them are leeches and goddamned turkey stupid. I'm surprised they don't drown when it rains. I thank God Beatrice's boy found his way back here, because at least he's got a

44

damned brain. So I don't give a shit if you found him dancing in the middle of dead babies covered in blood and flossing his teeth with their guts. I will fight like hell to make sure that boy walks free. Because that's what my family's come down to, two faggots and a bunch of drooling idiots squatting over me and waiting for me to die. And I can only depend upon the faggots to keep this family going."

"One thing you forget, old man," Rook growled at his grandfather as he strolled into the room, his fingers hooked into the waistband of his low-slung jeans. "Us faggots can still have kids, but no matter what you do, you can't ever fix the stupid. So how about a little respect there." His odd eyes gleamed behind his dark lashes. "Hello, Detective. Imagine meeting you here. Did you find another dead body you want to pin on me, or was it you just couldn't get enough of my ass?"

Six

ROOK STEVENS was a punch to Dante's balls.

Dante'd been punched there before. A cop didn't work the streets of Los Angeles without taking a shot to the nuts more than a few times, so he was very familiar with the sickly sweet curl his stomach made when he was at his most vulnerable.

When Rook Stevens walked into the library, Dante Montoya's stomach reacted as if he'd just taken a line drive to the groin by a cannonball.

He tried shaking the feeling off, but no matter what he did, the tingle was still there. A telltale frisson of nerves, lust, and want that made Dante wish he could roll up into himself and set it on fire in the middle of a crucible so nothing else would be caught in the raging flames. And as much as he longed to blame his discomfort on anything but an attraction to the oddly-eyed man prowling around the center of the library, Dante knew he couldn't.

Squaring his shoulders, Dante inclined his head toward Stevens. Knowing how squirrelly the thief was, Dante'd expected him to be nothing but dust in the wind, and he'd nearly choked on his own tongue when his suspect ambled into the library as if he were showing up for a tea party with his grandfather. The men were definitely two of a kind, predators in their own way. Stevens went for the con, manipulative and charming, while the old man was definitely a take-no-prisoners aggressor.

One he could deal with.

Two he'd have to be very careful around.

Dante stopped himself from clearing his throat. The carrion hunters were definitely circling, and any sign of weakness, however accidental, would throw Rook and Archie a psychological advantage he wasn't willing to give up. "We were actually wondering where you were, since apparently throwing you in jail doesn't seem to keep you in check. Luckily, here you are, since Detective Camden and I have some follow-up questions for you."

"You don't have to say shit to them, son. Not without a lawyer. If they want to talk to you, they can make an appointment." Archibald nearly spat on Hank's shoes as he spoke.

"I've got nothing to hide, Archie." Rook met Dante's gaze. "They're just going to have to listen to me tell them I didn't kill Dani. And I don't know who did."

The glittering hardness in Rook's eyes challenged Dante on so many levels, he wasn't sure if he wanted to punch the man or bend Rook over a table to fuck him. A primal need reared up in Dante's mind, ravaging away his reason. He was about to call Stevens a liar when Hank's phone rang.

"Hold up a second. Let me get this. Don't start anything until I get back." Hank quickly flashed his screen at Dante. He frowned at the number, recognizing LAPD's outgoing trunk line. Hank mouthed a "fuck" as he turned his back on the men, whispering as he went by, "Betcha this is someone yanking our asses out of here. You hold them back."

With Hank gone, he was outnumbered, and Dante braced for the attack he knew was coming. Unsurprisingly, it was Archibald who took the first bite, confirming what Dante would have expected from an old man who'd spent his life carving out people's guts to amuse himself.

"So, my grandson tells me you two have a history." Archibald's eyebrows danced over his beaked nose.

Dante couldn't help but shoot Stevens a startled look, and damned if the man didn't quirk a cocky smile back. Their shared history was dangerous—more so if Archie was made aware of it—and Dante didn't like the edge it gave the thief. The old man would twist anything he got into a weapon, and the case didn't need Archibald Martin brutally dancing through it.

"Grandpa knows you're one of the detectives who tried to arrest me a while back. You know, when the LAPD thought I was a thief." Rook shucked his disheveled mane away from his face, and for a second, the resemblance to the elderly man beside him was uncanny.

"We still think you're a thief," Dante replied smoothly, a tingle of satisfaction warming him at Rook's tight glare. Two could play at the mind-fuck game, and he guessed Stevens was going to hold his trump card close to his chest until he needed it. "We just know you're a murderer too."

The woman who'd let them in walked in, pushing a rattling tea cart in front of her. Dante had to give the old man credit. He might have resented having cops at his front door, but he didn't do courtesy half-assed. A silver coffee urn stood proud among a cluster of heavy white mugs, and a smattering of delicate pastries did a pretty dance on saucers around a cream and sugar set. The mugs were odd, but from the housekeeper's practiced filling one of the mugs with a stream of steaming, fragrant black brew, then handing it carefully over to Archibald, the thick-walled cups were a house staple.

"I'll get my own, Rosa. Thanks." Rook sidestepped his grandfather's cane as the old man made a jab at his thigh.

"I *knew* her name was Rosa. God, you're a damned pain in the ass," Martin grumbled. "Help yourself, Detective. Looks like your partner's going to be a bit. Might as well get some Kona into you before I kick your ass out."

Archibald's hand shook slightly, and the man's fingers lost their grip on the mug's handle. As it tumbled to the floor, coffee splashed everywhere, mostly on the floor but enough—frighteningly enough—on the old man's trousers, probably scalding his flesh beneath the fabric.

Rosa and Rook beat Dante by a second, the woman daubing at Archibald's legs with a dish towel as Rook cleared the mug's shards from the floor, folding up the edges of a runner from under the old man's feet to catch every speck of broken porcelain.

"I'm fine." Archibald's grumbles grew coarser, peppered with profanity when Rosa disagreed. "I'll go change out of these clothes and be right back."

"I'll call the nurse to see if you've been burned—" Rosa stepped back when Archibald hefted his cane and shook its silver-tipped head a few inches beneath her nose. "Mr. Martin, she should have a look at you."

"I don't need that vulture to tell me if I've been cooked." He snapped a growl at Rook. "You keep the cops entertained while I'm gone. Or better yet, let this one finish his coffee, wrap up a danish, and kick them the fuck out of my house."

Stevens hovered for a second around the old man, earning himself a thump on the shin. Pulling back, he threw his hands up in surrender. "Fine. Fuck you. You want to turn into a *chicharrón*, go right ahead. Just make sure you leave me that fucking stuffed fox in your will."

"I hate that damned thing," Archibald muttered, hobbling toward the library door.

"Yeah, I plan on shoving it into your coffin right before they toss you into the dirt." Rook sneered at his grandfather's back. "Let Rosa get the nurse."

"Fine… fine. Call the fucking nurse. See if I care." The elderly man shook off his housekeeper's hand from his arm. "Just don't get yourself into too much trouble while I'm gone, or I'm not going to be the only one sitting in a dirty hole before too long."

Dante waited until the man left the room before turning to face Rook. "Charming man. I see where you get your winning personality."

"Cute." Stevens sidestepped the folded-up rug to fill two cups with coffee. After handing one to Dante, he added cream and sugar to his, then took a taste. "So, wait for the crimson Sasquatch you brought with you, or do you want to get right into it?"

Dante took the cup from Stevens only to set it down on a table. "You and I need to have a talk about—that night. In the club."

"*That's* got you worried?" He shrugged smoothly. "What about it? We were having a good time, then bam, lights on, and neither one of us finished. Pretty much all there is to say. Worried I'll spill the beans you weren't at peak performance?"

Stevens studied him over the edge of the mug, his ocean-sky gaze curiously wary behind his shroud of dark hair. He said nothing, waiting for Dante to make his next move, so Dante plunged forward, wary of his partner lingering out in the hallway.

Grabbing Stevens by the arm, Dante pulled him closer. "It's already on my record. I told Internal Affairs about it, but I don't know if my captain knows, but he will soon—"

"Look, even after all the shit you tried to drag me through, you should know I'm not that kind of person. I don't fuck with other people's lives like that," Stevens said quietly, his voice low and soft between them. "And I am *never* going to out you that way. Even if everyone on the goddamn police force knows. What happened there at the club was just something between us. Nothing to do with you being a cop and me being… well, me. If anyone finds out about it, it's not going to be from me. I promise you *that* much."

"LAPD knows I'm gay." Dante tried ignoring the strength he felt in Stevens's arm and the delicious masculine scent of freshly showered skin and vanilla soap. It was bad enough he'd pulled the man close enough to feel Stevens's breath on his face and see the slick moisture he'd left behind on his upper lip as he licked off a stray drop of coffee from his sip. He wanted to trace where Stevens's tongue had been and follow it back to where it lay in wait. "They just don't all know I almost fucked a suspect. And while I intend to keep it that way, if it comes out, it comes out. Just warning you."

"That was then. This is now. You're not planning on fucking me, and if you do, let me know so I can avoid it." Stevens hissed a bit when Dante tightened his grip. "Because you're a complication I don't need, Montoya. A fucking hot complication I'd love to slide down into my throat and up my ass, but still, not one I need. So either let go, or I'm going to make a mess of your pants with this coffee."

He really didn't know whether or not to believe Stevens. Not consciously. Yet some part of Dante's mind knew Stevens was serious about keeping his mouth shut. For all of his lying and thieving, Stevens had an honesty about him, an odd moral code probably only he understood but lived and breathed by.

Dante knew the power in the man's body, muscles and sinew hidden under loose shirts, but he'd felt Stevens's strength under his hands. He'd only had his hands on Stevens for a few minutes, barely fifteen in all, but they'd burned into his memory, molten seconds seared into the very grit of his being.

There'd been an odd trust then, in that moment of unknown between two men looking for something alive in the dead of night. He'd have to trust again, with something greater than his pleasure—his life as a cop.

Dante's captain still needed to be told. There were too many nontruths lingering around Vince's old cases, and the last thing Dante wanted was to be one of them.

"Tell me one thing, Stevens." Dante loosened his grasp but still held Stevens's arm lightly. "Did you know it was me? That night? Did you purposely put yourself in front of me?"

"You want the truth from me, Montoya?" Stevens chuckled, a low, husky roll hot enough to tickle Dante's already aching balls. "I didn't know it was you. Shit, I didn't even know you were gay. But that night, I saw someone I thought looked like the hot detective gunning for my ass and wanted it. So yeah, while I didn't know it was you, it was you I was looking for."

Hank's deep, barking laugh startled both of them. Rook pulled back, sloshing his coffee over the floor while Dante grabbed at Stevens's arm, yanking him to the side and out of the way. Hank didn't seem to notice the nearly guilty look they exchanged. Instead, he barreled into the room, took one look at Dante's hand on Rook's upper arm, and grinned.

"Good, you've already got a hold on him." Hank's grin grew wider. "Now turn him around and cuff him. We've got another murder."

THEY DROVE him to Potter's Field, then parked right in front, a near miracle most days in Hollywood, but when wielding the power of sirens, lights, and police batons, apparently pretty easy to accomplish. Rook sat quietly when the detectives got out of the car and pretended to consult with one of the crime lab people. But he sighed with disgust as, a few feet away, another cop stood with the same transient who'd tried to stop Rook on the night of Dani's murder.

As setups went, it was spectacularly bad, especially when it became overtly obvious they were asking the street-sleeper to identify him as he sat in the rear seat of the unmarked police car with his hands cuffed behind his back.

Rook didn't know what made him feel stupider, sitting patiently while the cops framed him for yet another murder he didn't commit or that he didn't get himself out of the cuffs a while back and on the run before they'd gone a block away from his grandfather's house.

"This is what going straight gets you, Rook." He banged his head lightly on the clear partition between the car's front and back seats. "Sitting in a squad car while some guy stoned off his ass is telling the cops you—"

He stopped, straining against the cuffs slightly to lean forward. Montoya was approaching the car, and by the look on his face, things were not well in the land of tall, dark, and Hispanic. Or possibly Latino. Rook wasn't sure.

Montoya unlocked the car door, then jerked it open. "Get out."

"Hispanic or Latino?" Rook asked, wedging his foot against the doorsill so Montoya would have to fight to pry him out. "Which one?"

"What the fuck?" Montoya's scowl deepened. As glowers went, it was a pretty impressive one, but Rook ignored the man's attempted intimidation.

"Which one do you use? Hispanic or Latin American descent? Wouldn't want to fuck it up when I'm describing you to my lawyers."

"Both. My mother's Mexican. My dad's Cuban. Either one works. So does *sir*." Montoya hooked his hand under Rook's arm and pulled, easily dislodging Rook from his perch. "Now shut the fuck up and come with me."

Rook stumbled a bit, trying to keep his feet under him. "Hold up. Let me repeat what I told you back at the house. Lawyer. Law-*yer*. Maybe even more than one. Shit, they're probably waiting for us. Hopefully with stun guns for you assholes."

"Shut up. I want to see if you can ID the bodies. Something's weird here. Weird even for you." Montoya's grip was nearly as punishing as the pace he set, dragging Rook across the sidewalk, then down the narrow alleyway toward the back of the building. "And don't think this is a get-out-of-shit card for you. I'm going to catch crap for doing this, but three dead people in a week is high, even for a troublemaker like you."

"Wait, bodies? Three?" Rook stammered, but Montoya didn't answer him. "Total or including Dani?"

There was a stream of cops they rode past, like skipping rocks over a mean blue wave. Their faces were mostly blurs. Some in uniforms, others in suits, but all with the same damning judgmental expression Rook'd been running from ever since he could remember.

Montoya's redheaded partner was there waiting for them, stepping aside when Montoya pulled Rook up past a cinder-block enclosure the surrounding buildings used to store their trash dumpsters and to the graffiti-tagged charity bin next to it. If the front was swarming with cops, behind the building was a murmuring of nearly every breed of civil service Los Angeles had on its payroll.

The parking lot and side alleys by his building weren't normally places he spent a lot of time. There'd never been a need to. A few trips to toss out his trash once in a while and a couple of steps across the sunbaked gray asphalt to get to his SUV parked in one of his three designated carports pretty much made up Rook's entire experience with the back lot.

Still, Rook was fairly certain he'd have remembered if there'd been blood splattered on the donation bin a few feet away from Potter's Field's back door. And he sure as shit would have recalled if it'd been stuffed full of legs and arms when he'd snuck by the cops to get into his apartment in the early hours of that particular morning.

One of the legs was female—or to be fair to the general populace in Hollywood, a very attractive indeterminate-sexed leg in a silk stocking and wearing a mauve pointy-toed high heel sharp enough to pierce litter if its wearer wanted to. The other limbs were poking up out of the box's large donation hatch, gnarled fingers tipped with bright green nail polish tangled in with a broken halogen lamp and cracked window shutters. Blood matted a shock of vivid gold-white hair dangling over the lip of the hatch, but Rook couldn't make out if the hair was real or a wig someone'd tossed into the bin in the hopes of brightening the day of a bald cross-dressing Carol Channing impersonator.

Rook was suddenly stuck on the shoe. Staring at it, he lost the ability to breathe. He'd seen that shoe. He'd teased Charlene about how they'd cut off the circulation in her toes, laughing when she'd told him they'd been on sale at the fetish shop near the Kodak. His legs didn't know if they wanted to pitch him forward or fold in on themselves. The drying blood seeping out of the wooden box's uneven seams drove Rook on, and he broke free of Dante's grip, shaking off the cuffs before he took three steps away from the detective.

There was noise, lots of buzzing, irritating noise, but Rook paid about as much attention to it as he did the arms struggling to hold on to him. He fought off the binding hands, a dirty brawl of punches, kicks, and bites he'd learned while growing up rough and untamed. His world spiraled down to a single pinprick of blood-splattered flame-red leather and its wearer's delicate pale foot sticking up out of a smashed-together twister of body parts and trash.

With the noise came a blow to his head, and Rook snarled, furious at being unable to reach the box. A strong pair of arms locked around him, and the sky tilted briefly into Rook's view as he was lifted off the ground. The world spun a bit, taking him away from the bloody box, and Rook twisted in the embrace imprisoning him against a solid wall of muscle.

"Stevens, take a breath. Please. I don't want to bring the paramedics over to tranq you. I *need* you here. Shake it off." Montoya's accent tickled Rook's brain, sending licks of reason to splash cold water over the rage burning through him. "Breathe, baby. Just breathe."

"Char.... Montoya, I think that's.... Charlene. Fuck. No." He choked, and his stomach rebelled, tossing up the coffee he hurriedly drank before joining the cops in his grandfather's library. Montoya cradled him, holding Rook's back into his hard belly, his arms pressing dangerously into Rook's tender stomach. "Fucking let me go. I've got to go... see."

"Listen to me. I need you to look at a few pictures. We've got faces, two women, and I want to see if you can ID them. We can do this here or at the station, but—I've got a guy over there that says you were here last night, and now I've got two dead women here. Something's off here, Stevens," Montoya muttered into Rook's ear. "So get your shit together and help me out."

"You think *I* killed Dani, you fucking asshole. And now Char?" Rook swallowed the sour tide washing up from his belly. He refused to puke in front of the cop holding him, but it was going to be close. "Fuck you."

"You might have had something to do with Dani Anderson, but I don't think you'd kill your assistant. Yeah, you're a lot of things, Stevens, but killing someone you've taken in? I've got doubts there. Now I'm going to let you go, and Camden's going to show you their faces, got it?" Montoya gently lowered Rook to the ground and grabbed him again when Rook's legs almost gave out. "Hey, I've got you. No worries. Okay?"

"You two done doing the salsa there, Montoya? Or are we going to do this thing?" Camden's disgusted look was met with a steady glare from his partner. "What?"

"That some kind of racial thing or gay thing?" Montoya asked in a low voice. "The salsa?"

"Shit, it just was a crack about the two of you whirling around the parking lot like you're at a prom," his partner spat back as he thrust a sheaf of papers at Rook. "Crimes took these a little bit ago. They tried to get just the women's faces, but it's hard to get some good angles. Whoever did this just shoved them in hard, so shit's a bit crazy in there. Take a good look, Stevens, and tell us what you know."

The photos were bad, dark and smeared pixels across a thin roll of paper used in portable printers. Resembling a heat-imprinted receipt more than an actual photo, the women's faces were lines of horror and overbright spotty grays, but Rook could make out enough of their features to welcome the sickeningly sharp feeling of relief he got when he realized neither one of the women were Charlene.

"Fuck, it's not Char. Neither one of them is Char." His stomach's taint was back, and he gagged on the taste in his mouth. "Jesus, thank fucking God, but… that's… a shoe. Charlene had those shoes on…."

"When was the last time you saw them?" Montoya pressed.

Rook looked up from the photos and did the one thing he never thought he'd ever do with a cop—be straight-up honest. "Last night. Well, more around three in the morning. I broke in. I was planning on red-lighting. Well, I was going to take care of Char. Wouldn't do that shit to her, but… she was already there. Picking through the closet because she wanted a costume."

"Jesus fuck, wasn't anyone watching the place? We had two cars here last night," Camden grumbled.

"Yeah, don't take this wrong, but most cops are blind, deaf, and dumb when they're sitting in a patrol car." Rook shrugged at Camden's disgusted hiss. "If they saw her, chances are they were too busy watching her boobs bounce around to see anything else. Hell, she makes straight women horny."

"Red-lighting. I take it that means you were planning on jumping bail and taking off?" Montoya asked. "What happened?"

"Char happened. She kind of talked me out of it. Told me to grow some balls and stick up for myself." There was a wall behind him, sticky with Los Angeles's grime, but Rook didn't care. He leaned back, grateful for the support. "She's blonde. Really blonde. I thought that was her."

"The blond is from a wig," Montoya reassured him. "It was probably in the bin when they were dumped. It doesn't look like either of the victims was wearing it."

His nerves were shot, and he was shaking, probably from lack of food and shock, but something bothered him about the photos. Shuffling the papers, he stared at one of the faces, studying the woman's slack-eyed expression and folded-in features.

"Recognize one of them?" Camden stepped closer and tapped the paper Rook held up.

"Yes. Maybe?" Rook squinted, trying to see through the blurry lines and into his past. "This one looks like one of the Betties, but I can't be sure. Hell, for all I know it could be both of them in there. It's been a while since I've seen them, and these are for shit."

"What's a Betty?" Montoya shushed his partner when Camden snorted. "Besides a hot chick."

"You know about Betties but not about the six-fingered man? Montoya, you've got shit taste in movies, dude." Rook shook his head and handed the papers back. "The Betties are… were… a couple of women who do whore stings. They work in teams. This is probably one of them… teams, I mean. Maybe?"

"Explain. In English." Camden motioned for Rook to continue.

"It's where a girl, or a guy, connects up with a rich, married guy and blackmails him for cash. Usually you'd want it to be a quick hit. Hanging around means the guy gets too used to the fear and finally says fuck it one day and either blows you away or calls the cops. Not my thing." Rook shook his head. "Seriously, this could be one of them. Char was friends with one of them… maybe both, but it's not like I keep track of everyone Char knows. That's like trying to find good literature off of the bathroom walls at Griffith Park."

"You're talking but not making much sense, Stevens." Camden took the page, folding it in half. "Give us something to go on if you've got it. This Betty got any connection to Dani Anderson?"

"The woman who ran the Betties' stings hated Dani. So did the couple of Betties I've met in the past. They used to run cons off of each other's marks if they could. That's how much they hated each other. Dani wasn't good at making friends." Rook frowned, looking up to see a man dressed in a bubble suit slowly ease a woman's arm out of the donation box. "But killing Dani and then the Betties doesn't make any sense."

"It does if you're the mark," Montoya murmured, grabbing one of Rook's wrists and cranking a cuff down on it. "I think you've got something in that shop of yours, Stevens. Something people are willing to kill for… or kill to prevent someone getting before they do."

"Dude, do you really think I murdered them?" Rook gasped when the cop wrangled his other wrist into the cuffs. "Shit, for a second there I thought one of them was Char. How fucked-up do you think I am? I didn't *do* any of this. What the fuck do I have to do to get you guys to believe me?"

"It's not that we don't believe you, Stevens," Montoya practically purred. "It's just that we don't trust you. And somehow, I don't think there's anything you could say or do to change our minds."

Seven

"I ALMOST fucked Stevens."

It felt good to finally say it. In retrospect—as their unmarked slid across two freeway lanes while Hank fought to keep the car under control on the slick road—Dante could have chosen a better time to confess his sins than when his partner was driving them from the station to the coroner's office.

Horns blared, and for a moment, the unmarked hydroplaned sideways, skimming over the oil drawn up from the misting rain. A second later, the tires caught traction, and Hank spun the wheel into the turn, narrowly avoiding a lumbering old Buick held together by rust and duct tape. They were nearly in the clear when a motorcyclist skirted the slow-moving behemoth, nearly plowing into the front of their car. Hank hit the brakes, smoking the air with a thick, stinking gray cloud before jerking them to the relative safety of the slow lane. Easing them off the freeway, Hank swore as a rush of air from a passing semi buffeted the heavy car as he coaxed the shuddering vehicle to a taco stand's half-empty parking lot.

Los Angeles continued on with its day, churning cars and people about on a carousel of noise, clutter, and rain-soaked chaos. A few blocks away from Union Station, the causeway was packed with tourists and locals hurrying to reach the train platform and avoid the grimy slush splashing up from passing cars. The walk-up taco stand's makeshift tin roof chimed low tones as the rain struck it, the water running down its length and splashing onto the uneven asphalt below. An old Mexican woman peered out at them from the shanty's side window, her hands moving quickly as she worked a flour tortilla into a flat round. She ducked back into the darkness when Dante smiled, but he could hear her scolding someone in rapid-fire Mexican about salting a pan of cooking pork.

The sedan rumbled softly, and Dante felt his heart finally slow down from its panicked beat. Shaking his hands out, he asked softly, "We going to park here and talk, or do you want to get a free shot in while I'm carsick from your driving?"

Hank turned off the engine, waited a moment for the car to settle down, then turned to Dante, practically spitting as he struggled to speak. "What the fucking hell?"

"Stevens. Me. In a club." Whatever relief he'd been expecting for his confession seemed to be missing, and Dante was left with the heavy push of his stomach cresting into his throat. "Before this. Way before this. Back when Vince and I were chasing down the whole damned ring Stevens was a part of. I was looking for a hookup, and shit, it was almost him. Well, it was him. We just didn't… it didn't get that far."

"The case Vince fucked up. Crap. Is that why he did it? Vince, I mean. Did he plant that shit on Stevens to protect you?"

"Vince—I don't know why Vince did it. He didn't have to protect me. I didn't *do* anything. Shit, even IA barely blinked, but I don't know. Maybe he knew we were going to go down and thought if he put their eyes on him, they'd ignore me." Dante rubbed his face, tired and worn-out from the day. "And before you ask, the captain already knows. I told him before we left the station, but—"

"He knew from before. It's why he didn't want to give us the case. Because he already knew you had an almost thing with Stevens." Hank opened and closed his mouth several times, wringing his hands around the steering wheel. "Jesus, Montoya."

The captain'd been hard. Going into the man's office ready to eat crow and be kicked off the case had been a given. Book's annoyed expression and grunting dismissal had been like standing in front of his father and admitting he'd been the one to crash the family car. Internal Affairs had done their job, smearing his record with veiled references to inappropriate behavior, and Dante couldn't say one damned word to the contrary.

He'd been the one to walk into that club looking for a piece of ass to take his mind off the man he'd been hunting. It was just bad luck he'd found out exactly what Rook Stevens tasted like that night.

Even worse, he hungered for yet another sip from the man's mouth, despite knowing down to every single cell in his body that Stevens was nothing but bad news.

Finally, Hank sighed. "I don't know what the fuck to say, Montoya. This is…."

"I should have told you as soon as I took him down, Hank. I just didn't…."

"Just tell me there isn't anything else, Dante. Spare me any more revelations." Hank groaned softly. "And for God's sake, are we still primary on the case? Or has he handed it over to his favorite pet, O'Byrne?"

"We're on the case. Captain's got no one to give it to. O'Byrne's stacked up, and so is everyone else." Dante gave his partner a rueful smile. "And no, there's nothing else. But truthfully——"

"God help me. What else have you got up your sleeve, Montoya?"

"I don't know if Stevens did it. The murders, I mean," Dante ventured. "I want him to be…. Fuck, you have no idea, but…. Camden, I don't know."

He'd stared at Stevens's face when Rook broke down in front of him. There'd been fear in the man's odd eyes, fear and horror at what he saw before him, then the spark of relief when he realized his friend wasn't among the dead. Dante'd seen his share of liars and cons, smooth-talking actors able to fake nearly everything but the fluttered rush of a panicked heartbeat and the sting of terror under their gulping inhales. Stevens feared for his friend's life, mourned her in an instant of heartbreak and sorrow. Dante felt the pain in Stevens's body as it worked through him. A man couldn't fake that ache—not without being soulless and cold.

And for all his flaws and cunning, Rook Stevens was definitely not cold.

"I don't think it's in him. It all feels… weird… off-weird. I can't explain it." Dante shrugged. "My gut says we're looking at it all wrong, but he's the one covered in blood. So that's my take. He's not who we're looking for."

"Yeah, I kind of figured that," Hank grumbled. "You thinking he's innocent. Could have called that before I found out you played grab-the-weasel with him."

"Oh?" Dante frowned. "I *just* decided that before you tried to kill us."

"You called him *baby*, Montoya." His partner shot him a dirty look. "I was just trying to figure out how the fuck to bring *that* up. Thought maybe you'd gotten soft on me. Didn't know you'd already gone hard on *him*."

"Didn't get that far," Dante protested. He tried to recall what he'd said when Stevens fought him, but for the life of him, all Dante could remember was the feel of Stevens's long, hard body against his and the warm scent of vanilla soap on the man's skin. "And shit, I didn't—baby? Really? Damn it."

"Between you and me, not a problem." Hank started the car, prompting the *abuelita* inside the taco stand to pop her head out again. This time both men waved, and her returning scowl made Hank laugh. "I'm not convinced Stevens isn't ball-deep in trouble with this shit, but I guessed you'd say he was good to walk. As much as you want to nail him for what happened back in the day, you wouldn't pin him for this if you weren't sure. I just didn't know you wanted to nail him for other things too."

"You sure it's not a problem?" Dante asked. "'Cause I'm having a problem with it all on my own. He's… a complication."

"Nope, not a damned problem," Hank replied. "Just don't put your prick in him until after he gets clear of the charges. Got it?"

Snorting, Dante said, "What makes you think I want my prick even near him?"

"Because I saw your face when you called him baby, Montoya." Hank put the sedan into drive, then checked the mirror to see if the car was clear to go. "You want in his ass so hard, *I* can almost taste it."

THE CORONER'S brick building dominated its corner on Mission, an officious-looking edifice built with a nod to East Coast architecture. Solid and red, the main structure was the center of the coroner's compound, a stamp of authority among lesser pale gray buildings squatting at its stone foundation and swallowing up a good portion of Los Angeles's milky blue sky as the partners drove in.

Dante thought the place stood out like an angry ruffled cardinal among the pale, sparrowlike city buildings surrounding it, a disgruntled preening autocrat forced to wallow with the area's toiling peasants.

They drove to the back, narrowly missing a meandering pack of visitors intent on shopping at the department's gift store. A tour guide smiled tightly, then mouthed *take me with you* as Hank eased the sedan by. They kept driving, leaving the woman to herd her charges up the main building's enormous steps.

Inside the cold rooms, the playful macabre atmosphere changed, growing serious and heavy with the smell of the dead. Hank coughed as they walked toward the examination rooms, bringing out a tin of strong peppermints from his jacket pocket. Shaking a few out, he handed one to

Dante and sighed happily when he popped a couple into his mouth, obviously relieved at the mint oil's effects on his nose.

Dante was smart enough to slide the mint into his mouth and suck on the pungent lozenge. No matter how cold the morgue kept its hall, the dead worked their way through the building, reminding everyone who worked there or visited of their existence. Under the bitter cold in the air lingered a flat, oily smell, an unpleasant aroma subtle in its presence yet acrid enough to trigger a primal fear of decay and rot in the most primitive corner of his brain.

Rochelle O'Rourke was already hard at work on the women from the crime scene when the partners walked in. A British import, she hummed and half sang as she walked around the room, her startling purple hair pulled into a ponytail and tucked up into a cap to avoid contaminating her work. Her scrubs were visible through the thin layer of protective coveralls she wore, bleeding dancing lavender and red cats through the white fabric. Compared to the room's sober grays and steels, she was an eye-stunning block of color nearly vibrating across their line of vision as she moved.

"Hey, Rochelle, what do you have for us?" Hank edged into the coroner's peripheral vision, startling her.

"Camden. God, you're an arse. Warn a girl." She nearly edged Hank with her elbow, giving Dante a quick smile. "Why haven't you killed him yet? I'd have done him in a long time ago if I had to share a car with this git."

"Because everyone would know I'd done it?" Dante quipped.

"Shit, you're not killing him here, are you? 'Cause if you are, I'm going to go on break, and you can do it without any witnesses. I'll even turn off the cameras for you." Rochelle stepped closer to the table she'd been working at before they'd come in. "Stay out there. Mind the line, now, and what the hell are you two doing here anyway? It's too early for me to do anything on these two. I don't even know which piece goes to what head yet."

"Just wanted your prelim," Dante reassured her. "We weren't even sure there *were* two."

"So far, based on the legs, arms, and heads I've got, I'm going with two. If something doesn't match up once I'm done matching the bits, then I'll revise." Rochelle reached under a bled-gray limb and lifted it up carefully, turning it around to see if it matched one of the trunks she'd laid flat on a nearby work table. "Not as much mess as I'd expect. Too much damage to the skin and flesh but not a lot of blood."

"So killed elsewhere," Dante commented softly as Hank began to take notes, "and then brought to the scene."

"Scare tactics?" Hank muttered under his breath. "The other one, Anderson, she was killed onsite?"

"I think so, but I didn't catch that one. Could have been just killed and dumped on the scene. Are these all connected, then?" Rochelle turned the leg, carefully manipulating it into place. The squeak of latex on skin was disturbing, and as Rochelle aligned the limb, she checked the torso. Frowning, she sighed. "God, whoever did this is very sick. Get out of the way, Camden."

"I'm not even near you." Hank shuffled back.

"I can see you. That's enough." The examiner bent over, skimming her finger inches above the severed leg's end. "Rough cuts. Someone didn't know what they were doing. I have to wait until tox gets done with their runs to know if they were drugged, but what I can say is the cutting happened after they were killed."

"Definitely not at the scene." Dante's partner rocked back on his heels. "We're going to have to shake Stevens's tree a little bit. See if he knows anyone who'd want to kill these two. Processing should be done with him by now. If some asshole hasn't let him walk out the front door."

"Can we get the pictures as soon as you get them done? We've got the prints, but those are going to take a bit. Walking through facial IDs helps. That assistant of his might know who they really are if Stevens doesn't." Dante examined one of the severed heads. Unable to step in closer without suiting up, he squinted, trying to get a better look at one of the victims' faces. "Are they identical twins? Or did the women just try to look alike? The one on the right seems a bit off. Different from the other one?"

"Women?" Rochelle looked up from her leg matching. "I don't know how to tell you this, Montoya, but that one? That's a man, baby."

IT'D TAKEN a bit longer to shake himself out of the cops' hold than Rook would have liked. Too many protests and a phone call got him wiggled free before Montoya and Camden returned to pull his teeth, but the whole ordeal left him uneasy—and indebted further to his grandfather.

Sliding past a patrol car parked too close to his back door for his liking, Rook muttered desperately, "Fucking Archie is going to own my soul if I'm not careful."

Archie was Satan, complete with contracts and fiery hells. He liked the old man, but Rook didn't need his mother around to figure Archie out. The more threads and obligations the old man could wrap around someone, the better he liked it, and Rook was at his own breaking point. One more favor called in, and Rook was going to ask the cops to just throw him into a prison cell and lock the door behind them when they left.

"Rather go to prison than dance for *anyone*." He dug his keys out of his pocket, eyeing the wall of blue uniforms standing near his SUV. "Fuck, that's not a coffee table. Don't put your damned cups on the hood of my car. Assholes."

The lot behind the shop was definitely off-limits. Even with the clearance to go into the shop so he could assess the damage done to the front room, Rook's skin itched when he spotted the sea of people combing the parking lot behind his building. From what he could make out, investigating a crime scene mostly involved wandering around and talking up a bullshit storm while a couple of people crawled about on their hands and knees looking for needles in a haystack.

Working his key into his shop's back door lock, Rook breathed a sigh of relief when the tumblers clicked apart. "Now to get out of this mess and see what kind of shit hole they've left me in here."

Potter's Field was silent. Too silent for Rook's liking. Even from the back of the building, the eerie quiet of the front salesroom reached through to halls and seeped into the storage areas near the rear door. The main storage area seemed untouched except for a few large boxes someone'd taken down and left open. Most of the toys had been moved around, shuffled about on shelves and tables, but for the most part, it was a disorder he could deal with.

The front would be a different matter altogether, especially after Dani's life was left drying on the floor. The hallway to the front seemed like a long walk to a fate Rook wanted to avoid but couldn't. His Converses made squeaking noises with every stride he took, and he paused to take a breath before taking those final few steps. Beside him, a knockoff 1960s robot standing at the end of the corridor slowly flashed away the seconds, and Rook braced himself for the damage, then stepped out onto the main floor.

It was worse than he could ever imagine.

The first time he'd snuck in, there'd been no time to take a good hard look at what the cops and their ilk had done to Potter's Field. Even before hitting the switch to the storefront's floodlights, Rook could make out the devastation to his shop's interior.

Turning the lights on made him want to weep.

Dani's blood streaked black and flaky swaths near a smashed-in display case, smeared out from a curved negative space where her body had been. Speckled with glass from the window, the floor sparkled with tiny diamond-like shards, the tempered scales throwing back the white and blue beams caught on their edges. Nearly every case bore some sign of distress, and at least two were total write-offs, bullet holes shattering their frames and glass. The small ticket items he'd used to chum casual browsers were ruined, dusted with the same residual fingerprint powder that coated nearly every surface in the shop.

They'd also shot the shit out of his Wookie.

Rook ached inside. He'd poured every bit of his life into the shop, nearly every second of his time, working to bring Potter's Field to a point where he could say he'd made it. On his own. With no help from anyone else and not a con taken.

Now it lay in ruins at his feet, and he was suspected of killing people he might have actually wanted dead in his not-so-recent past.

"Why Dani? And why the Betties?" He skirted the blood smears, his Converses squeaking as he made a quick turn. "Dani, sure. We've got some history, but the Betties? I don't even know if the dead ones are the ones I know."

The large case he'd set up as a wall between the front and the back of the store was broken as well, but from what he could see, the movie props he'd placed there were intact, although he couldn't say the same for the enormous papier-mâché griffin he'd found at a Harryhausen tribute auction. Peppered with bullet holes, its body and head were marred with crumbling white holes, a scatter pattern large enough to make Rook's stomach turn.

"Shit, they were trying to kill me." He leaned back, trying to do a visual count on how many bullets pierced through the window and into the shop while he'd been plastered to the floor to avoid being shot.

"Go in but do not touch." Rook echoed what his grandfather's lawyers told him, trying to absorb the destruction. "I can't even move without touching something. And how the hell am I going to document the damage? What isn't damaged? Fricking lawyers."

"Are these the same lawyers that told you to return to the scene of the crime and screw up any residuals that might be here?" Montoya's deep voice rumbled out of the darkened doorway leading from the storefront to the elevator up to Rook's apartment. "If they wanted you to be thrown into jail, they could have just left you there instead of this catch-and-release program we've got going."

Montoya looked… good. Again. Too good. Too ruffled, too scruffy hot, with broad shoulders and his burned-honey eyes fringed with thick, long lashes. A hint of a dimple threatened to spread when his mouth quirked to the side, and Rook had to swallow around a lump in his throat when Montoya shoved his hands into his jeans pockets, sliding his black leather jacket back with his elbows to expose his gun harness.

Even from a few feet away, the man was a tall, dangerous complication in Rook's life. One he wanted as badly as he didn't want him around. Rook wasn't sure what was worse—being accused of murder or being tailed by a man he'd gladly bend over for but who wanted him in handcuffs instead.

"What are you doing here, Stevens?" Montoya's rumble tickled Rook's belly, licking hot flames down his crotch and over his ass. "You shouldn't even be here. What were you thinking?"

Rook had just the smartass answer to throw back at the detective. A burning slap of a sting mingled with a bit of a flirtation hot enough to make the man blush. It would have been an epic moment. One to balance out the unbearable want Montoya seemed to rake up inside of him and caustic enough to push the man's buttons while pushing him away.

"You can suck my—" Rook's face exploded with pain, shearing a line of hot red along his right cheek. Another followed, pushing him around as it pierced his arm, overloading his nerves with a shock wave of anguish.

There was a flash of mottled colors, a gold and ebony weight hitting him so hard Rook saw stars, then felt the ground slide around to slam into his shaking body. He blinked, trying to wash away the sticky red clinging to his vision, but the world turned viscous, miring him down with a heavy suction he couldn't fight. For a split second, he caught sight of Montoya's handsome face pressed in close against his and then the barrel of a gun silhouetted against the store's overhead lights.

Rook fought to recall what he'd been about to say, but the pain was too deep, burrowing down into his belly, washing away everything he'd been thinking of except for the odd, comforting heft of Montoya's body on his. Then the agony took him over, and Rook let the encroaching darkness eat him alive.

Eight

THERE WAS a split second of chaos followed by mayhem.

In the moments between Stevens's come-fuck-me smile and a burst of blood exploding across his cheek, Dante lost a decade of his life under a tidal wave of fear and confusion. Another shot rang out, slicing through Rook's upper arm, and Dante dove across the distance between them, slamming the lanky man to the ground.

Bringing his gun up, Dante covered Stevens with his body, resting his hand across Stevens's face to protect his eyes from flying glass and wood when another bullet broke through the boards nailed over the empty panes from the last shooting. Beneath him, Stevens moaned, twisting under Dante's hips in a profane mimicry of sexual release.

The shots came sporadically, a single, then two booms, right after one another. Plywood splinters peppered the air, arcs of sharp, acrid darts thick enough to sting where they struck. Dante ducked, shielding his eyes by burying his face in Stevens's thick hair. He could feel Rook's frantic heartbeat pounding away, beating out an unsteady tattoo on Dante's jaw.

It was over after one final boom. Then a silence settled down, breaking apart in a rush of noise as the sounds of loud voices and screams rippled over them. The scent of blood—Rook's blood—was in the air, the smell of terror and metal too familiar for Dante's liking, and he waited until he was certain the shooting was over before he lifted himself up to check on Stevens.

Dante did not like what he found.

They were both sticky with Stevens's blood, trails of dark red pouring from a deep crease in his arm, and Rook seemed to be in shock, his long lashes fluttering madly as his pupils blew outward, turning his odd-colored eyes almost a demonic black. He mumbled something as Dante turned him over then fought any attempt Dante made to lift up Rook's bloody shirtsleeve.

Sirens sounded nearby, drowning out the mewling noises Stevens was making. There were footsteps, pounding leather on cement, and the familiar chatter of cops working through the scene, calling out when areas were clear. The sound of a rolling metal door going up rattled behind Dante, and he gave a quick glance over his shoulder as a pair of cops crept around the doorway he'd just come through.

"You okay, Detective?" Another detective, female and looking young enough to make Dante feel old, swept the room with her eyes, gun held up at the ready to give Dante cover. "Are you hit?"

"No, civilian's down. Need a wagon in here. Two GSW, one probably serious." Dante rattled off the address. "Call it in. I'll see what I can triage."

Tugging the shirt made the wound bleed more, and a sliver of fabric slipped out of the hole when Dante finally was able to work the sleeve up Rook's arm. A quick glance at the man's cheek reassured Dante the arm wound was the one to worry about, but the lump forming on Stevens's temple made him pause.

"Great, trying to protect you, and I bash your head in." Dante tore at Rook's thin T-shirt until he got a long strip he could tie around the bullet wound to stave off the bleeding. Rook's eyes followed Dante's face, but as far as he could tell, the injured man was drifting in and out of consciousness. "Hold on. I hear the ambulance coming. I'll go with you when they take you."

"'Toya." Rook's head lolled forward, sending his hair cascading down over his face. Strands caught in the blood splatter, smearing threads of red across the man's pale skin. His hands clenched at his side, kneading the air like a cat. Then he reached up and grabbed Dante's jacket in a surprisingly strong grip. "Hurts."

"You're not going to die, if that's what you're worried about. Just try to stay awake until the EMTs get here and they can get a look at you." The lump on Rook's forehead swelled up enough to form a ridge under his hair, and Dante frowned, not liking the man's unfocused expression. The cotton scrap he'd fastened over Rook's upper arm began to drip crimson, saturated by the leaking wound. "And they need to hurry the fuck up."

"Shhhhh, trying to tell you something," Rook muttered darkly. "Listen, fucker."

Keeping one eye on the door, Dante leaned in. "What?"

"Next time you throw me down, there better be a damned bed under us, not the floor." His voice was a soft whisper, and his body slackened against Dante's arm, but Rook held on as he tried to focus on Dante's face.

"First time you fuck me, there'd better be warm sheets and a soft pillow under my ass. Forewarned, Montoya. Forewarned."

"HERE, WIPE the blood off of your face." Hank sidled up to Dante, holding out a damp towel. "Medics check you out? You didn't get hit, did you?"

"Nah, blood's his." The towel was cold, a shock to his overheated skin, and the wet terry cloth felt good as he rubbed at his jaw. "I'm fine."

Dante wished he could somehow do the same to his nerves. His innards churned into a knot, refusing to loosen even when the medics assured him Rook would be all right. The gunshot wounds were minor, and the bump on Rook's head was more than likely a very mild concussion, nothing cataclysmic, and after a small whimpering confession on the woozy thief's part, they'd discovered he couldn't stand the sight of his own blood.

And there'd definitely been a lot of that.

Hollywood seemed determined to empty itself out into the street. The sidewalk became a partial carnival of uniforms and supposed witnesses, half a dozen stories being told all at once and with conflicting results. According to some of the people he'd overheard, the shooter had been either a tall black man with a red beanie or a slump-shouldered Latino driving a Buick. The forensics team fell on the front room like locusts, and as they buried themselves in discussions about telemetry and blood splatter, Dante realized it would be a very long time before Stevens got his shop back.

Hank nudged him gently. "They say where they're taking him?"

"Yeah, they're getting him over to St. Vincent's. I gave them his grandfather's contact information but told them I'd make the call. I left a message with the housekeeper. Archibald Martin is out with friends and doesn't carry a phone on him. She's going to call his driver."

"Must be nice. I feel like I can't even take a shit without the thing."

"That's something I could have lived without knowing." Dante made a face. "I'm about done here. Want me to drop you off before—"

"Let me guess. You'll be heading over to St. Vincent's to hold Stevens's hand," Hank drawled. "Don't give me that look. You were all ready to sing Celine Dion to the fucker from what I could see when I came in. All you needed was a damned iceberg and a diamond necklace."

"Is that another gay crack?" Dante stopped wiping his face and glared at his partner. "'Cause it if was…."

"No, if it was a gay crack, I'd have said something about ruby slippers, but I couldn't work it in." He stepped aside to let a workman carrying plywood pass by. "It was about me finding you making goo-goo eyes at a guy you know is a piece of shit."

"Not arguing about him being a piece of shit." Frowning, Dante peered at his reflection in a squad car's side mirror. "Just don't think he murdered anyone."

"Yeah, neither does the captain. I was coming to tell you he'd called when hell broke loose. Stevens's been cut loose. DA's dropping all charges on your boyfriend." Hank shrugged as Dante turned in surprise. "Yeah, shocked the shit out of me too."

Dante whistled low, shaking his head. "What happened? Stevens's grandfather has that much pull?"

"While I don't doubt that, no," Hank replied. "Someone ran his plates for warrants. Standard procedure before they impound it to forensics. Your boy apparently caught the end of a yellow in Santa Monica twenty minutes after O'Rourke called time of death. Camera snap shows his entire face. So unless he's got a twin brother we don't know about, there's no way he could have killed her."

"And he definitely didn't transport Anderson here. It was confirmed she died on-scene. What about the vics in the bin? Do they have anything else besides pieces and parts? We dragged him in on that because it looked connected."

"Gore squad was focusing on Stevens's SUV because it was a kill-and-carry, but nothing pinged on their machines. Doesn't look like it was used for transport, so he's clear of the Bert and Betty murders. Martin and the housekeeper gave him an out, but until we know when and where those two were killed, it's still kind of shaky, but they're not looking at him for it."

"Change of game." He grimaced, trying to look at the case without Stevens in the middle of it. "We're back to square one. Only thing we had was Stevens. Might be all we have now. Shooting today confirmed it."

"Yeah, unless he paid someone to fling bullets at him to make him look innocent, but if we start going down that route, might as well make some tin-foil hats and wait for aliens. Kind of grassy knoll shit there."

"Too big of a risk, Camden. Stevens takes risks but not that kind. Up until a couple of days ago, he'd steered pretty clear of anything violent." Dante frowned. "Might want to go through the old files I've got stashed. It's been a while. Vince might have had something sketched out on Anderson. I was focused more on the break-ins. He caught the associates and connections."

"Yeah, good place to start if Stevens can't give us anything." Hank nodded toward the building. "Why did he come here? What was he looking for? Do you know?"

"Didn't get a chance to ask a lot of questions." Dante made one last swipe at his face with the towel. "Shooter lit the place up, but from what I caught, lawyers told him he could come by. I think he wanted to see what was left of his shop."

"Yeah, hard to tell what was from the rookies going crazy because they saw Chewbacca in the window and whoever is after Stevens." Hank grinned at Dante's confused look. "One of the babies in blue coughed up that he thought he saw a gun. Turns out it was that furry mannequin Stevens had by the counter. Guess in the dark and with lights flashing around, you could mistake a Wookie for a viable threat."

"It's a fucking seven-foot-tall hairy dude with a crossbow thing. How could you *not* know it wasn't real?"

"Don't look at me. I'm not the one who went Duck Hunt on Stevens's ass." Hank threw his hands up in mock surrender. "So, word of advice, once you go kiss Sleeping Beauty awake, see if you can get him to tell us anything about the weirdos someone stuck into the Goodwill box. Between the chopped-up bits and their brilliant use of acid on their fingertips, we can't get a good ID on who those two actually are. Lab's going after dental, but that'll be a long time coming."

"He kind of left me with the impression they were grifters. Definitely a Vice game. We should see if Rackets got any papers on them. Might be something to chase down there." Dante mulled over the possibilities. "His assistant's got priors. Mostly soft cons and a supposed solicitation, but that went the way of Stevens's convictions—wiped clean of everything but an honorable mention. Rook seems to be the only thing connecting Anderson and the pair we found in the back. I'd give my left nut to get a hold of this Canada woman. She's got a lot of information we need."

"Think Stevens told her to run?" Hank leaned against the squad car, his eyes roaming the crowd. "Wouldn't be out of character for him to split, although he's wedged in pretty tight here. She might not be."

"I'll ask him that too," Dante offered. "So, you coming with me or asking one of the blues to drop you off at home, *culero*?"

"Nah, you go get on your white horse and gallop to the hospital. I'll find my own way home. Just a bit of advice for you, don't be surprised when your Prince Charming turns out to be a frog." Hank tsked as Dante flipped him off. "Being honest here, Montoya. I don't want to see you get hung up on a pretty face, then have your heart broken."

"Don't worry about me, Camden," Dante reassured him. "I'm not looking to fall in love. And if I did, it sure as hell wouldn't be with Rook Stevens."

THE AIR stung Rook's lungs, biting through his chest to leave a searing icy burn down his torso. There were more burns, too many for him to keep track of, and he lay still, his eyes closed in an attempt to keep the warm darkness close. Unconscious was better than the frigidity waiting for him, and he grunted, fighting off the wakefulness threatening his sleep. Something went tight around his arm, and Rook shifted, uncomfortable at a chilly bite.

Then a much-too-familiar golden voice poured over him, chasing the chilly licks on his skin away with a sensual heat Rook longed to sink into.

"Come on, *cuervo*. Time to wake up. I can hear you thinking under there."

"Don't want to. You'll arrest me for murder or something," he grumbled back. "Just let me sleep."

"Can't do that. The hospital people will want their bed back at some point." Montoya jostled him lightly. "And do you want your grandfather to find you like this? The old man will sell your kidneys or something if you're not awake to catch him."

"God, it's like you know him. Trapdoor spiders hang posters of that man on their webs as inspiration." Rook opened his eyes and immediately wished he hadn't. The room was searing bright, digging into his eyes and gouging out what little sense he had left in his skull. Blinking, Rook made out the Hispanic detective looming over him. Smirking, he muttered,

"Nice as you are to wake up to, if we've fucked, I don't remember. Shit, I feel like I've been microwaved to death."

"Yeah, you'll be fine. You're already complaining." Montoya shook his head and pulled out of Rook's view. "You were starting to swear at someone in your sleep. I figured it was time to pull you up out of it."

As hospital rooms went, it was a nice one. There were comfortable armchairs and fine art on the walls, a private sanctuary Rook was certain his grandfather's name had a hand in securing. For all he knew, the old man was somewhere nearby, pulling strings as Rook lay in a stupor, strung up like the puppet he was becoming. Still, it was better than most places he'd recently been, including the dull green cell he'd had courtesy of the Los Angeles Police Department.

But it was just another prison—although it certainly came with better eye candy than the vomiting heroin addict he had for company while Montoya and his partner tried to pin Dani's death on him.

"What happened?" He tried sitting up, propping himself up on his hand, but his elbow folded in on itself, plopping him back into the bed. His memory fuzzed in and out. He recalled walking into Potter's Field, then Montoya sneaking up on him, but the rest of it was caught behind a gray veil. "Shit, a bit dizzy here. Why am I in here?"

His arm ached, and his face seemed stiff on one side. Touching his cheek solved the question of why he couldn't move his nose. A stretch of gauze and tape went from his jaw up to his cheekbone, and from what Rook could tell, Boris Karloff's makeup artist had gotten a hold of him, wrapping him up tight with yards of bandages and more tape.

"You were shot." Montoya skirted the bed again, reaching for a cup of ice chips. "Nothing serious. Crease on your cheek and a dimple on your arm. Went through the meat—"

"Went through the *meat*?" Rook felt the blood leave his face. "Like through my arm? Then what?"

"Then you fainted. Manfully. It was very manly. Medics thought you might have passed out from the pain. Or it could have been when you hit your head on the floor. They've checked to see if you've got a concussion, but other than a lump, nothing major. Just rattled your already shaky brain." The detective jangled the cup at Rook. "Here, bend your head forward. I'll tilt it up so you can get some in you. No food for a while."

"Screw the… whatever the hell that is. Who the fuck shot me?" It wasn't pretty, but Rook's voice suddenly jumped a couple of octaves. A brief flicker of memory slithered around Rook's brain, mostly the painful hit he took when Montoya took him down. "Wait a minute. I hit the floor because you *tackled* me. What happened to just screaming *duck* or something? Next time I'm under you, I better be fucking awake for it, Montoya."

"Chances of that happening are none to never, Stevens. And I tackled you because someone was shooting at us. Well, you in particular. We don't know who the shooter is. By the time the uniforms got around to the front, the place was chaos. Guy could have been standing right there in the crowd, watching the whole thing, but we'll never know." Montoya jiggled the ice again. "Get some of this in you. You're dehydrated as it is, and IVs only do so much."

Rook took the ice chips, slurping up a mouthful when Montoya angled the bottom of the cup. Chewing was difficult. The gauze and tape sculpture on the side of his face felt like he was a fossil being prepared for transport, and chewing only made things worse. Rook swallowed and shook his head when Montoya brought the cup back up.

"No, I'm good. Too fricking cold." He shifted in the bed, then reached for the bandage on his cheek. "Stitches under here?"

"Butterflies, I think. What are you—?"

"This." Rook tugged at the bandage, steeling himself for the eventual pain, then ripped it clean off his face. He got a quick thrill out of Montoya's wince. "For my next trick, I'm yanking this needle out. Now who do I talk to so I can get out of this place?"

"You are going nowhere, Stevens. The doctors want you in here for observation. I'm hoping it'll stick." Montoya's expression went unreadable, but his eyes were hot. "Would kind of be nice to know where you are for at least twelve hours. Can't seem to keep you in jail long enough to question you, and now it looks like someone's trying to kill you."

"Yeah, it's a laugh a minute around me." Rook gestured to the stack of machines near him. "This doesn't work for me. I want out. Or am I under arrest again? Still? Again? I'm not even sure what the hell is going on anymore."

"What's going on is your car was picked up on a traffic camera as the light was turning red about the time Dani Anderson was being killed. The timeline for you killing her doesn't add up, so you're free and clear." The detective pulled a metal chair up, then sat down. "So you're either the luckiest son of a bitch, or you can somehow drive from Santa Monica to Hollywood in thirty minutes."

"Not at nine o'clock at night on a Saturday. Shit, I don't think you'd be able to do that even after the apocalypse and all the roaches are left driving Dodge Darts." He lay back, unsure about the lightness in his chest. Dani was still dead, and someone killed her in his shop; that much he knew. Relief was a great thing, but the hole in his arm told him he wasn't out of the woods yet. "Fuck, then who killed her and the Betties? And why the hell shoot me?"

"Don't know," Montoya admitted. "And that diamond she had? They're testing to see if it's fake. One of the lab guys called shenanigans on it."

"Yeah, usually more than half of them are. You'd be surprised how many fakes I got doing jobs—" Rook blinked. "Shit. What the hell do they have in that IV?"

He'd broken. A cup of ice chips, a set of hard broad shoulders, and a rolling hot accent and he'd broken. Montoya grinned at him, catching the bandage Rook flung away. Montoya's sweet act and the lump on his head did him in. That or he was getting soft and lazy. He'd been so careful, denying everything and admitting nothing, refusing to give the cops even a whiff of maybe to latch onto. And he'd just handed Montoya a thread to hang a confession on if the detective chased it far enough down the rabbit hole.

"I know you're a thief. That's not a surprise. I might not have caught you at anything, but I'm not stupid, Stevens. You're just slippery," the detective informed him. "I just didn't think you were a murderer. Hank and I... well, mostly me at first, but something was off from the beginning. I wanted it on you. I did. For all the shit you pulled in the past, but this one—this one isn't on you. So while formal charges aren't dropped yet, it looks like Camden and I are back at square one."

"And the cops shooting at me? At the store?"

"*That* is under investigation. Call came in that there was a gunman. You were there, and someone saw... something." Montoya had the grace to look abashed. "The first detective on the scene thinks it was one of your props. There's a few issues. IA is going nuts with it."

"Told you I didn't kill her." Rook scratched at his cheek, careful not to dislodge the butterfly bandages affixed to his skin. "Any of them. I just don't know who did or why."

"What can you tell me about the Betties? You said your assistant, Charlene, knew them, but she's been hard to find." Montoya rested his elbows on the edge of Rook's bed. "Tell me where to go, Stevens. Who knew them? Who *are* they?"

Rook eyed the IV needle piercing his arm and nodded to the door. "The Betties? Shit, spring me out of here, Montoya, and I'll tell you everything I know. Hell, most of it might even be the truth."

Nine

ARCHIBALD MARTIN proved to be Montoya's savior. The elderly man arrived just as Rook was mounting his campaign to be set free of his hospital bed, and a flurry of angry words from Stevens's grandfather quickly set the matter to rest. Satisfied his now informant would be someplace he could be found, Dante headed home, leaving Stevens behind in his hospital room.

It was Dante's bad luck that Rook Stevens didn't stay there in spirit. Out of sight and out of mind didn't seem to apply to Stevens, and despite everything Dante did to distance himself from the long-legged thief, Rook slithered right back into view.

The man clung to his thoughts, flashes of sexual heat and frightening worries mingling in Dante's mind until he was left marinating in a perplexing soup. He wanted Rook. There was no denying that. Being around the man made Dante's skin itch, and even as bullets were slamming through the air inches above his head, his body responded to the press of Rook's spine and shoulders against his belly.

Rain drops spun wet pinwheels on his windshield as Dante turned onto his street, noticing his next door neighbor hadn't brought in her trash bin. After parking his truck, he retrieved the elderly woman's cart before shuffling his back into place by the garage. Shaking the rain off his jacket and hair, Dante let himself into the back door and smiled when he smelled Manny's *carne guisada* simmering in a Crock-Pot on the kitchen counter.

"*Mijo*, is that you?" his uncle called out from the living room. "Are you staying for dinner?"

"I was planning on it, *tío*." He toed his shoes off, then slid them into the plastic shoe hanger hooked over the mudroom's back door. Padding into the front room, he spied his uncle sprawled out in a recliner, his feet tucked into a ratty pair of bunny slippers. The television was on, but the sound was muted, leaving Dante with a silent tableau of two older Latino women overacting a scene involving a red vase. "How long until it's ready?"

"About an hour. I thought you'd be later, but here you are." Manny looked up from a word-search puzzle book, peering over a pair of half-moon reading glasses. "Are you busy, or do you have time to help your old uncle?"

"Find me an old uncle, and I'll be happy to help him."

"Flatterer, but I shall take it." Manny preened, patting at his silver-shot hair. "I need some help with my hair. I always miss the back. Silly, no?"

"Let me go change, and I'll be right back down." Dante shrugged off his jacket. "Anything you need, *tío*."

TWENTY MINUTES later, he found himself snapping on a pair of latex gloves and waiting for Manny to settle on a short stool. His uncle ruffled the hem of the plastic cape he'd draped down his shoulders, then swung up onto the seat, wiggling until he was comfortable.

"I am ready." Manny flung his arms out. "Do your worst to me, for I shall not talk."

"Can we not say things like that?" Dante admonished his uncle. "Don't you remember having a black streak down your nose for two weeks the first time I helped you do this?"

"Ah, I remember that. Try not to do that again. It's bad enough I can't do my own hair. Evidence of incompetence doesn't reassure clients." His uncle sniffed. "I just told everyone it was an elaborate ash ritual gone horribly wrong. Hair only, *mijo*. Hair only."

Armed with a comb and a brush, Dante parted his uncle's thick hair and began to dab hair dye along the line. A few minutes in, Manny began humming an old song from the '70s, and Dante joined in for a moment, stopping when Manny sneezed. Dante blessed him absently, murmuring in Spanish as he daubed the brush back into the dye for another pass.

"Thank you for doing this for me. I know this isn't how a young man should be spending his Friday nights. There are a lot better things to do besides help a fat, old Mexican get rid of his gray hair." The tinge of sorry in Manny's voice made Dante stop.

"You're not fat or old." Dante made a show of examining Manny intently. "The Mexican I can't refute, and I don't know why that would be a bad thing, gay or straight. Weren't you the one who told me there isn't just one type of gay? Just like there's no one kind of person?"

"*Mijo*, look at me. I became your *abuelita* when I wasn't looking." The older man rubbed a hand over his chest, crinkling the plastic. "I even had the breasts, but, well, the cancer took those. Which I suppose is a good thing, *no*? Or I'd be catching them in my belt when I put on my pants, just like Mama's."

Dante pulled out another stool, then straddled it, ignoring Manny's alarmed protests of getting dye on the vinyl seat. Facing his uncle, Dante leaned in, tugging at the cape to catch his attention.

"I am going to say this again, and I want you to remember this, *tío*. I am here because I want to be here. We are *familia*. I am a better man for having you in my life. The day they closed their hearts against you is the day they threw away a gift God gave them, proving they are blind and stupid." Montoya lightly tapped his uncle's head with the brush as he began to protest. "Uh-uh, I hear you talk like this, and I think I hear my grandfather or my own father, and that is not who you are. Remember, *tío*, they tried to bury us. They didn't know we were seeds."

"I know… I know," Manny murmured. "I feel… old sometimes. It's hard sometimes to look in the mirror and see… *me*. That old queen, you know?"

"You say queen like it's horrible to be that. If you want to be a queen, then be one. If you want to be a go-go boy, be that too. You are who you are, Manny." Dante placed a hand over his uncle's, gripping the man's fingers tightly. His uncle sniffed again, then wiped at a tear on his cheek with a twist of his arm. "I am proud of the man I call *tío*. And if he wears high heels sometimes, I just wish he wouldn't break his neck going down the porch steps, but I will kill anyone who says anything against him."

"You're a good boy, *mijo*. Even if you've just turned my hands black like a beggar." Manny snorted despairingly at Dante's distress. "I'll rub the leftover dye on it when we're done. It'll come right out. Should have done that with my nose that time. Finish up, and I'll feed you. When was the last time you ate?"

"Okay, in some ways, yes, you are becoming Grandma." Dante reached for the brush again when his cell phone chirruped from where he'd left it on the table. Frowning, he stared at the unknown number as he tugged off a glove. "Hold on, Manny. Let me get this."

"I'll put dinner on simmer. Phone calls usually mean you go out and I end up watching bad telenovelas," his uncle grumbled.

"Montoya," Dante barked into the phone.

A woman husked a breathy whisper, barely audible above the traffic noise on the other end of the line.

"I'm sorry. I can't hear you. You have to speak up. Who is this?"

"God, I can't believe I'm calling the *cops*," she rasped, lifting her voice up loud enough for Dante to make out what she was saying. "You're that detective that arrested Rook, right? Do I have the right number?"

"Yes, this is Detective Montoya." His brain clicked, adding Rook to a column containing a woman wary of authority. "Charlene Canada? Did Stevens tell you to call me? I need to talk to you about a couple of people Stevens identified as the Betties—"

"Here's the thing, Detective," Charlene replied in her half whisper, all-sex-kitten voice. "Rook's gone. Like gone from the hospital, vanished. He just walked out when no one was looking. That gargoyle he calls a grandfather is having puppies over it, and I don't know where Rook went. So if you want to talk to me about the Betties, help me find Rook. Before that guy who shot him finds him first."

LEAVING THE hospital seemed like a good idea at the time. Standing in the chilly wind whipping through downtown Los Angeles wearing only a thin T-shirt and a battered pair of jeans made Rook rethink his life choices, especially after the painkillers in his system went the way of the dodo and he was left feeling battered from head to toe.

Los Angeles rumbled a sleepy growl from its perch on the California coast. There were parts of the city that churned and bubbled no matter what time it was, and Rook was walking right into its belly. The Fashion District was the best place to get lost in, or at least on its edges where it ran into Little Tokyo. Long spans of empty, weed-choked lots lay at Downtown's feet, land too valuable to give away but too expensive to develop. Even parking structures, a much-desired commodity in LA, weren't worth the effort. Nothing viable or profitable was nearby, and until Little Tokyo took another yawning stretch to absorb another few blocks, the worn-down area wasn't going to see gentrification any time soon.

It was the perfect place to get lost until he was ready to be found again.

"Fucking Montoya. Seriously, yelling *duck* works. No need to relive old football days." Rook rubbed at his bare arms. "Okay, Stevens. Get the fuck going and go under."

The fight with Archie had been quick and brutal, a slash of words and anger. Rook found a dark place within him, and he'd flung them out with a deadly aim. His grandfather fought back, hemming Rook in until he felt like he couldn't breathe. Advice was one thing. Having his life taken over by an old man with an agenda was something entirely different.

Suing the cops for a fucked-up arrest was out of the question. In Archibald's world, doing something that stupid was apparently like shooting a warning shot off someone's bow. For Rook, it was slapping the wolf in its face after he'd missed the first time. All it did was piss the wolf off, and it would be right back on his ass, right after it was done sharpening its teeth.

Nothing whetted a wolf's appetite for Rook-ass like a long round of sharpening teeth.

His cell phone was practically dead, and since most of his things were at the Castle Martin, Rook had to be conservative with what little energy it had remaining. Calls from Charlene went unanswered, as did the numerous jingles from Archibald's house.

It was late. Or early, depending on how he looked at things. Breaking out of a hospital was harder than he'd thought it would be, but then Rook had little to no experience with health care. Living on the show circuit meant skirting too close to the bone on money, and by the time he'd found a use for his flexibility and quick fingers, he'd already learned how to walk off a broken arm.

The rippling anguish from the gunshot wound was a sign he was getting soft. Confessing to Montoya he'd pulled fake diamonds on a job was another chink in his armor. He'd been an idiot to turn to Archibald and a moron in thinking he'd be able to control their relationship as he'd done countless others.

Never give away the upper hand. A bitterly learned lesson. One he'd learned before and one he certainly wouldn't be repeating with Montoya. No matter how much the man pushed every single one of his buttons and made Rook want to spend a lot of time doing filthy, sticky things to him.

"Hey, man, you got a dollar?" A grimy man stepped out of the shadows when Rook passed by a slim alley.

He shook his head and kept walking, keeping an eye out to the side as he turned the corner. The beggar's profanities chased him down the street, and as if on cue, another man, larger and dirtier, slid out of a dress shop's doorway.

The element of surprise shifted on Rook's side, because he evaded the man's initial grab with a spinning twist that took him one step onto the street.

"Got no time for trouble, man." Rook held up his hands, more dismissive than apologetic, as he kept walking. "I've got nothing on me."

His long legs gave him enough distance away from the second man before he had time to recover, not sticking around to hear if the man decided to play the sympathy card or would have strong-armed him into giving up his wallet.

A wallet holding a few burner cards, just like the ones he'd given Charlene.

They were the sum total of his temporary independence and the pieces of plastic Rook had no intention of giving up. He needed space to think—time to breathe. Hurrying past the Angel's Flight station, he spotted what he was looking for, an old W-shaped brick-and-concrete hotel sitting on the corner a block and a half away. Bristling with fire escapes and broad windows, the four-storied hotel was the perfect place to set up shop and hunker down.

If his arm hadn't been killing him, Rook would probably have seen the tiny speck of a car screaming up the hill as he crossed the street. The red domestic was barely a thimbleful of glass and plastic, but its driver caught the slope at the right speed because it jumped off the asphalt and careened toward the sidewalk. The car grazed him, its passenger-side mirror clipping Rook on his hip, and the momentum of the hit spun Rook about, slamming him to the street.

The blacktop gouged at his palms, and his knees screamed in pain when his jeans were torn open on the rough street. Twisting, he rolled over onto his shoulder and tucked himself into the curb. Another car passed by, the wind knifing a stinging kiss to his torn-up hands and raw knees, and Rook covered his head, trying to avoid getting hit again.

Off in the distance, the tiny red car continued to careen through the street, its wee engine screaming with the effort of climbing the hill.

A heart-pounding eternity later, he creakily got up and stared out at the empty dark street. If he'd hurt before, he'd gone into full agony.

Lurching down the sidewalk, Rook made it to an all-night convenience store. A few minutes and many odd looks later, he headed to the hotel, trying to keep scraped-up hands from sticking to the plastic shopping bags he'd packed with what he needed.

At some point in the six months since he'd spotted the hotel and buried its existence in his memory, it'd undergone a semirenovation. Brighter and cleaner than the last time he'd walked through its doors, the place was still staffed by smiling people who seemed oblivious to the fact Rook hobbled into their lobby dressed in road-rashed clothing and whose only luggage was four plastic bags smeared with a bit of blood.

The room was everything he expected, musty and a bit worn around the edges. Stripping the bedspread off the mattress, Rook resisted the urge to fall face-first into the pillows and sleep off his pain. His hands were shaking by the time he got four ibuprofen out of the bottle he'd purchased at the store, and a glance in the mirror was enough to convince him bribing the clerk to let him buy a bottle of whiskey had been one of his better life decisions.

Lack of sleep and food dragged his skin down to a pasty gray, and the bandage on his arm was beginning to lift up at the edges, probably from when he'd rolled around in the gutter to avoid getting hit by another car. After stripping as quickly as his injured body would let him, Rook twisted his shoulders to get a good look at the triangular bruise forming over his rib cage. It was a glorious splash of watercolor purples and blues with a promise to go full spectrum in a matter of hours.

"Well, at least not another scar." He examined the area again. The skin was tender and a little bit hot, but bruising he could take. His hands and knees were another matter.

His body definitely wore its time on his skin. Living in a roaming trailer park with temperamental carnies was an experiment in Darwinism best looked at with *Lord-of-the-Flies* spectacles. Small nicks marbled his hands and feet, bits of meat chewed out by equipment, ropes, and boards. Training to be a knifer, he'd sliced his hands and arms more times than he could count, and spending his childhood lacing and working the midway hadn't helped.

But Rook couldn't remember a single damned time when he'd felt as worn and beaten as he did right then.

Peroxide helped clean out the scrapes, and Rook carefully plucked away any bits he saw embedded under his skin with a pair of sharp tweezers. His ribs were beginning to hurt by the time he was done, and his arm was nearly numb from pain. Gently easing off the filthy bandage around his shoulder, he grimaced at the line of stitches marching across the muscle. They pulled when he reached into the shower to turn the faucet on, and Rook hissed at the nearly unbearable sear of pain when the hot spray hit his torn-open skin.

"Fuck, that's maybe a nick. I've been knifed deeper than this." It was a small consolation but one that bolstered his tender ego. "I probably passed out because you slammed me into the goddamn floor, Montoya."

He wasn't sure what drove him out of the shower first, the water turning icier with each passing second or that he couldn't stand up any longer.

His phone continued to sing and dance its way across a nightstand, happy to be connected to an outlet and getting juice. A few more from Charlene and a string of texts from his grandfather, coldly impersonal and abrupt orders to call the house so he could be retrieved and brought back into the fold.

"Yeah, got one of your monkeys to send those, didn't you, Archie? Like you'd know how to work a phone." Rook collapsed onto the bed, grateful for the mattress's thick padding. Whatever corners the hotel cut to keep costs down, pillow-tops apparently weren't on the list. "This is damned comfortable. Either that, or I'm so fucked-up I don't give a shit anymore."

Cradling the phone in his hand, Rook eased onto his back, naked and welcoming the heat kicking up from the unit next to the bed. He had a half thought about closing the room's drapes but realized he really didn't give a shit if anyone saw him.

"Not like I'm filming pornos or something," he muttered. "Fuck, what the hell is going on?"

Hunger was a fleeting thing. Swallowing the analgesics on an empty stomach guaranteed he wouldn't want anything for a while, a bitter afterwash climbing back up his throat to sour his tongue. His head hurt where he'd struck it, and his brain seemed folded into layers of cement he couldn't break through.

"Okay, figure this out, Rook. Who the hell would kill Dani and the Betties? And who the fuck would leave them on your front porch?" There were too many names and faces connected to grudges, but he'd always dealt fairly with everyone he'd run jobs with. Even Pigeon, the Betties' handler, would *never* kill off two of her assets just to rattle Rook's cage.

"One thing, that woman's all *these are my children*. Once a Betty, always a Betty." Rook stared up at the ceiling, counting the cracks radiating out from one of the overhead pendant lights. "Dani, though. She pissed a lot of people off, but murdering her? Shit, why? And why me? 'Cause she was the one who backstabbed *me*, not the other way 'round. What the hell connects all of us?"

They'd never all worked a con together. He barely knew Pigeon, and he'd given the hive-mind Betties as wide a berth as he could.

"That diamond. Setup on Dani's part? Did she bring that to plant in my place to fuck me over?" Rook frowned. "She didn't work doors. Needed someone to trip locks and alarms for her. Who'd she trust to bring into my place? Unless they were looking to rip me off, but shit, none of this makes any damned *fucking* sense."

The sick hit hard, wrapping around Rook's stomach and cutting through his body. He tried to roll off the bed, but he only got as far as the edge of the mattress when he lost the battle with his innards. Choking on a rush of bitter water and half-dissolved pills, Rook gagged on his own tongue when he tried to spit out the last dregs. Another wave rose, and he couldn't hold back, nearly screaming as his retching twisted his abused body. The room dimmed, and Rook felt the bed slide out from under him, but he'd not moved an inch, clinging to the edge of the mattress.

Another burble from the phone in Rook's hand, but this time he fumbled to answer it, not caring who was on the other end. The world went sideways again, and he finally tumbled, collapsing into a heap on the room's scratchy, cheap carpet. It was damp on his skin, and for the life of him, Rook couldn't figure out why, but he definitely knew the voice shouting his name through the phone's tiny speaker.

"Stevens!" Montoya's silken rumble dissolved into a roll of hot Spanish, prickly words Rook learned from the transient workers on the circuit. "Where are you? What's going on?"

"'Toya, think I'm sick." His muttering was nearly lost in another course of water he'd somehow had left inside of him. "I need some help, man. Shit, Dante, I really need you."

Ten

"*DIOS*, STEVENS, you look like shit." Montoya sighed, hooking his hands under Rook's arms, then lifting him back up onto the bed. The floor was wet and smelled. While the damp was probably Rook's fault, the smell probably came with the room. "Well, at least you're alive."

"Hello, my name is Montoya. You killed my suspect. Prepare to die." Stevens wiggled his fingers as if he expected Dante to know what he was talking about. "Come on. Really? You *really* don't know that movie? Best movie ever. Maybe. God, so many movies. If my last name was Montoya, I'd totally want Inigo as a nickname or something."

"You're not a suspect anymore, and I have no idea what you're talking about, but if you get up on the bed, I'll watch the damned thing." Moving Rook was like handling a greasy wet noodle. Six feet of bendable, bruised, and sensual body, a naked Rook Stevens was proving difficult to maneuver. "Help me out here, Stevens. Get up on the damned bed so I can take a look at you."

"Dude, I'm not wearing any clothes. How much more of a look do you need?" Rook slurred.

Dante didn't like the heat coming off the man's skin or the pale tinge of green on Stevens's face. In the time it took him to find the hotel Rook mumbled over the phone line, he'd given himself an ulcer wondering what the hell his former suspect had gotten himself into.

The hotel's location hadn't done Dante's already tortured nerves any favors. Sitting like a misplaced mole on skid row's temple, the brick building did its best to hide its flophouse origins but to no avail. The cramped, musty room reeked of old skin and bleached-out mold, and Dante was less worried about Rook's gunshot wound than he was about the bacteria Rook smeared over his body when he hit the carpet.

Rook gave a halfhearted roll with his hips, brushing Dante's thighs, then oozed onto the mattress. Throwing his arms up, he shot Dante a silly grin. "Ta-da!"

Despite the splatter of bruises, dried blood, and stitches, Rook Stevens was adorable, and Dante hated himself for noticing.

"Are you drunk?" He was trying not to look at Rook's thickening cock as it lengthened down Rook's thigh. "I thought the hospital said you didn't have a concussion."

"Probably not when I left. I probably smacked my head again when that car hit me." Rook's gleeful expression was quickly replaced with panic. "Gonna throw up again, Montoya."

Dante got the trash can to the side of the bed in time, just as Rook rolled over onto his stomach. If the bruises on Rook's hips and shoulder were startling, the massive tracts of purples and blues on his back were horrifying. He rubbed at Rook's shoulders as the jerking retches took over, stopping only to offer a bottle of water when Rook gasped for breath.

"I'm going to have to get you to a doctor. What car hit you? Where? Did you see the driver?" Dante peppered Rook with questions, throwing a blanket over Rook's hips. Dante angled the bedside lamp's shade up to get a better look at the man's pupils and was relieved to see they were relatively normal. "Talk to me, Stevens. What happened? Why'd you leave the hospital?"

"You want car or hospital?" Rook sipped at the water bottle, his hand shaking so much Dante helped him tip it up.

"Both. Someone tried to kill you today. Where did this happen?"

"No one I knew. She ran the red light and screamed up Third. Or at least I think it was a she. I didn't get a good look. I don't think she was *trying* to kill me. Just kind of almost happened. I ended up on the curb." Rook shrugged, and pain poured into his eyes. "Shit, okay, I might have hit the street kind of hard, but dude, I needed to… get out of that place. So I left."

"Checking out against medical advice—"

"Yeah. I didn't wait for that either. I just walked out when no one was looking," Rook confessed softly.

"God, you are the—" Dante didn't hold on to his English and slid into a round of curses his mother would have been ashamed to hear him say. "I'm getting clothes on you and taking you to the ER. No bitching or complaining. Understand?"

"Fine." There was a bit of muttered grumbling, but Rook appeared resigned to the trip. "Just one thing. I kind of don't have anything to wear."

"HE'S NOT breathing." There'd been no mistaking the blond bombshell in the hospital lobby for anyone but Charlene Canada. Built like she should have been painted on the side of a World War II bomber, Charlene was a teetering tower of bright yellow hair, red lipstick, and curves. "Do you breathe when you throw up? He was throwing up when they took him. Isn't that how people suffocate? Because I don't think you can breathe if you're throwing up."

"He'll be fine. Did you bring clothes with you?" Dante wasn't going to question how Rook's assistant got to the Urgent Care before he did, but she'd already set up camp with two comfortable chairs, a table, and cups of steaming coffee.

"Oh, yes. Let me give it to them." She pursed her lips. "I'll be right back."

Somehow she'd also managed to talk someone into giving her actual plates to put a stack of homemade cookies on, and from the appreciative look on the male clerk's face as they walked past the front desk, Charlene Canada definitely made an impression. She tottered about, her generous hips swaying as she walked over with cookies and a duffel bag to the nurses' station. Smiling benevolently, she leaned forward to give the duffel to one of the male nurses.

"It's for my boss, Rook. He's back there." A few seconds and a cookie later, the duffel was on its way to where Rook was being examined and Charlene was heading back toward Dante. She settled into a chair, then picked up one of the coffee cups from the table. "They're going to make sure he has it. I even bought him some underwear, but he'll probably hate it. He only likes boxers. I keep telling him those do nothing for his ass. Don't you think?"

What Dante'd seen of Rook's ass, it didn't need much help from a pair of underwear. Pushing aside the image of a naked Rook spread out over a cheap hotel bed, he shook off the stream of confusion Charlene seemed to weave around him as she spoke.

The Urgent Care intake area ebbed and flowed with activity. There were long minutes of solid noise. Then a whispering silence crept in once people were moved back to the examining rooms. Double glass doors swished open periodically to let new patients into the beige and powder-blue cocoon, most wearing the dazed expression of someone caught in things they weren't quite ready for.

Dante knew that look. He had it on his face when he'd found Rook lying naked and crumpled into a ball in his grubby hotel room. Now with Stevens in the hands of doctors who could possibly talk some sense into him, he turned his attention back to his case and the blonde actress Rook seemed fond of.

"How about if we talk about the Betties?" He'd hoped by bringing Charlene to the hospital, he could leverage some information out of her. "That was the deal, right? I find Rook, and you tell me what you know?"

"He's still… you know, hurt. Suppose. he needs something and I—" Charlene's lashes fluttered hard enough to ghost a breeze across the small table. It was either her lashes or the breathy whispering she affected, but the look on his face must have told her she wasn't going to get very far, because she sighed hard, and her shoulders slumped. "I don't know what I can tell you. Not really. I mean, there's—you're a *cop*, you know?"

"That's what my paycheck from the city says," Dante agreed. "I also know Rook's in a bad place because someone is trying to frame him, kill him, or both. You can either help me catch that person, or you can stay quiet and help them kill Rook. Your choice, Charlene."

He'd hit the right note because Charlene nearly crumbled in on herself. Picking at her cup's zarf, she began to peel away a layer of cardboard as she kept her gaze pinned to the floor. "Pigeon will know I talked to you. It's just not… you don't talk to cops."

"Will this Pigeon person do something to you if you talk to me?" He pressed in, leaning forward to reassure Charlene. "Rook said something about Pigeon working with the Betties. If you tell me about the Betties, is Pigeon going to hurt you?"

"Hurt me? Pigeon wouldn't hurt a fly. It'll just screw up anything the Betties have going. Well, she's not running them anymore. She went clean too. Do you know how hard it is to run a long con?" Charlene's remorse was gone in a flash, replaced by an incredulous smirk. "It's not that I don't want to talk to you. Well, I don't. I mean, no offense, but it's just not… we don't talk about stuff like this. It's just not right. You don't know—"

"I know that they're dead, Charlene. Someone killed Dani Anderson. And maybe the same someone killed your friends. It's not just about Rook. Three people are dead, and I need to catch their killers."

"Because it's your job?" She looked up at him through her lashes. "Now that Pigeon's out, the Betties work too—"

"It's more than a job, Charlene. I *owe* these people the peace they deserve. It's my... I can't explain it to you better, but it's what I *have* to do. It's a part of me. They need justice for what's been done to them."

It was difficult explaining what was a fundamental truth, something so ingrained in him Dante couldn't imagine *not* being a cop. The only time he'd not stood up for what he believed in was the day his father beat him out of the family, throwing him away from the only home and life he'd known. If anything, those final moments of blood and pain cemented his resolve. He was going to love another man, spend his life with someone who had a dick, balls, and probably as many issues as he did. He was going to wear a badge and fight for anyone who couldn't fight for themselves. With each shuddering, painful breath, Dante *knew* he'd die without any reservations about who he was or what he wanted to be.

Justice, no matter what the victim had been or did. Murder was murder, and if Dante had anything to say about it, no one with bloodied hands would walk away without paying the price for someone's life.

"If someone murdered you, Charlene, wouldn't you want someone like me to catch them?" He took the cup from her hands, setting it down on the table. "I don't know which Betties were left behind Potter's Field. No one does. Not really. But that doesn't mean I'm not going to find out who killed them. Because no one deserves to be forgotten and thrown away. *No one* deserves to die unnoticed."

Charlene sat so still Dante wondered if he'd gone too far, shared too much with the woman. Then she gasped, pulling in a body-shivering breath. Nodding once, she finally raised her head enough to meet Dante's gaze, then said, "Okay, Mr. Montoya. I'll tell you about the Betties."

"FIRST THING you should know is, the Betties you found? They're not the ones I know, because I called Jane and Madge and they're still alive," Charlene confessed over her coffee. "So those two? I think they're new or something. You'll have to ask Pigeon, but I don't know if she knows them either. They might have just riffed off of what she did. You know, making it their own. People do that all the time."

"Does Pigeon have a real name?" Dante looked from the notepad he was using to jot down Charlene's information. "Or is she like Rook and named after a bird?"

"Rook? I don't get it." Confusion muddied Charlene's blue eyes. "I thought he was named after a chess piece. The little castle one, you know? Anyway, Pigeon's real name is Deb. We all call her Pigeon because her last name sounds kind of like it but...." She paused. "You probably don't want to hear all of that."

"How about if we stick to the Betties? What did you mean those weren't the ones you know?" Dante began to diagram out the relationships, starting a box with Deb/Pigeon and working downward to his two murder victims. He called up the close-cropped photos of the latter two victims' faces on his phone and showed the images to Charlene. "Are you sure you don't know them? Stevens said you might."

She studied the images, then shook her head. "I mean, they all try to look alike. It's part of the scam, right? But you totally can tell which one is which if you know them. Those two look like Betties, though. So either they're Pigeon's, or someone's running the same con."

"What kind of con?" Dante sighed as Charlene shook her head. "Okay, so say if a con was going to be run. How would someone do that?"

"Oh, like explain how it all happens without saying for sure Pigeon's doing it? Rook talks like that sometimes. All pretend. Okay, sure." Charlene's smile glittered. "So say someone like Pigeon runs a bait and switch. She finds a really rich mark. Then one of the... B-women gets up a relationship with him or her... 'cause we're all about equality these days. After they've been together a bit, they figure out what's good to take, and then one day when the first one is out with the guy, the second B-woman comes in like she's been there a thousand times and takes what they agreed on. Then it's a split because the P worked out who to get close to."

"So if there's a doorman or security, they're used to seeing this woman coming and going." Dante sat back in his chair. "What about the fingerprint erasing? Do they all do that?"

"Like what? Like the whole sandpaper thing?" Charlene wrinkled her nose. "Why? People just wear gloves. Rook used to do gloves or superglue, but the Betties don't run jobs like he used to. Fingerprints aren't going to... shit, I just spilled the beans on Rook. He's going to kill me."

"I spent three years trying to get him into a jail cell. You're not telling me anything I don't already know." It was a shameful truth but a truth just the same. "Let's just say I'm happier in Homicide. I'm leaving chasing after cat burglars to someone else now."

"Well, they won't be chasing him," she sniffed. "He's gone straight. Okay, not like sexually straight, because you know, he's kind of a waste for us girls, but he doesn't do B and Es anymore. He wants to be a businessman. And he's a good one. People call him all the time to get them some of that weird sci-fi stuff, and he knows how to get his hands on it. Kind of like a con but totally legit. You know?"

"Yeah, I know." Dante finished up his diagram, then drew a box to the side. "So what about Pigeon and Dani? Any way they're connected? Bad blood? Good friends?"

"Oh, Pigeon wouldn't give Dani the time of day. Dani was in it for herself, but Pigeon isn't like that, so they fought a lot. I don't know if they even really talked anymore. But if Dani needed something, Pigeon would be there for her. I know it." Charlene glanced over her shoulder when an orderly came out of the back. "Do you think Rook's almost done? How come no one's come out yet?"

"They needed to see if he broke his head open." Dante grimaced. "I'm pretty sure he didn't. It'd take a nuclear bomb to get anything through that thick skull of his. Charlene, I need you to focus for a second. Why would Pigeon help Dani out if they didn't like each other?"

"Because they're sisters." The look Charlene gave him left Dante with no doubt she thought him dim. "And even if you hate your sister's guts, if she needs you, you have to be there for her. It's kind of what family is all about."

"DON'T SEE what was wrong with the last hotel. It had walls and a bed," Rook grumbled at Dante as the cop led him out of the elevator and onto his room's floor.

"And roaches to hold the door for you when you came in. Maybe I just wanted you in one with less vermin." The sarcasm in the cop's voice barely stung, but Rook felt it just the same. He pulled a plastic key out of his jeans pocket, then paced off the room numbers, dragging Rook behind him. "Ten fourteen. Here you go."

Unlike his previous room, this room was large enough to swing a cat in. Not that Rook would swing a cat, but the saying could only be stretched so far without seeming silly. He actually could have given a shit about the amount of space he had, cat-swinging or otherwise. The only length and width that mattered was the king-sized bed up against the suite's bedroom area and how soon he could get to lying on it.

He ignored the view out over Los Angeles's bustling streets and even the single-cut expensive coffeemaker on the kitchenette counter, focusing on the bed nearby, then contemplating the soft-looking couch set in the middle of the loft-style suite to break the area up into two rooms. Sure it was nice but definitely more expensive, and he felt... accessible, traceable even. One thing Rook did have to admit—to himself—the place definitely smelled better, but he'd be damned if he gave Montoya that much to hang his smug grin on.

And man, that cop's grin was smug.

Rook ignored that too.

He was tired down past his marrow, but Montoya lingering nearby made Rook's skin itch, chasing away any stray cobwebs he might have had in his brain. At the hospital, he'd been reluctant to hand over the cop's leather jacket, half convincing himself it was for the warmth, but the rational part of his brain quietly informed him he was a fat liar that lied, because the moment Rook went to shuck the garment off, his heart began to pound furiously.

Because tossing the jacket aside seemed like he was peeling Dante Montoya off him. And Rook Stevens, thief and heartless con, did not want a damned husky-voiced, hot cop to let him go.

"Fucking pansy." The room swayed, and he reached for anything to hold onto, narrowly missing a solid grab on the room's love seat. He tumbled forward only to find himself slamming into Montoya's back. "Shit, sorry. Fuck."

"When was the last time you ate, Stevens?" Montoya's hands were hot on his waist, sliding under the oversized leather jacket and over the stupidly expensive T-shirt Charlene'd brought for him to wear out of the Urgent Care clinic. "I can call up room service. The front desk said it's staffed around the clock."

"Nah, coffee's fine." He wanted to step back. Step away. Step anywhere away from the cop who'd shoved himself into Rook's life like he belonged there, but there wasn't a single muscle in Rook's body agreeing with the rational part of his brain. "I don't know if I can keep anything down yet."

"How about less coffee and more tea? You need to get some of those pills they gave you down, don't you?" The heat was gone, stolen away when Montoya slid him onto the couch, then left to investigate the kitchen area. "Might help you sleep. The doc said if you've got a concussion, it's so mild they really can't tell, but your blood sugar was low. Probably that, lack of sleep, and adrenaline fatigue made you loopy."

"Yeah, they gave me some juice after they were done zapping me." Rook watched Montoya intently when the man leaned over to poke around in a minifridge hidden behind a cabinet door, and he wondered how the hell his life got so fucked-up that he was wondering what a cop would taste like in his throat. "I feel better."

"Hah. Found something for you." Montoya came up with a bottle of pomegranate juice from the wet bar, and Rook winced, not wanting to guess how much the hotel would charge him for it. "Don't give me that look. I'll expense everything out to the department if you want. They'll pay to feed you while I ask you a couple more questions."

He couldn't take it anymore. Not for long. Rook'd been rolled over by life and shaken down to his core. Between the battles with his grandfather—fights he no longer even knew what he'd been fighting about—and the delectable rub of Montoya's body near his own, Rook was tired of fighting. He was sick of running, and most of all, he just wanted a bit of *normal* in his life. It'd been the dream he'd been chasing. A chance to wake up in the morning, get some coffee, and then maybe go back to bed and have sex with someone he liked, someone whose name he remembered.

Hell, he'd even been ready to get a dog or a cat, just to make the whole domestic thing real, but the thundering arrival of police, bullets, and then a sloe-eyed man who'd been a wet dream of his for years put an end to all of that. Now Rook just wanted… he wasn't even sure anymore.

Except for the wet dream.

His tall, bulked-up Hispanic cop he'd seduced in a club once as a self dare, only to discover the man's kiss whispered too many promises for Rook to ignore. He'd known who he was hooking up with that evening. When the cop stalked out of the darkness surrounding the dance floor, Rook's stomach clenched as his ass practically begged to be spread apart. Shit, he'd wanted Montoya to fuck him against the wall until he couldn't breathe, but something broke in him then. He wanted more than a single night. More than a con or a grift. He wanted to fucking wake up next to someone and have them be *glad* to see him instead of showing him the door.

That night, Rook realized he'd never have the white picket fence and calico-curtained bungalow. Not if he continued on the path he'd been walking. That was the night he'd gone clean. It was also the night he'd seen himself reflected in Montoya's eyes, and he hadn't liked the disgust he'd found there.

"Answer me something." Rook tried to work his sneakers off but gave up.

"Sure, what?" Montoya put the juice bottle on the table in front of the sofa, looming over Rook. The man was too close, too tight in for Rook to do anything but inhale him. A second later, Montoya shoved the bottle of juice aside and sat down, his legs straddling Rook's. "What do you need, Stevens? You thinking of taking another run?"

"Truthfully, I can barely *walk* as it is," Rook replied derisively. "Besides, if I took a run, you'd just chase me down again. That's what you do. You're a cop."

"And you've broke more laws than a body has bones," Montoya replied.

"Broke, yes, but once again, caught, no." Rook tried to tease, but it went flat, stopped short by the unreadable expression on Montoya's face. "I haven't had sleep in about three or four days, little food, and there's this fucking hot cop chasing my ass but for all the wrong reasons. Now someone's tried to kill me, some asshole accidentally ran me over, and I still don't know who dropped Dani's body on my front porch, but all I can think about is how I think we should either fuck or kill each other, preferably fucking, because I just can't get rid of you."

"So you want to get rid of me?" Montoya's smile was a saturnine blend of pleasure and sensuality, a wicked combination hot enough to tickle Rook's tired dick awake. "After all I've done for you today."

"It would be the worst thing that either one of us should do because, well… reasons. So many reasons. Like… the whole you're a cop thing, and I am… so not a cop. So yeah, I want something, Montoya. But it's not like you're going to give it. So maybe you should go, you know?"

"Huh."

Montoya was quiet, that still silence Rook'd seen in him before. When Rook was finally about to burst apart, Montoya spoke, shattering everything built up between them with a rumbling sigh.

"What makes you think I don't want to fuck you, *cuervo*?"

Eleven

THE COUCH was their first victim.

Dante lunged forward, pinning Rook to its cushions, and their weight tipped the sofa over, sending it crashing backward to the floor. They hit the ground hard, spilling over the cushions and sliding across the carpet. Rook gasped with explosive pain, and Dante began to roll away, startled he'd forgotten about the other's injuries when Rook's hands dug furrows into Dante's shirt.

"Shit, we can't do this—"

"You fucking leave me like this, and I will hunt down your entire goddamn family and kill them," Rook growled. "You said it yourself. I'm not a suspect. Shit, if anything, I'm just some guy you know, because I ain't shit as a witness. So come on, Montoya. Let's just get this thing out from between us and get on with our damned lives."

The aggression in Rook's voice was strong, grabbing at Dante's balls and twisting them hard. Spread out under him, Rook looked wanton, needy almost, and Dante had to admit there was some part of the man's helpless sprawl that flipped on every single one of his switches.

Rook looked—battered. There was really no other word for it. His T-shirt rode up over his ribs, exposing blooms of bruises and cuts, and Dante knew beneath Rook's sleeve lay a weave of stitches and abused flesh. If he were honest, he didn't know if Rook could survive being fucked, not with as much as Dante wanted him.

Hell, Dante wasn't sure if he'd survive it, but he was willing to die trying.

They were wrong for one another, polar opposites of worlds and experiences, yet Rook Stevens dug in deep beneath Dante's psyche, hooking in and holding on while burrowing down into every layer of Dante's mind.

He wasn't even sure if he *liked* the man, but he sure as hell wanted to be buried deep inside of him. As worn down as Rook appeared, there was something about him Dante *needed*.

"On the bed." Dante grabbed at Rook's hips and lifted him up from the floor. "We do this, it's going to be on a fucking bed, *mi cielo*. Shit, condoms. We can't—"

"Wallet," Rook grunted as he twisted to get at his back pocket. He tossed a leather billfold at Montoya, then shucked off his T-shirt. "Don't know how long it's been in there. Do they go bad?"

"Is it old enough to vote?" Dante dug through Rook's wallet, finding a pair of foil packets. "They're fine."

He was about to unbutton his pants when Dante caught sight of Rook slithering free from his jeans and forgot how to breathe.

Whatever—whoever—Rook Stevens was, one thing was for certain. He was everything Dante ever wanted in a man.

Probably without the bruises and cuts, but outside of that, Dante's cock certainly took notice. His heart took in the scrapes and bandages, begging to kiss away the aches and pains plaguing the lanky former thief. His mind, however, had other thoughts.

The naked man standing at the edge of the hotel bed was prey. Clear and simple. Dante'd spent days on end hunting the man down, hoping to corner him, but each time, Rook slipped away—a mocking reminder of how sometimes justice was subverted by the cunning. His brain threw up nearly every instance he'd seen Rook in the past—being led past the bullpen, handcuffed and shoved along by Vince, to the horror on Stevens's face when Dante'd slammed him into the cement sidewalk after running him down.

Funny how catching Rook now meant something totally different than slamming a cell door in his face.

Powerful and lean, Rook moved with a careful grace. His long limbs were more muscular than Dante'd expected them to be, stretches of pale skin marbled with strength. His chestnut brown hair lay tangled about his throat and down to his shoulders, creating shadows across the strong planes of his face. Even if he hadn't seen where Stevens came from, the man looked… rich, expensive. As if his blood had been poured into his body through gold and emeralds, captured in an ivory-cream skin, and polished to a glistening, beautiful statue.

A statue not untouched by time and trauma.

There were little hints of Rook's past life on his skin, old scars run white over his ribs and back. A bluish-black curl on his hipbone turned out to be an inked feather, its spine and fringe rendered so perfectly, Dante half expected it to tumble from the man's body and onto the floor. A wider scar cut across the small of Rook's back, inches away from the bubble of his ass, and Dante reached out to caress it, startling the odd-eyed man.

Dante took a step into Rook, pressing himself up against the man's spine until Rook's ass nested into his crotch. Sliding his hand over Rook's silken flesh, he stroked at the keloid and tucked his mouth into the curved hollow between his neck and shoulder.

They said nothing. The air was thick with their breathing and heavy with their want, but they remained silent even as Dante stroked his hands over Rook's body, exploring the arcs and dips of his torso, then his sides. A hiss escape Rook's parted lips when his belt buckle dug into Rook's ass and then another when he scraped at Rook's left nipple with his fingertips, pressing the tender flesh in with a hard twist.

His own cock was damp, pressing against the inside of his clothes, begging to be released so it could bury itself between Rook's taut asscheeks. Dante licked at Rook's shoulders, dragging his teeth over the wetness he'd left behind as he reached between Rook's legs to cup the man's pulled-up balls.

"Why the fuck are you still dressed, Montoya?" Rook pressed into Dante's embrace, gasping when his balls were rolled between Dante's hard fingers. "Jesus Christ, what the hell—"

"Tell me you want this, Stevens." He pressed harder, ignoring Rook's bobbing cock to pull at his sac until Rook's trapped balls churned in his palm. "For once in your damned life, try telling me the truth."

Rook pulled out of Dante's hold, hissing when Dante held on a second too long for comfort before he let go. Hooking his hands in Dante's hair, he pulled them together, their mouths clashing in a brutal kiss. Rook's teeth scored across Dante's jaw, and he dropped one hand to Dante's waist.

"Take these off." Rook bit again, rolling a piece of Dante's cheek between his front teeth, then letting go. "And fuck me, Montoya, before the damned painkillers wear off and I feel every single fucking bruise on me."

Dante shoved the man back, bouncing him across the mattress. Rook scrambled to get away from the edge, but Dante reached down, gripping his ankle tightly. He struggled a bit, but Dante refused to let go, unfastening his belt with one hand, then working the buttons on his fly loose. The condoms he'd found in Rook's wallet were riding a fold in the sheets, and Dante nodded toward the packets.

"Get one of those open, *cuervo*." With his pants unzipped, Dante took another step forward while yanking Rook down to the end of the bed. "Put it on me."

"Think I'm just going to bend over and take it?" Rook's eyebrows nearly buried themselves in the shock of burned cinnamon hair falling over his forehead. "Not my style, Montoya."

The rising sun pinked the edges of the sky, and a bleed of light murmured into the room, catching on the jeweled flecks of green and gray in Rook's odd eyes. Beard burn had scraped trails down Rook's throat and over his shoulder, and Dante rubbed at his own chin at the sight of the marks, feeling the thick, heavy rasp of his shadowed skin on his palm. Rook's mouth was swollen from Dante's nibbles, and one nipple stood out red and pouty on his chest, plucked hard and tight from Dante's fingers.

Dante stepped out of his pants, kicking them to the side. In the long hours since he'd left the house yesterday morning, his life'd been turned upside down and inside out by the man he held to the bed. Defiance set Rook's jaw into a stony ridge, and the thin scruff on the man's normally clean-shaven face added a vulnerability to his pretty, aristocratic features.

"I'm not taking here, Stevens," Dante said softly. "I'm going to finish what we started a long time ago in that club, and after that, we can both walk away if that's what you want. You want to give me as much as I want to give you. Deny that. You can't tell me you don't want me to push you into that bed with my dick and make you feel every damn inch of me. Can you?"

"Fuck you," Rook ground out, looking away. "God fucking damn it."

"Yeah, I thought so," he murmured, snapping his waistband with his fingers. "Now get that thing open while I take this off."

He was bigger than Rook. In nearly every way. Dark burnished gold against Rook's paler skin, Dante marveled at the differences in their bodies as he ran his hands over Rook's shoulders and sides, carefully avoiding any tender areas. As Rook rolled a lubed condom down Dante's heft, he reached out to stroke Rook's leaking cock, smearing its liquid over Rook's tip and down over the shuck of skin around its head.

"Go easy with this thing, 'Toya. You could put a man's eye out if you're not careful."

"I don't think it's going to be your eye I'm aiming for, Stevens," Dante replied, running his fingers through Rook's hair.

The condom was warm and stretched around his cock, snugging up against the root of his shaft. Rook's fingers danced over his length, stroking him along the ridge of his cock and then down the length of the vein running hard beneath the thin skin. His balls were already tight up into his body, and his stomach jumped as his muscles tensed with anticipation.

Standing at the side of the bed, Dante spread his legs slightly when Rook nudged them apart with his shoulder. Half expecting the man to punch him in the nuts, he was pleasantly surprised when Rook pressed a kiss on the inside of his thighs, then snuffled through the soft hair running down from Dante's belly button to his groin.

"I like the fur on you. Not too much but enough to play with." Rook grinned as Dante squeezed out the last drops of lube from the condom packet. "Shit, that better be for me."

"Lay back," Dante murmured. "Let me see you."

There were words for how Rook looked. Words Dante only knew from the romance novels his mother read out loud to his grandmother until she realized her sons were listening in.

Lascivo.

Disipado.

Dispuesto.

The sheets were white, a stark canvas for Rook's flung-out form. His knees were raised, his heels dug down into the mattress as he tried to get a better purchase on the bed. Looking up, he caught Dante watching him, and Rook's familiar cocky smile turned sensual with a heady promise.

"God, you are so fucking hot," Rook whispered. "Jesus, what the hell was I thinking not fucking you sooner?"

"I don't know, *cuervo*," Dante murmured softly, climbing onto the bed to rest his knees between Rook's spread legs. "*¿Estás listo?*"

Rook nodded, and Dante slid his lubed fingers down the cleft beneath Rook's taint. He grunted when Rook's hips rose up off the bed, pushing Dante's hand back. Leaning over Rook's hips, Dante forced Rook's legs apart, spreading him open to take his fingers in. Pressing against the puckered dip hidden between Rook's cheeks, Dante slid in, hooking over the ridge of Rook's hole and deep into his soft clench.

The agonized hiss Dante pulled out of Rook as he worked his fingers deep into his ass was nearly enough to make him lose himself before they'd even begun.

"Let me turn over."

Rook tried to pull away, but Dante pinned him down.

Resting his weight on his knees, Dante leaned over and cocked his head. "Why?"

"Why what?" The fire in Rook's eyes burned hotter, and something hard slipped into the man's expression. Shaking his head, Rook pushed against Dante's shoulder. "Just let me turn over."

"No, *cuervo*." He bent his head down, kissing Rook's parted lips. "I'm not having your back to me."

"I don't—" He bit his lip, squirming on Dante's fingers. "This—us. Shit, it's too much, Montoya. I don't know—"

"I do," Dante whispered over Rook's mouth. He rested his weight on Rook's chest, delicately balancing himself as he smeared his thumb across Rook's chin, then grasped his jaw, forcing Rook to look him in the eyes. "I want you to know it's me inside of you. I want you to know who's fucking you. Who is making you come. I want you to feel me deep up inside of your body, and I want to see your face when you give in. Understand me, Rook?"

"Yes." Rook nodded slowly.

"Good." Dante gave him one final punishing kiss.

Then plunged his hard cock deep into the heat of Rook's body.

IT WAS too much for him to take. Everything closed in on Rook, and at the same time, his mind was being blown open. Montoya's cock was thick, nearly too thick to take in, but he didn't have a choice, not when the man cuddled into the curve of Rook's spread legs and slid in. There was too much of him—of Montoya—of *Dante*—for Rook to wrap his brain around.

Because he'd never in his life had a man's cheek against his own during sex. Never once on a bed. And never ever face-to-face.

He'd been fucked at clubs, in the backseat of cars, in semi cabs, and once in a horse trailer, but the intimacy of Dante's face pressed against his was too much to take. It overrode the pain in his shoulder and the aches of the bruising along his back.

There'd never been a man who'd wanted to see him. Not really. There'd been some who'd pulled his head back by his hair so they could come over his face or mouth, sometimes even deep inside of him when he'd not been smart enough to demand a condom. Those days were long gone. He'd turned into the user, the one who'd decided how and when he'd be fucked, and each and every time, he'd insisted on being taken from behind.

It was safer that way. There was never a question of vulnerability and intimate whispers. On his knees or up against a wall with his legs spread, Rook never had to see who was making him feel pleasure. He'd not had to pin a face to the sensual threads of want coursing through him, and he didn't have to know who was tearing apart his control, making him lose his hold on his body to release everything he had inside of him.

Not until Dante Montoya. And Rook almost wished the car had killed him, because the length of Dante pushing in and out of him in long, slow strokes was going to be the death of him.

He felt *everything*. Dante's fingers stroking his face and then the push of Dante's shoulders against the back of his thigh as he dipped his cock in again. The slap of their bodies sounded like a feverous kiss, turning wet as Rook's dick wept with pleasure. With every tug out, Dante sent a caressing tingle through Rook's core, reaching up into places along his belly and chest Rook couldn't absorb.

It was too much to take in.

And far too dear to push away.

The rasp of Dante's scruff on his cheek matched the burn of the man's dick working through him. There wasn't enough lube on the condom, Rook was sure of it, but the ache of his rim being roughly stretched apart was a welcome one. It made him feel *real*, as if Dante would be there in the morning when he woke up or stumble back into bed with him the next night after he finally got some rest.

Dante's breath on his neck was damning, an erotic enticement for Rook to want more than one single fuck. More than he'd gotten before.

It was stupid to dream. It was stupid to want. A fuck and then maybe a kiss good-bye was all he was worth.

Especially with the past they had between them. Once Dante had his fill, he'd be gone. Just like the others who Rook never wanted to stay.

And damn him if he didn't want the man to linger.

Clenching down hard on Dante's cock, Rook was pleased to hear him hiss in surprise. Dante's fingers were in his hair before he could do it again, and he arched his back in response, pressing his hard, wet cock into Dante's belly. The light trail of hair along Dante's muscled stomach tickled Rook's shaft, and he wiggled again, hooking his ankles around the small of Dante's back.

They rode one another, catching into a rhythm that demanded nothing of them but the fierceness of their thrusts. Rook stretched up to meet Dante's cock. His balls slapped against Rook's sweat-damp skin, and Dante shifted, sliding his hands under Rook's ass to spread him even farther apart until Rook felt himself opened up to take every inch of Dante's dick.

His thrusts changed, going deeper and faster. Another shift and Rook's body lit up, sending him into a spasming roil. Their bodies rocked, moving up across the mattress until Rook's shoulders were pushed into the headboard and he needed to bend his head forward to avoid being slammed against the hard wood.

He lost track of everything but Dante's body on his. A second ago his stitched arm ached, and then the next he was riding a lightning storm raised up from inside his blood. Rook couldn't hold back any longer. Grunting, he clung to Dante's broad shoulders, reveling in the power of the man's muscles as he craned to reach deep into Rook's ass. Dante lifted Rook's legs until his calves rested against his chest, folding them up as he bent forward and laid in harder.

The bed rocked and creaked under them, and the headboard rattled, chips of plaster and scraped-off paint falling onto Rook's shoulder. He didn't care if the hotel tossed them out on their asses so long as Dante carried him the rest of the way.

A heartbreakingly tiny cry escaped him, and Rook panicked, wondering if Dante heard him moaning for more. He was fairly sure he'd whispered Dante's name, a bubbling pop of sound nearly as private as the kiss they'd just shared. Before Rook could deny its existence, he was lost in the maelstrom slamming into him from Dante's shattering slide inside of his ass, and Rook flew apart.

His climax hit hard. Too hard to do anything but ride it out on Dante's momentum.

"God, coming. You're so damned—" Dante slipped into a Spanish too hot and hard for Rook to follow.

It stung as sharp as Dante's kisses. He didn't need to understand what the man was saying. He caught enough of it to know Dante was going over the edge, and then the hot push of Dante's cock came again, piercing his reason once more, and Rook fell over with him.

They came together, wet and filthy, but Rook wouldn't have had it any other way. Dante's lips were on his, and then the press of Dante's tongue invaded him, licking at him until his mouth was as thoroughly fucked as his ass. Dante kept up a slow circling rhythm, milking out the last of Rook's softening cries until Rook was left gasping for air.

When Dante pulled free, Rook whimpered at the hard pull of his skin being dragged alongside of Dante's softening cock. He was worn out, and the pains he'd left on the couch were back, crawling down into his bones and leaving him tired and broken. Lying on the bed, he could only watch Dante get up to toss the condom away, then pull the curtains across the windows, shutting out the Los Angeles morning with a plunging darkness only broken by the green splatter of numbers across an alarm clock on the nearby nightstand.

The bed gave under Dante's weight, and Rook let himself be maneuvered around on the mattress, murmuring in complaint only when Dante pushed his shoulder. Rook's eyes adjusted slowly to the black, turning the room into cat-grays. Sleep fought with the pain, and he groaned, sitting up carefully.

"Here. Take these." Dante held out a glass of water in one hand and a pair of pills in the other.

Swallowing hurt nearly as much as sitting up, but Rook welcomed the quenching chill of the water going down his throat. Handing Dante the water, he flopped back down on the bed, tensing when Dante slid in behind him.

"You going to be here when I wake up?" Dante moved in close, pulling Rook back until they were spooned chest to back.

"Yeah." Rook sighed. "Sure."

"That as much of a lie as you not knowing it was me back then in the club?" Dante's breath was hot on Rook's neck, as scalding as the pain ratcheting up his back and over his ribs.

"What makes you think it was a lie?" Rook whispered. He'd told no one about seeing the detective that night. Told no one of how he'd wanted Dante Montoya since the first time he'd laid eyes on the cop bent on taking him down. And if there was one thing he knew how to do besides slither in and out of a place without anyone knowing he was there, it was lie.

"Because you've done nothing but lie to me since I first laid eyes on you, Rook." Dante pulled the duvet up over them, settling the linens against their bodies. "But no more. I want the truth from you from now on out. I don't lie to you. You don't lie to me."

"Got it, Montoya." The pills were kicking in, and Rook nearly wept as the pain leeched out of his body. "Sure. Whatever."

"And one more thing." Dante pulled him back, then rubbed his knuckles over Rook's cheek. "You call me Dante. If it's good enough to say when you're coming, it's good enough to say when you're talking to me. Now get some sleep. And you better be here when I wake up, because we've got one more condom, and I intend to use it."

Twelve

DANTE KNEW the moment Rook surfaced from his dreams. There was no mistaking it. As Los Angeles screamed along its merry little way, shut out by thick curtains across the hotel's soundproofed windows, Rook's skin began to hum beneath Dante's hand.

It was as if he'd stuck his fingers into a fast-moving current, a stream of energy catching on the ridges of his fingers and palm. There was no change in the man's breathing, not a shivering flicker of lashes over his cut-glass cheekbones, but something *intangible* fired on inside of Rook's being, and Dante wondered if his hand would cook beneath the buzz slithering through Rook's nerves.

He took a chance and kissed the nape of Rook's neck, taking a moment to catch his teeth on the fine hairs there before pulling slightly away, waiting for Rook to respond.

There was nothing big at first, nothing overt, but there was a skipping pulse under Dante's wrist where he'd laid his arm over Rook's uninjured shoulder and over his chest, the quick stamp of a heartbeat caught up in its own excitement.

"I can *feel* you thinking, Rook," Dante whispered, nibbling on Rook's earlobe until he got a hissing response. "Don't pretend you're sleeping. What do you think is going to happen if you don't wake up?"

"Like you'd have the good manners to sneak out and pretend nothing happened between us."

Typical Rook. Shove away. Deflect, then stab Dante with a hint of something soft and longing beneath the bravado. He didn't rise to the bait. Instead Dante found the spot on Rook's ear he'd discovered last night and delicately blew on it.

"Stop that. It tickles, and I hurt when I laugh." Rook moved slowly under him, too carefully for Dante's liking. "God, I fucking hurt everywhere. Wasn't like this a couple of hours ago when I got up to piss and brush my teeth. Shit, it was only a damned Ford speck."

"That speck was enough to bruise you something fierce. It's time for another round of pills." He was about to pull back when Rook dug his fingers into Dante's thigh. "What? No?"

"No." Rook shook his head, twisting slightly in Dante's embrace until his shoulders rested on the arm Dante slung underneath him. "I don't like what they do to me. Make me all fuzzy. I've got to watch my wits when I'm around you, Montoya." He hitched his breath once, then murmured, "Dante."

"I'd rather have you fuzzy than in pain. How about some ibuprofen?" Rook's subtle nod spilled his chestnut hair over Dante's arm, and he tugged at a lock as he slipped off the bed. "Wait here."

He was mildly amused to find Rook still there, in bed, waiting for him.

With the sun in full possession of the sky, the ambient light creeping out from under the room's curtains was more than enough to illuminate the space. Their clothes were everywhere, and neither one of them had given a second thought to the couch lying on its back in the middle of the room. Sofa cushions were scattered across the carpet, and Dante was nearly certain it was his underwear dangling from one of the sconces hanging above the headboard. It was a scene best used to illustrate a rock star's enfant terrible behavior.

Or the aftermath of two men finally giving in to something larger than either one of them wanted to admit.

Like the room, Rook looked worse for wear but still too damned expensive for Dante's budget. His faint injuries from the car were now full-blown bruises, and the gunshot wound lay bare and naked in the faint light. The stitched-up flap looked raw, too pink for Dante's liking, and he tenderly touched the skin around the area, testing it for heat.

"They shot me full of shit twice last night. Antibiotics or something. Shit, they could have given me bubonic plague for all I know. Who checks that shit for them? Kind of dangerous if you think about it. One guy with a needle wandering the halls, looking for someone to fuck up."

Rook gulped down the pills, following them with a mouthful of water. Dante took the water glass from him, and Rook fell back into the tangled sheets, his arms spread out about him.

"Are you heading out to fight crime with Camden the Ginger Wonder, or do I have to share the bed again?"

It was the closest thing Dante was ever going to get out of Rook in the way of asking him to come back to bed, but Dante took it.

"Day off today, but I'll be running some things down. Like your friend, the Pigeon." He climbed onto the bed, tucking his hand under Rook's hip, lifting him easily aside so he could slide in next to him. "And I've already talked to Hank and my uncle Manny. I left things with him… half-done, but he said it turned out all right. Move over."

They were still naked, and from the tender way Rook moved his legs to let Dante under him, he knew the other condom was going to remain on the nightstand where he'd left it. It didn't matter. He was more interested in hearing the man… breathe and talk. For now at least. But Rook seemed unsettled, shifting as Dante pulled the covers up over them.

"Come closer," Dante ordered softly, and for a moment he thought Rook would resist. "I'm not going to hurt you."

That moment came quickly enough when Rook's jaw set. Then more resistance trailed after it in Rook's soft grumble. "You know, you and me—we're a really fucking bad idea. I should just go—"

"Yeah, as bad decisions go, you're definitely one of the worst—and best—I've made." Dante propped himself up onto an elbow so he could see Rook's face. "We both knew it was going to get to this. You're lying to yourself if you say it wasn't."

"No, I only lie to other people." His laugh was touched with a tincture of bitterness, but Rook gave Dante a rueful smile. "If it hadn't been for Dani showing up dead on my floor, we never would have ended up here."

"From what little I know about you, I can safely say you're trouble enough that I'd have ended up on your doorstep no matter what, Stevens," he teased. "Now, come here. You know you want to."

He could see it in the man's oddly beautiful eyes and the set of his full mouth, but then as slowly as he'd eased into the bed, Rook slid up against Dante's body, leaning into the crook of his outflung arm.

Pulling the covers up, Dante waited until the tenseness left Rook's body before moving his arm down to cradle Rook back against his chest. Nearly a minute passed before Rook's shoulders loosened, and Dante felt, rather than heard, the soft sigh when Rook finally let go.

It was odd lying next to a naked man, their cocks soft and vulnerable, silken velvet between their thighs. Rook's skin was warm, healthy, and firm to Dante's touch, and he explored the planes of his lover's stomach, tracing out the muscles he found there. There were tender spots, unseen because of the duvet covering them, but all Dante had to do was close his eyes to find the memory of Rook's body burned into his mind. He knew where to avoid, mostly the lower edge of Rook's left side and then under his right shoulder blade. His arm was tender from the shot, but from what Dante could tell, Rook soldiered on past that pain.

The slice across his cheek seemed barely worth mentioning, especially since Dante'd kissed it after they'd collapsed, and Rook mocked him for being soft.

Lying next to Rook Stevens was akin to trying to take a nap on a bed of nails. A lot of practice, a seemingly futile exercise, but once accomplished, a sliver of nirvana from its mastery.

Not that he considered himself a master in Rook Stevens. Not by a long shot. Hell, the only reason Dante knew Rook'd gotten pleasure the night before was because he'd been there when the man surrendered his control, splattering them both with the sticky gush of his release.

He waited a heartbeat, then another before speaking again. "After all the times I've seen you run away, I was surprised to see you stay, *cuervo*."

"Yeah, don't get too used to it, Montoya. I'll most likely kill you in the morning." Rook glanced over his shoulder. "Really? Nothing? Jesus, you have *got* to watch the damned movie."

"*Dante*."

Rook took a second, then murmured, "Dante. You're woefully ignorant of pop culture."

"Yeah, I don't get to watch a lot of television and movies. Most of my time's spent on my house or trying to find people who kill other people." He kept stroking at Rook's skin, reveling in the soft flush of pink he brought to Rook's cheeks. "I'm glad you stayed."

"God, you are such a chick."

"Pretty sure with what I did to you last night, I'm not." He slid his hand down and brushed at the nest of curls above Rook's dick. "And a true man is one who can talk to his lover. Anyone can be all macho and hide behind a wall of silence. You want a real man? Find one who'll say the scary things and try to work them out. A man faces fear. He doesn't swallow it and then choke on his pride when it goes down the wrong way."

"What fortune cookie did you pull that out of?" Rook snorted. "Really, life's not a Disney movie. There's no wacky sidekick—despite what you think about Charlene—and there sure as hell isn't any fairy godmother."

"My uncle Manny told me that. In a lot of ways he's kind of my fairy godfather." Dante tweaked Rook's nipple lightly, mimicking what he'd done with his teeth a few hours before. "He'd like you. He likes lost causes and broken boys. God knows he surrounded himself with enough of them."

"I'm not broken." The assertion was quiet but strong, a thread of hot steel cloaked behind the velvet purr of Rook's voice. "Don't mistake me not giving a shit about other people as being broken. There's nothing *wrong* with me because I'm different from you."

"You run, Rook. Every time it looks like someone's getting close to you, you rabbit." Dante tightened his hold on the man, and as if on cue, Rook tensed up to push away. He held Rook tighter, refusing to let go, keeping his breath shallow when Rook remained on edge but in his arms. "Don't you get sick of running? Don't you get tired of always having to look over your shoulder? What's so hard about just... staying?"

"Because everyone wants something, Montoya." Rook's breath was a hot, slithering wind over Dante's bare arm. "No one does anything without a reason—"

"Even your grandfather? Man seems to be chasing after you like his head's on fire, trying to keep up."

"Fuck, *especially* my grandfather." He shifted on the bed, finding a comfortable spot, but Rook's muscled ass ground into Dante's crotch, sliding his dick into Rook's cleft. "See? Right there. Even you."

"Your ass practically gave my dick a cheek job." Dante sank his teeth into Rook's shoulder, letting go when he heard a small yelp of surprise. "Just because you make me hard, doesn't mean I'm going to roll you over and fuck you. Not now. Tell me why you run from your grandfather. And yeah, he's a mean old man, but he's your mean old man. From what I can tell, he cares about you. Maybe even loves you."

"He sees me as a way to fuck over my cousins. They're idiots. I'll give him that. Well, not Alex, but he's gone and said fuck you to the old man in his own way. Owns a comic book shop. Apparently that's worse than what I do, but go figure." Rook grumbled at Dante's exploratory fingers over his ribs. "You want me to talk to you, or do you want to fuck, because this whole touchy-feely only can happen verbally or physically. I can't do both."

"So no chewing gum and walking at the same time?" Dante teased.

"Hard to talk when my dick is hard enough to cut a diamond." He hissed softly. "Shit, I'm still on the hook for that diamond Dani had on her."

"Did she find it in your place? And be honest. Did you have it there, and was she walking out with it?"

"I haven't seen that thing in fucking years, Dante. There's no way in hell my prints are on it. I never touched the damned thing with my bare hands when I had it to *begin* with. And that's not a confession." Rook struggled to turn around, and Dante loosened his hold so Rook could face him. "Statute on that job is almost up if I'm counting from when you guys walked away from the case. It's one of the last damned things hanging over me, and I've worked too fucking hard to get free. I'm not going to let Dani or whoever else is fucking with me screw it up."

"I'm not going to take it as one," Dante assured. "But if I'm going to catch who's killing your... past associates, then I'm going to have to know how you're connected to them. Good distraction, though. Moving on to the diamond instead of your grandfather. I've got to give you that."

Rook at least had the decency to fake a little bit of shame in his expression. "Yeah, well... it wasn't on purpose. I... fuck, Mon—Dante, this is too damned hard."

"Then do something easier on you. Tell me how a kid who grew up on the carnival circuit ended up selling dolls on Hollywood Boulevard." Dante prodded him lightly. "Tell me *something*, Rook Stevens. It can be about you grandfather or, hell, why you gave Charlene a job. Just between you and me. It goes no further than this room."

"Dude, I think I'd rather go to jail," Rook ground out, turning around so his back was to Dante's chest again. "Seriously. And for your information, they're called *action figures*. Not dolls."

WHAT MONTOYA—Dante—wanted was worse than standing on the edge of a high-rise with only a thin steel braid stopping him from becoming a splatter on the street below. He didn't *share*. Sex was something to have and be done with, like eating a pot of ramen over the sink so he didn't have to do dishes.

And much like gulping down hot noodles, the idea of *talking* about things to a cop—even one whose dick had been inside of him—gave Rook heartburn.

The problem with Dante Montoya was that he was *good*. Not the tiptoe through the forest, sing to forest animals kind of good, but a more brutally real, honest-to-God, throw himself into the line of fire for someone he didn't know kind. Rook didn't have it in him to even understand that kind of good, yet there he was, cuddled up against a white knight as if they were starring in a Hallmark commercial for Valentine's Day.

"Think less. Talk more, Stevens." Dante nudged Rook's shoulder with his chin.

"Why is it I have to call you Dante and you can still call me Stevens?"

"Because I have a gun."

"Nice."

Dante snorted. "Anything. This is a trust thing. If we're going to be—"

"Tangled," Rook interrupted. "If we're going to call this fucking mess anything, it's going to be tangled. We'll ride this out for as long as it takes us. Then we walk it off, right?"

Dante was silent behind him, and Rook swallowed the prickly anxiety rolling up his throat. The cop finally sighed and hitched Rook even closer, molding his body against Rook's back until there was barely enough space between them for air to move.

"There's a lot of things I don't understand about you, *cuervo*. I get that your mother wasn't—"

"Around? Sober?" he suggested quickly and tried to remember the last time he'd actually spoken to Beanie. "*So* many words to choose from."

"I was going to say maternal." Dante's hands were moving again, a soothing caress over his belly. "I don't want to put words in your mouth."

"Dude, there are so many words to describe Beanie—Beatrice. Stupid's one. That's the one I come up with the most, you know?" He thought back on the day when he'd first seen the mansion his mother called home. "She went off to join the goddamned circus because she didn't want to finish up high school. How screwed up is that? But that's Beanie. She'd get this brilliant idea about making jam—which she doesn't know how to make—come up with this soupy, fruity crap but won't have anything to put it in. Typical Beanie."

Dante stopped his stroking, and Rook wrinkled his nose, hating that he missed the touch.

"I take it you aren't close, then?"

"You have to see someone more than a few times a year to get close to them, right?" Rook asked. "What kind of stupid bitch walks away from being rich just because she can't keep her legs together or a thought in her head? That's my mother for you. Don't know what surprises me more. That she had me or that I'm the only one she's had."

He'd finally gotten to Montoya, because Dante's breath stopped, and his chest jerked beneath Rook's shoulder blades. *Mothers* were important to Montoya—or at least his mother. He added that bit of information next to the uncle Dante spoke of earlier.

"She didn't have you to think about then. When she left home," Dante replied. "You walk away from things easily enough. Maybe that's where you get it from?"

A small cut with a knife, not deep enough to do serious damage, but Dante's smooth response was sharp enough to prick Rook's temper. He shoved the irritation aside, hating that his walls crumbled so easily when Dante touched them.

Maybe he was beyond soft. Spending the past few years as legitimately as he could was wearing down his defenses. Gone were the days when he could callously walk by something or someone, not caring if they were bleeding out or crying at his feet. The world was a hard place, and he'd learned long ago that suckling at its stone teat would only leave his mouth raw.

Then why did Dante's touch unsettle him so much? And why did he hate himself for not reaching out to Archibald to tell him where he was?

"God, I fucking hate you. This crap you're—" Rook winced as Dante's nails flicked over his chest. "There's nothing to tell you. I grew up, did some jobs, then got sick of it. So I opened up a shop. There you go."

"I'm assuming you got the money for your place off of those jobs you did," Dante surmised. "And before you bitch, we agreed nothing said here would be used against you. Or I agreed. Besides, the case we had against you was thrown out. Both of them."

"Yeah, your partner really fucked that up." He grimaced. "Sorry. That came out wrong."

"No, it's true. Vince screwed up." Dante leaned away, pulling Rook down onto his back. "I'm going to be honest, *cuervo*, I wanted to nail you and the guys you ran with so badly I could taste it. Vince knew he was living on borrowed time, I guess. Maybe he thought he had nothing to lose, but he did."

"He should have taken care of you at least." His hair was in his face, and Rook pushed it aside, only to have it slither back. Dante gently brushed it away, another one of his secretive, wise smiles plastered on his rugged face. "Don't look at me like that. You're the one who's all family this and friends that. Fucker should have had your back."

He'd been out of the state when Dante's former partner said he discovered a stash of stolen items in Rook's trailer at the carnival's winter spot. The fallout had been ugly, played out on a stage where Rook couldn't see the players, but he could hear the whispering and the shouting, rumors reaching him through a loose network of people. There'd been news of the older cop's shameful dismissal and how the younger detective almost lost his balls over it.

At the time he'd thought about paybacks, karmas, and bitches, but seeing Dante ache ruffled a darkness Rook didn't know he had inside.

The sorrow in Dante's face hurt. His eyes bled pain, and Rook needed to get away from the raw outpour of betrayal and confusion rolling off Dante's body.

"Yeah, he should have. But I understand why he did it. Don't agree with it, but that's what it is." Dante leaned over, touching his nose to Rook's. "What about you? Who did you depend on, then betrayed you? Because no one is born as cynical and bitter as you are. Who was your Vince?"

"No one's ever had my back, Montoya. No one. And I don't expect that to change. Ever," Rook shot back, shoving Dante away with a hard push. "Right now I'm going to get some more sleep. Then I'm talking to Pigeon about you so I can say I'm done with this."

"We're not done with this, Rook, and I don't know if we'll ever be *done* with this," Dante said softly as he rolled over onto his back. "You were right the first time. You and I? We're tangled. So whether you like it or not, I'll be here. Because God knows, someone needs to take care of you. Especially since you're doing such a shitty job of taking care of yourself."

Thirteen

ANGUISH FORCED Rook to emerge from the depths of his sleep. His thoughts were fragmented, minnows scattered before the ravenous hunger pursuing him, and his lungs burned as he fought to catch his breath beneath the rippling agonies rolling under his skin and through his bones. There wasn't enough oxygen in the air, and Rook fought to surface the rest of the way, anything to shed the coat of thorns he seemed to be wearing.

Opening his eyes made it worse.

There was glass in the light. Sliver wide and razor sharp, each drop of sun dug down into his eyes, twisting further in until his brain couldn't absorb any more pain.

Then he blinked, and the agony began anew.

"Come on, *cuervo*. I need you to wake up the rest of the way. I want to get some meds in you before I leave."

Rook knew the voice calling to him. He loved that voice—Dante's voice. Its rum-dark pour smoothed away some of the dry roughness on his soul, and Rook forced himself to lift his hand to his face to rub at the prickly sand in his eyes.

"He's not going to die, is he, *mijo*?"

That was definitely not Dante Montoya. And Rook shoved himself off the sleepy cliff he'd been walking to plunge into full consciousness. He struck the hard, flat surface of awareness with a clattering headache and a realization there wasn't a single inch of skin on his body that was left untouched by pain. Even the faint dusting of hair on his arms crinkled in distress, but as soon as he shook off one ache, two more took its place.

Sitting up was an exercise in futility. Nothing in his body moved as it should have, and Rook wondered if Dante had somehow fucked his spine loose, leaving him an unresponsive sack of meat and bones on the hotel's expensive sheets.

"Let me help you. Don't try to move without someone helping you up. Not until after you take a painkiller."

Dante emerged out of the watery background, coming into focus in startling detail. A light scruff darkened his jaw, and as he sat down on the bed, light from the window struck Dante's face, casting shadows from his long lashes onto his cheeks.

"I'm going to help you sit up. No fighting me."

"Fighting you? Shouldn't have fucked you," he grumbled at the man he'd let have him a few hours before. "You broke me."

"You were broken when I got you." Dante wedged his arm under Rook's shoulders, lifting him up. "And if you remember, I told you… it was a bad idea. The fucking. *You* are not a bad idea, *cuervo*."

Sitting up was almost as big a mistake as opening his eyes. Sure enough, his spine wasn't having any of Rook's upright nonsense, and his shoulders seemed to be on crooked. Straightening himself out only made things worse, and Rook nearly toppled forward, saved at the last second by a judicious block of Dante's hand on his chest.

"*Mijo*, what do you need me to do?"

Somewhere out in the fuzzy ether beyond the bed, another man spoke up, reminding Rook they weren't alone. He got the impression of a shimmer of colors and a white smile before the man ghosted back out of his sight.

"Water would be nice, *tío*. He needs to take some meds. Warm would be better on his stomach, but I think you'd have to run it through the coffeemaker for that." Dante spoke to the murmuring outline at the end of the bed.

"That I can do. And once we're done drugging him, you can tell me why you broke him."

Rook liked the censure in the man's voice, a barbed sting in his sweet, rolling tenor.

Waiting until the man's blurry shape faded out of his sight, Rook said softly, "If you're thinking of getting up a threesome, you're shit out of luck, Montoya. I don't play the *guess-whose-dick-is-in-you* game."

"Let's get a few things straight, *mocoso*. That is my uncle Manny. I called him here so you wouldn't be alone while I go interview a few people about the murders at your place." Dante sat down on the bed, then eased a pillow behind Rook's shoulders. "And secondly, I don't share. If you have a problem with that, then… well, get over it. As long as we're doing… what we're doing, there will be only you and me. Got it?"

"Sure you don't have a class ring or something you want to give me?" Rook tried going for a sneer, but his face didn't seem to work properly. His belly, however, pitched a fit, and Rook rubbed at his stomach. "Who thought this was a good idea?"

"We both did. Last night. This morning, I'm beginning to reconsider my actions."

"Too late now." His skin began crawling again, sending off little pings to his brain, and Rook sighed. "Really, just kill me the rest of the way."

"Maybe later," Dante promised. "Not in front of my uncle. He gets squeamish around blood. Just like you."

"Low blow, Montoya. Very low blow." The room slowly got clearer, and Rook spotted the plump older Mexican man coming toward him. "Your uncle, huh?"

There wasn't any question about Dante's blood tie to the older Latino. Even with his impossibly black hair and rounder face, the man's features held a strong resemblance to the cop Rook ached for. Where Dante's clothes ran to practical and earthy hues, Manny preferred a more vivid palette—one that included dark red pants and a yellow T-shirt stretched over his slightly rounded belly. The clash of maroon and buttercup was startling, and Rook wondered how out of it he'd been if the man's loud clothes hadn't woken him up as soon as Manny walked into the hotel room.

"Yes. My favorite uncle." The hard edge to Dante's tone was definitely a warning for Rook to behave. "*Tío*, this is Rook. Pain in the ass, this is my *tío*, Manny. He'll be staying with you because he's a very nice guy. Try not to be too much of an asshole while I'm gone."

"I can see where you get your smile, 'Toya." There was a tiny spark of satisfaction when Manny preened a bit, squaring his shoulders before handing Dante a mug. "Looks better on him too."

"Ah, Dante said to watch out around you because you'd charm my wallet out of my pocket." Manny's grin was a near echo of his nephew's. A bit softer around the edges and without the sexual aggression Rook swore Dante saved up just for him. "You take your medication and sleep. I brought a book."

"Hell, you could probably dance on the bed. Pills knock me the fuck out." Rook picked up one of the two pills Dante held out on his palm. "One only. I want to wake up at some point this week. Fuck, even my tongue hurts."

"Both, *cuervo*." Dante pulled on his cop face, failing to hide the spitting fire in his eyes. "Two is what the doctor ordered. That one you took the last time didn't last."

"I'm a lightweight." Rook nearly shook his head, but there was a real fear his brains would leak out of his ears. Instead, he dry swallowed the pill and chased it down with a sip of water. "Don't argue with me. I don't like what this kind of shit does to me. I'm old enough to know that, Montoya."

"Dante," he corrected, then looked over his shoulder at his uncle. "He has a hard time remembering my first name."

"That's 'cause your last name is so cool."

His hands were trembling, so Rook knotted his fingers into the bed linens, hoping to hide his shaken state from Montoya's sharp gaze. He might as well have held his hands up to the man's face, because Dante's expression turned from teasing to deadly serious.

"I'll take the other one if I don't feel better soon."

"Deal. And don't think Manny won't pin you to the bed and shove it down your throat," Dante warned. "I've watched him pill the neighbor's five cats in three seconds flat without getting scratched. You'd be nothing to him."

Lethargy began to creep through Rook's marrow, and he inhaled slowly, testing his lungs and ribs out before sighing in relief. He could handle the fatigue that came with the painkillers, but falling asleep would be—dangerous. He didn't know Manny, and as the pain slipped away from his body, Rook could barely grasp that he'd fallen asleep in Dante's arms.

Not something he did. Not a situation he'd ever wanted to put himself in, but somehow the cop went and dug down under his skin. As nice as it was to have the pain leaving him, the drugs also brought a silky stickiness to his brain, and Rook fought to stay awake.

From the long black span across his eyelids and then the startling jump of Dante sitting on the bed to standing by the now upright couch, Rook knew he was losing the one battle he'd chosen to fight that day.

Time shifted again. Or space. Rook wasn't certain, but he'd only taken another breath when Dante appeared at his side again. Gone were the worn jeans and paint-splattered T-shirt he'd been wearing a moment before. At some point between one second and the next, Dante'd donned his cop face, a pair of black jeans, a white button-down shirt, and the brown corduroy jacket he'd worn a few days ago.

Rook got another shock when Dante leaned over and his jacket fell away from his side, exposing a black shoulder harness and holstered gun.

He didn't like guns. Getting shot was no great joy, but guns themselves made him nervous. They were too volatile, too uncontrolled, and from his past experience, handled by people who really just wanted to kill things—or him. The smell of metal and oil made him queasy. His leg muscles clenched, his body remembering another time when he'd woken up to hot shards and torn flesh. The scars were small, the largest a dapple of dark brown on his hip, but even after more than fifteen years, he still hated the smell of guns.

Of course, Rook reasoned, his most recent gunshot wound wasn't a parade through the park either.

"You okay?" Dante brushed his fingers through Rook's hair, bringing him back to the present.

"Yeah, just… what's the saying? Goose walking over my grave." He tried for a smile but failed. His mouth was too tired to do much more than purse automatically when Dante leaned over. Their lips touched briefly, but the caress warmed away the chill down Rook's spine. "Just tired."

"Get some sleep," Dante whispered into his ear. "And you can trust Manny. The worst thing he'll do to you in your sleep is cover you with a blanket. You're as safe with him as you are with me. Okay?"

"Don't think I really want to be safe with you, Montoya," Rook mumbled, trying to stay conscious for a second longer, but he was quickly losing the battle. "Don't do something stupid while you're out there. We've got another condom to go through."

"*Cuervo*, as soon as you get better, I'll buy you a whole damned case," Dante promised. "'Cause one is just not going to cut it."

"ONE JOB, Montoya. You had one damned job." Hank's disgust thickened the air in their unmarked police car. "No fucking the… shit, witness? Informant?"

"Not a person of interest. If anything, he's now considered a victim in this case. Breaking and entering. Which is kind of ironic." As reminders went, it was slim. "Things got away from us… from me. It was an accident. Sort of."

"How do you accidentally fuck a guy? You're sitting naked on the bed and he trips, impaling himself on your dick?"

"I said sort of. And accident's the wrong word… look, I knew what I was doing. He and I—there's something there." He sighed, suddenly tired of the complications in his life. "He pisses me off, and I like him. I'm also the one he called after he got hit by that car. So it's not like I'm on a one-way street here."

"Someone hit him with a car? Okay, so let me get this straight. Yesterday he was exonerated of murder, shot twice—"

"Not badly. But definitely creased."

"Whatevers. More shot than I've ever been, and I'm walking around with a fucking gun." Hank waved away Dante's interruption. "He then sneaks out of the hospital he's supposed to stay in because he's got some serious control issues, where he gets hit by a car on the way to a hotel he'd picked out years ago to rabbit to in case things went to shit for him. Got sick because he hadn't eaten anything, then called you? Do I have that right?"

"Pretty much. Okay, I called him. But he'd been ignoring everyone before that." He nodded. "From there, I took him to the ER, where they said he was fine but needed watching. Then I took him over to a hotel without insects living in its walls."

"Where you fucked him senseless." Hank's laugh guttered in his belly. "Jesus, are you trying to get thrown off this case?"

"Not senseless but mostly… it was rough for him when he woke up. He's kind of bruised up. I left him with Manny."

"Of course, because this story *needed* an ex-drag queen to make it complete." His partner threw his hands up in surrender when Dante shot him a hot look. "Hey, no judging. Don't get mad at me. I've got a lot of respect for Manny and his friends."

"*Tío's* proud of who he is. And was. Mock him and pay the consequences, Camden," Dante warned.

"Dude, all women should have legs like Manny. I've seen him in heels. Deadly." Hank returned Dante's look. "A lot like your fuck buddy, Stevens."

"Don't call him that. It's… I'd say complicated, but that's a cliché. He calls it tangled. But I'm worried less about him than I am the case." Dante reached over to the pile of papers straddling the console between them. "We have more questions than answers here. And every time we turn around, one of our facts becomes a lie."

"Like that fucking diamond. Why'd it take them so long to figure out it was costume? Isn't that kind of shit obvious?" The other detective growled through clenched teeth. "Something's hinky in all of this. We've got three dead, one ex-crook with a target on his back, and we're going to go see a woman named Pigeon."

"A pigeon who's the first victim's sister," Dante reminded him. "The rock's a copy, so the original's still out there. And from what Rook told me, chances are good the owner either still has the stone, or it was swapped out when things got a little tight in their wallets."

"He's off the hook for it even if he did take it. Too much time's gone by, and no one's going to nail him for it," Hank pointed out. "Circumstantial evidence at best."

"It's what he was known for. Smoke and mirrors," Dante agreed. "Also, the DA has a hard-on for Stevens's grandfather. I might like Rook, but I have a feeling that even if I found him driving a pickax into a toddler's head, they'd let him walk because he's Archibald Martin's little boy."

"Something you guys didn't know back in the day when Vince was gunning for him." Hank appeared to mull things over, then cocked his head. "So where did our first victim get the fake diamond? And why did she bring it with her?"

"I don't know. He also said he'd never made contact with it, so his print being on it is odd. I asked the lab to see if there were DNA or oil traces on it." Dante debated with himself for a moment. He'd made a promise not to share what he'd learned from Rook the night before, but there was one key thing the former thief and Charlene said that kept coming back to him. "Stevens's assistant said something about using some kind of adhesive to mask someone's prints, but what if they could lift a print from that after it hardens? How hard would it be to transfer a fingerprint?"

"You're straying into cow abduction conspiracy theory shit here, man."

"Weirder things have happened," Dante pointed out. "Take a look at what the lab said."

"It's just too much fucking trouble to go through—the print thing. Not the lab work. And for what? Why pin something on Stevens?" Hank picked up the papers, then shuffled their order until he found the lab report. "Fingerprint was smeared, and the partial they got was from Stevens's pinkie finger. The thing is… what? Three or four inches? How the hell does someone pick up something like that with their little finger?"

"Still thinking aliens didn't get that cow, Camden?"

Hank frowned. "So Stevens is the cow? I thought he was the white whale."

"The biggest question isn't whether or not the aliens took the cow, it's why they took the cow." Dante turned down Washington, slowing as the traffic tightened up around them.

"It just doesn't make sense. There's a big fat fucking 'why' in the middle of this. I'm thinking we need to see how viable this theory of yours is before I commit myself to the crazy. And more important, is it worth enough to drag me out here on my day off?" His partner pointed at a traffic light ahead of them. "Make a right there. She's the third townhouse on the right. How are we going to play this?"

"She's the first victim's sister and, from all accounts, either knew the couple found in the bin or ran cons with them." Dante parked the car in a loading zone, then tossed a police placard on the dashboard to ward off zealous meter maids.

"She's got some priors. Mostly grifting stuff, but not much. Some petty things, but nothing earth-shattering. So either she skims in and out of the system, or she's so fucking good she doesn't get caught." Hank looked around the neighborhood. "Not rolling in dough here."

"If she's smart, then she wouldn't live high," Dante pointed out. "Sometimes the best criminals don't start spending money until after they can't get nailed for it."

"Kind of like Stevens."

"Hey, I've never said otherwise." Scanning the street, Dante noticed the overwhelming stillness in the neighborhood. "It's like a Stepford community here. Everything matches perfectly. How can people live like this?"

The street was riddled with a maze of townhomes, each section only slightly different from the one next to it. Ruthlessly green lawns were trimmed to an inch high, and each sidewalk leading up to the front door was pinned with a black mail box, their red metal flags pushed down at nearly exactly the same angle. A short flight of stairs led up to each front door, most painted brown or cream with an occasional rogue olive green thrown in to add a splash of variety. Mottled pansies circled the two-storied structures, half circles of purple and pink providing the only color to the drab landscape. Even the cars parked on the street were sand- or gray-hued, mostly smaller imports, although one turquoise late model VW bug stood out like a sore thumb at the end of the cul-de-sac.

"People like conformity." Hank shrugged. "Some people like living by rules. She might think she's safe hiding here. She's probably on the neighborhood watch and calls in cars who've been parked in front of her house for more than seventy-two hours. Blending in is the best thing for a con artist. That's why people always say shit like *but she seemed so nice* when their neighbors are caught with dead bodies in their basement."

"Probably, but I could do without the dead bodies," Dante agreed. "Let's go in to console her about the deaths. Captain said there was a next of kin contact made, but we were on the scene, so—"

The first boom shattered the car's windows, blowing glass inward into their faces. Another followed close by, too soon and too quick for Dante's hearing to recover from the ringing going off in his ears. Around them, the neighborhood rattled and fell, walls crumbling in as the reverberations continued to shake the street. The unmarked rocked on its tires, lifting away from the curb, then slamming back down onto the road.

To their right, a row of newer townhomes lay in ruins, crumbling inward as Dante tried to catch his breath. He had about a second of peace when a third, smaller explosion blew, and one of the shingled two-storied buildings spat out columns of black smoke and thin fiery tendrils, startling Dante into action.

Covering his face, Dante shook loose of the shock holding him frozen in place. He reached for Hank with one hand while smearing away a trickle of blood falling into his eyes from his forehead.

"Camden!" He sounded tinny, shouting at the top of his lungs, but there was nothing but the rushing echo of his breath in his ears.

Hank lay on his side, slumped down over the console, and was much too still for Dante's liking. Reaching under his partner's shirt collar, Dante felt for Hank's pulse, his fingers numb and shaken from his overwrought nerves. There was a heartbeat, strong and fluid, but the splatter of blood across Hank's face worried him more than Dante cared to admit.

A second later, Hank coughed, and his eyes opened, wild and frantic, as he pulled himself up. The glass had done a number on his face and neck, starbursts of blood speckling over his fair skin. His partner was groaning but moving, and Dante pulled at Hank's shirt, looking for more wounds. Pushing away Dante's hand, Hank shook a handful of tempered glass out of his ginger hair, then reached for the car's radio.

"Calling it in." Gasping, Hank grunted and pressed at his ribs.

The explosion had been powerful enough to bend the car's door inward, knocking the armrest into Hank's side. He could barely hear Hank, and he nodded, knowing anything he said in return would be lost in the buzzing hum affecting both of them.

"Survivors...."

"Going in." Dante motioned to the townhomes. "Stay here if you need to."

"Fuck that. *Go*," Hank ordered, his neck muscles bulging as he screamed to be heard through the noise around them. "Right behind you, Montoya."

Dante went in at a full run, ignoring the hitch of pain along his leg and ribs as he mounted the cracked steps to the townhouses' raised entrances. Not much was left of the cookie-cutter building, but Dante spotted a pale hand sticking up out of a pile of rubble near a fallen staircase. A quick glance at the townhouse's ironically intact front door, and he made a connection to the address and the woman they'd come to look for.

"*Mierda*." Dante waded into the falling debris, carefully picking his way to the lifeless limb a few feet away. "For fuck's sake, please don't be dead, Debbie Pridgeon. We need a goddamned break. Just one goddamned break."

Fourteen

THERE WAS someone singing.

It wasn't bad singing, just… *odd*. Especially since Rook didn't know anyone who liked '80s pop classics, much less knew about being like a virgin. Whoever was singing decided the song needed less bubble gum and more heat, because the lyrics snaked in and out of the singer's lower register, adding a growling camp to its melody.

He wasn't home. That much was certain. The light was very wrong, too little of it, and the wall he could make out was painted a soothing light green some asshole with a design degree would call celery. The bed wasn't as comfortable, but the pillows were nice and soft. He was wearing a much too large T-shirt and sweatpants, definitely not something he'd had on before he'd drugged himself to unconsciousness. They were freshly washed and a soft cotton purr over his traumatized skin.

Hotel—Rook remembered. A much more familiar smell to him than his own home, but there he was, confused by the strangeness of the light and walls.

Oddly, he also smelled of… sex. And when he moved, Rook definitely felt as if he'd broken his long dry spell.

He smelled of Dante Montoya.

A soft-bodied Mexican man with Dante's smile shuffled up to the bed. It took a moment before Rook remembered the man's name—Manny, Dante's uncle and his apparent babysitter. A babysitter with a paper cup of something delicious smelling in his hands.

"Coffee?" Rook croaked, nodding at the cup. "God, I'm throwing Dante over for you."

"Ah, now I know you hit your head." Manny chuckled. "Do you need help up?"

"No, I'm good." He slid across the bed, testing his body's reactions.

There was tenderness in some areas and a pulling along his arm, but for the most part, everything seemed in working order. It still felt like he'd been hit by something larger than a breadbox on wheels, but nothing screamed in crippling agony. His bladder did send up a warning flag, and any stiffness his dick might have had on waking up was shaken off by the pressing need to piss.

"Bathroom?" Manny caught Rook's arm as he slid off the bed. "Do you need help?"

"Doesn't hurt like it did when I first got up." The thick carpet beneath his feet poked up between Rook's toes. "Thanks, though. Be right back."

"There's toiletries in the bathroom if you want to take a shower. Dante made sure you had clothes to change into. But *mijo*, leave the door open a crack just in case you need help, okay?"

The older man's tender expression broke through Rook's stubborn instinctive response to lock the door behind him.

"If you fall, I want to be able to help you."

"Yeah, sure." With that, Rook left the bathroom door open an inch, then began to strip off the sweatpants he'd somehow gained in the middle of his minicoma.

Manny disarmed him. His body language was gentle, a sure sign of gullible and trusting, but there was a steely glimmer in his dark brown eyes, a remnant of battles fought and won. A curious blend of masculinity and feminine grace, Dante's uncle was definitely not a mark, and as Rook contemplated how he'd have approached Manny before he'd gone straight, he'd have avoided the man like the plague.

The man puttering around in the hotel room a few feet away was the kind of mark that made someone lose their way in a con, reminding the player of their humanity and probably stalwart enough to jump-start even the deadest conscience.

Showering was a slow and painful process. At some point, Manny cracked open the door and put spare clothes on the counter, but Rook only saw an outline through the shower's steamed-up frosted glass walls. The heat helped loosen the last of the tightness across his shoulders, and he tentatively scrubbed over his stitches and bruises, washing away the traces of blood on his arm he'd probably earned from stretching his wound too far when he'd tackled Dante.

"Fuck, what was I thinking?" Leaning his forehead against the tile wall, Rook let the multiheaded shower pound his back into submission. "Gotta cut him loose or something. Shit. A cop? Really? A fucking cop. Why not just frog jump over and fuck someone in the FBI or Homeland Security? Oh, I know, a judge! Let's go full out and fuck a guy in robes and call it a day."

Because Dante Montoya hits all my damned buttons, his brain whispered back.

He didn't want Montoya—Dante. He didn't want any of the crap Dante would bring into his life if he let him in. Each smile, every touch was another thread wrapped around his dick and balls until he wouldn't be able to move without Dante yanking on a leash Rook'd made for himself.

"Great, now I've got a goddamned fantasy of Montoya having me on a leash," Rook grumbled to himself. "Where the fuck did *that* come from?"

There were four ibuprofen and a bottle of water with the clean clothes Manny'd left on the counter, and he gulped them down. Padding out barefoot, Rook pulled the drawstrings of the sweats he'd been given as tight as they could go, then gave up when they rode down onto his hip bones.

And somehow in the time it'd taken him to shower, scrub his hair clean, and dress, Manny'd gotten housekeeping to change the bed and deliver a quesadilla and fries. The food set up on the coffee table smelled good, and Rook's stomach growled as Manny pushed him toward the table.

"Mine?" Rook plucked up a fry, blowing on it to cool off its steaming surface. "Because, dude, seriously, two of my favorite foods in the world."

Manny settled into an armchair, then reached for a mug on the table. "Yours. And there is more coffee."

"Okay, it's official. Dante's to the curb," Rook mumbled around a hot potato wedge dipped in jalapeno ranch dressing. "I only have room in my heart for one Montoya."

"Well, lucky for you I am not a Montoya. It's Ortega. I'm Dante's mother's brother." Manny shooed Rook to the couch with a flip of his hand. "Sit. It's not good for you to eat while standing up. And as you eat, you can tell me how my nephew went from hating your guts to having sex with you in a five-star hotel."

ROOK CHOKED on a fry.

There were tears and then a raw scratchiness he should have gotten from swallowing Dante's cock, but instead, the abrasiveness on the tender walls of his throat was from a goddamned potato.

And Dante's uncle, Manny, merely sat there watching him, a smiling Mexican Buddha sipping a cup of steaming coffee.

Rook tried to play it off, smoothing the potato's passage with a slurp of hot coffee. He cleared his passageway with a discreet cough, then smiled back at his interrogator. "So, he hated me, huh?"

"Maybe," Manny said slyly. "You tell me why else he has all of the files from your old case? He was mad at you, at everyone you were with back then, and now he's looking at you like you are the last piece of pumpkin pie."

"Huh." He bolted down another fry, then picked at the quesadilla. His stomach was rebelling at the thought of fried cheese and tortilla, and the potatoes were a heavy lump beneath a wash of coffee. "I figured after the case was dropped, he didn't give me another thought."

"That is something you'll have to bring up with him. Dante has never walked away from anything—even his family. Even me when I was... well, things happen. But he is always there. He's a good boy—a good man."

"Yeah, that's the truth. Too fucking good." Rook slid back against the couch. "Don't get too used to me. Pretty sure once this whole thing is done, he'll go back to... whatever it was he was doing before he ran into me again. I'm not exactly a guy you bring home to meet your mom and dad."

"In Dante's case, I *am* his mom and dad." Manny saluted Rook with his coffee cup.

Coffee seemed like a good idea, but then at that point, Rook was seriously considering faking his own death to avoid the knowing look in Manny's soulful eyes. "Is this where you ask me what my intentions are toward your nephew?"

"I know what his intentions are. He likes you. He didn't always like you, but he's always wanted you. Now he has you—"

"Had. Past tense, *'mano*," Rook pointed out. "Not looking for a ring and kids here. Shit, I don't even want to know where you guys live."

"We'll see." Manny patted the couch cushion. "Come here so I can put some cream on your stitches. Dante told me the hospital wants to make sure it is clean and covered. There's also more pills for you to take besides the ibuprofen. Antibiotics, I think, but it's almost time for pain medication if you want it."

"Antibiotics I'll take." The effects of the hot water were wearing off, and Rook found a cold stiffness had moved into his joints while he'd been sitting. "I'm okay right now, hurt wise. Just stiff."

"You *were* hit by a car, *mijo*," Manny reminded him gently. "*And* shot. No one's going to think you're weak because you take a pill to ease the pain."

"It's not being macho. I just don't like passing out. Makes me feel like I'm in one of those historical romances where women swoon because someone swears." Rook snorted. "I also pass out when I see blood. Usually mine, but I've been known to make exceptions. If I have a choice of fainting or running when cops start shooting at me, the chicken-lizard part of my brain apparently chooses *get-the-fuck-out-of-here* every time."

Manny waved a tube of ointment at him. "Come on. Let me see."

"'It puts the lotion on its skin.'" Rook slid over to sit next to the older man, staring at the blank look on Manny's face. "Does *no one* in your family watch movies?"

"Mostly, I read." Manny pulled up Rook's sleeve, then sighed. "Did you not see the bandage I left for you on the counter?"

"I don't like bandages. Skin's got to breathe to heal." He deflected Manny's skeptical look. "Trust me, spend some time on the circuit, and you see the kind of shit people do to themselves. If you can't see what's going on, it gets all gross and you die."

Manny's look went from skeptical to disgusted. "I worry about the woman who raised you."

"Dude, Beanie's the last person I'd want to kiss and make anything better." The lotion was cold on his skin, and Manny's fingers gently skimmed the wound. "I know some of the places her mouth's been."

Manny went in for the kill, but unlike Dante, the stab in was slow and subtle. "You call your mother Beanie? It's your mother, right?"

"Yeah, I couldn't say Beatrice." Rook tilted his head back, trying to read the man's next move.

It was harder to game someone when he didn't have a purpose. The whole point of interaction was to manipulate the outcome in his favor. Without an endgame, Rook knew he was floundering. He couldn't go on the offensive—no reason to alienate Manny other than on general principles, but Dante's uncle seemed unshakeable.

"What circuit? I used to do shows—a long time ago, before I got sick—but most of it was on stage. I guess you traveled?"

Manny slid the conversation in another direction, and Rook skipped a few thoughts to catch up.

"Circus or something? Do people really do that?"

"Carnival." Rook huffed in a breath when Manny touched a tender spot. "Beanie was looking more for... I don't really know what... but she hooked into a sideshow and carnival."

"And your father?"

"Anyone's guess. Beanie doesn't even try." He shrugged off Manny's concerned frown. "Dude, not an issue. Carnies kind of take care of their own. If anything, Beanie squatting to drop me in horse-shit sawdust gave me more cred than she could ever get living on the circuit for fifty years. Life wasn't so bad."

Manny absorbed Rook's words. "Did you go to school?"

"Define school." He laughed. "Sort of. Yeah. There's programs where you do schoolwork and send it in. Lots of that. I didn't do too bad. Got a GED somewhere. Not like I was planning on going to college."

"What were you planning?" Dante's uncle patted at the edges of Rook's stitches with a piece of gauze. "Did you think you were going to be a criminal? Or did someone there make you do it?"

"Let's get one thing straight, dude." Rook shoved his sleeve back down. "I knew what I was getting into. I knew what I was doing. Hell, I was good at it. Probably still am. I don't get lazy. I've had to be ready to walk away from everything all of my life. Stealing's what I'm good at. I keep limber and make sure I can hold my own weight on a line. Probably was the only thing that saved me when that car hit me."

"Probably," Manny conceded. The man's face went flat, nearly unreadable behind the sweet vulnerability he wore almost as a habit. "But don't you get tired of walking away from everything?"

"Only reason I stayed. Everything I've got now, I've earned." The fries were cold, but Rook picked at them anyway. Jalapeno ranch dressing went a long way in forgiving a food's sins. "So maybe that's the whole karma thing coming to bite me in the ass, because it sure as hell feels like someone's trying to take away everything I've built... so fuck it, I'm staying."

"And my nephew? How does he fit into this new life of yours?" Manny prodded, handing Rook a large adhesive. "Because now you're not running away from anything, you can have a home. A family. All of it."

"Look, I'm glad we're sitting around here braiding each other's hair and having hot cocoa, but life's not sunshine and kittens for everyone. Bottom line, I saw the chance to go legit, and I took it because it's hard to live your life looking over your shoulder." Rook snatched the bandage out of Manny's fingers, then peeled off its plastic backing. "Stealing kept me fed. Now something else does. That's pretty much all there is to it."

"There's more to life than being fed, *bebé*." Manny tugged the gauze out of Rook's grasp, then rolled Rook's sleeve out of his way. After laying the bandage down, he sealed its sticky tape edges to Rook's skin with a press of his fingers. "Don't you deserve more than that? Don't you respect yourself? Can't you dream a little bit bigger for yourself than that?"

"Manny, people like me don't get the two-point-five kids and the Sunday BBQs with the neighbors who don't return my weed eater. We're disposable, someone to slough off when people get tired of us." Rook frowned down at the bandage, wondering how the hell he'd allowed Manny to slap one on him. "Don't go measuring Dante for a tux or anything. After he gets his fill, he's moving on to someone else. Just like I will. It's how things are, Manny. Because no matter how much you polish up a trash can, it's still a fucking trash can."

"I don't know what to think then, *cuervo*, because my Dante, he doesn't throw people away. Not like you expect him to," Manny mourned. "I don't know what I find more pathetic and sad—that you'd think Dante would be like that... or that you believe that is all you deserve in life."

"It's all I'll ever be worth, *'mano*. A quick fuck and maybe a good-bye kiss." Rook rubbed at the bandage. "And if Dante isn't smart enough to realize, then he'll be the next thing I'm walking away from. 'Cause I'd rather do it to him way before he does it to me."

MOST OF the debris was drywall, paint, and wood, but there was enough of it to give Dante a struggle as he tried to dig out the woman lying motionless under the rubble. His hearing was spotty, tuning in and out as his eardrums tried to balance themselves. The sirens he heard through the falling crashes of the townhomes crumbling faded in and out, so it was difficult to know how far away the cavalry was.

There were others digging, mostly poking around the edges to look for the fallen, and one enterprising teenaged boy discovered a flat-screen television hanging untouched on one wall and took off with it, running clumsily away from the scene. Focusing on the pale fingers and wrist he could see, Dante kept excavating, his hands bleeding from the broken wood and twisted metal around him. It took a few minutes, but Dante eventually had a path through the mess. He waded in, flinging an enormous slab of drywall aside, then closed his fingers around the wrist.

Her flesh was cold, dead cold, and up close, Dante felt a rigid stiffness in the joint. Whoever lay under the rubble had been dead a long time before the townhouse went up. Shouldering a broken side table off the body, Dante finally got a good look at the corpse.

The young woman was pretty, slender, and with her short black bob haircut, nearly an exact match for the two dead bodies he already had in the morgue.

She also had a very large bullet hole in the middle of her forehead.

"Well, shit." There was little chance she was anyone but one of the Pigeon's Betties. In death, she looked much younger than most of the other grifters he knew. Rook's edgy prettiness lacked even a hint of innocence, even when he was passed out on painkillers. She'd been someone's daughter, and apparently, knee-deep in things too deadly for her to handle.

Torn between excavating the dead body or leaving it for the crime lab guys, Dante decided to move on, climbing over the remains of a floral-print couch to get to a pile of drywall.

"Hank, any sign of anyone else?" Dante shouted as his partner stepped into the debris. "This one's gone!"

"Going to see if there's anyone else in there," Hank screamed back at him, motioning toward another large pile. "Gas line's shut down!"

He waved Hank off and plunged into the rubble near him, scrabbling to clear out the larger piles in case someone was buried under the debris. A few seconds later, he came up with a dusty gray cat, its flat face dripping with distaste as he pulled it from under an overturned recliner.

"Oh God, Mr. McGee!" The high pitch of the woman's squeal must have been enough to cut through the buzzing in Dante's ears, because he heard her crying out what he presumed to be the cat's name over and over again as she tried to get through the rubble. "Oh thank God, he's alive. Please let him be okay."

The cat's owner was older than Dante by about a decade or so, with a soft, plump body and a pleasant face made for gentle expressions and loving smiles. Despite the slight nip in the air, she wore a pair of purple capris and a matching print top, and her casual tousle of graying ashen blonde hair had been gone through with probably frantic fingers because it stood away from her head as if she'd been caught in a wind tunnel.

"Stay there, ma'am. I'll bring him out. He's fine." He came out with the cat, spotting Hank being joined by a battalion of firemen and a few paramedics. Once he stepped out of the townhouse and into the sunlight, he recognized the woman holding her hands out for the cat. "Debbie Pridgeon?"

"Yes?"

Her reply was automatic, and then Dante waited for her to respond to the situation unfolding around her.

A second later, there it was—that little twitch of personality in the depths of her guileless hazel eyes. A moment later, it was followed by a slight hardening in her face and a sudden tenseness in her shoulders as she swayed back a step. It was a slip of the mask, the glimmer of the real person behind the construct Dante'd been staring at. In that split second, Dante could almost see her weigh her options as she spotted the badge hanging in clear view from his belt and then looked to the squirming cat he held in his arms.

It was the cat that broke her, and the con artist grimaced as she held out her arms to take Mr. McGee from Dante.

"I take it you weren't just passing by and stopped to get my cat out."

Her voice was still pleasant, but the cookies-and-milk tone was stripped clean, leaving behind a watery alto. When Dante handed her the Persian, she buried her face in its soft, dirty fur.

"Thank you for saving him. He's all I've got. I suppose you're here about the dead Betties. Truthfully, I'm kind of glad you guys showed up. There's another dead one in my house I've got to get rid of, and I'd like nothing more than for you to take her off my hands."

Fifteen

FOR SOME, home was where they went after a long day of trudging through the routines of their lives. For Dante Montoya, home was a maze of beige corridors, enormous bullpens of cubicles and cops, and the scent of bitter, burned coffee in the air. Home had a hint of gun oil and profanity. Nothing challenged his mind like the puzzle of a crime, and there was no finer feeling in the world than when he cornered his prey, taking them down to pay for what they'd done.

The first time he donned his badge, something stirred deep inside Dante, a calling that humbled and honored him to answer. And he'd been determined to never let anything or anyone persuade him to step off the path he'd placed himself on.

But then, Dante mused, that was before he'd fallen for an oddly eyed former cat burglar and sat across of a Romper-Room-sweet woman who apparently had, at some point, run one of the largest bait-and-switch cons in America's history.

After boarding the cat with a neighbor, Pigeon dutifully climbed into a patrol car and left the partners to deal with the dead body lying among the remains of her home. Two and a half hours spent with the crime lab people, paramedics, and another detective on the scene and Dante was ready to climb the walls.

"Jesus, I thought we'd never get out of there." Hank brushed at his hair as they walked into Homicide's bullpen. "Did I get all of the drywall out?"

"Yeah, I think so." A uniform strolling past winced, and Dante grimaced an apology. "Shit, I think we're still screaming at each other."

"Can't hear a damned thing," Hank confessed. "Well, not without the whole buzzing sound. Ambulance guy said no eardrum damage, but shit, it feels like I've got a wasp or something in my head."

"Montoya! Camden!" Their captain stuck his head out of his office and stabbed his forefinger at them. "Get in here."

It was a short and thankfully muted scolding, and more than once Dante caught Hank grinning foolishly as their captain turned his back to them to rail about something neither one of them could catch. The man's low bass growl thrummed and dove, dropping most of what he said beneath anything they could hear. Near the end of the man's rant, Dante's ears popped, and he was blasted with a wall of rumbling complaint. Hank continued his grinning, and the captain turned, catching them staring at him.

"You didn't hear a damned thing I said, did you?" he growled at the partners.

"I caught the end of it," Dante admitted with a helpless shrug. "Something about our day off, chasing down rabbit holes, and finding dead bodies."

"Jesus, the two of you are going to give me an ulcer. Tell me why you two idiots headed out there, and who's the broad sitting in Room One?" Captain Book eased into his chair then reached for a bottle of antacids sitting on his desk. "And Camden, quit grinning at me. You look like fucking Howdy Doody."

Dante laid out the case for their captain, starting with Dani's death, the discovery of the first set of Betties, then Rook's shooting. The man sat through all of it, chewing on the end of a pen and nodding at a few places. He'd just gotten to why he and Hank were going to talk to Pigeon when Captain Book held his hand up for Dante to stop.

"Back that up. You took a witness to a hotel." Book leaned over his desk. "Don't think I didn't catch that little bit of it."

"Technically, not a witness, sir." Dante caught Hank's eye roll and sighed. "Stevens and I have...."

"I know your history with Stevens, Montoya. I read the reports, remember?" The wet end of Book's pen bobbed about in the air as he gestured it at the partners. "He's still key to this case. You shouldn't be... doing whatever the hell it is you guys do in... shit, I don't want to have this conversation. I don't have this kind of talk with my own kid when he brought his boyfriend home for Christmas."

"You probably should, Captain." Dante elbowed Hank in the ribs when his partner snorted. "In all fairness."

"In all fairness, Montoya, I let their mother deal with the whole sex thing," Book rumbled back. "I don't have that kind of talk with my daughter either, and she's done married the last one she brought home. But this isn't about my kids. It's about you and Camden here fucking around with a case."

"I'm not doing any fucking, sir." Hank raised his hand. "I'm married."

"Shut up, Camden." Book didn't spare Dante's partner a glance as he rounded in on his target. "I can't tell you who to get in bed with, Montoya, but what I can do is take you off the case. O'Byrne's freed up a bit—"

Hank definitely heard that because he was up on his feet as Dante rose to protest. "Captain…."

"Stevens's involvement in this case is crucial. He's the one who led us to the woman who ran the Betties, and he's our in to talking to anyone else involved." Dante stood shoulder to shoulder with his partner. "We're still trying to figure out who the players are in this. Giving it to O'Byrne will restart the clock."

"No way in hell would Stevens talk to her. He's a squirrel. Look at him wrong, and he's up a tree."

Hank's booming voice was cranked up to eleven, and Dante winced at his partner's volume.

"We definitely need him, sir. No one's going to get any traction without him opening a few doors and pointing people out. When it's all said and done, he trusts Montoya here."

"He's shot straight with us from the beginning, Captain, even after those assholes on patrol tried to kill him," Dante pointed out.

"Shit, don't remind me. There's a bloodbath brewing over that. Stevens's lawyers are fucking sharks, and damn it if those fucking uniforms didn't chum the waters." Book leaned back in his chair and stared up at the partners standing in front of his desk.

"They've got cause, sir." Dante caught the full heat of Book's glare. "They shot up a Wookie statue, Captain."

"We've also got a theory that the fingerprint on that fake diamond isn't real either. Did some preliminary digging on that, and there's ways of getting it done," Hank piped in. "So someone's definitely got it in for Stevens. It'll be a good idea to keep him close and safe. Don't know how safe he'll be with Montoya, but you know—"

"Respectfully, Captain, I'd like to tell my partner to fuck off," Dante muttered at Hank.

"You two can take that shit outside. Right now, I'll let you keep the case if you two agree to step carefully. Camden, take a day to get your hearing cleared. You're not going onto the street with compromised senses." The captain tapped his pen on the desk. "Montoya, no running rogue. You document every single damned conversation you have with any witness Stevens drags up for you. Someone left us three—no, four— dead bodies, and you two aren't any closer to figuring out who the fuck that someone is. I want this case closed… and by all that is fucking holy, don't get Archibald Martin's grandson killed in the process."

"CAN YOU state your name for the record?" Dante set a cold bottle of water in front of the woman Rook called Pigeon.

More schoolteacher than seductress, the older woman thanked Dante for the water, then spoke clearly into the flat microphone set on the table between them. She spelled out her last name, then added, "But they call me Pigeon. Everyone does. I don't really answer to anything else."

"Do you understand your rights as they were read to you?" He glanced down at the reports the on-scene detective e-mailed him before he'd stepped into the room. He could hear Hank shouting through the wall, and Dante resisted the urge to look over his shoulder at the one-way mirror behind him.

"I'm not under arrest, am I?" She laid her hands on the table, ignoring the water. "Because if I am, I'd like a lawyer."

"You're not under arrest, but you're welcome to representation at any time, Ms. Pridgeon." Dante found the paper he'd been looking for. "Your alibi for the murder's a strong one. We've confirmed you were in Chicago for the past two weeks, but according to the airline, you'd landed in Los Angeles two hours before your house's exploding. Want to tell me where you were? I'm guessing you came home and found Jane already dead. Why didn't you call the cops?"

"I certainly didn't kill her. I hired her to take care of my cat." Pigeon sniffed, and her eyes moistened. "And yes, I came home and found Jane. As for the police, I needed a moment first. So I took a walk. Nothing nefarious, and it wasn't as if Mr. McGee would chew on her while I was gone. He's a very picky eater. I just couldn't… I'm a practical person, Detective Montoya, but it does take one aback when someone I knew and cared for is stiff and blue in my foyer after I come home from a long trip."

"I am sorry for your loss. I gather Jane was a friend." Dante got a packet of tissues out of his jacket pocket, then slid them over to Pigeon. "And people do odd things when they find a dead person. While we'd preferred you'd called us immediately, I'm more interested in talking about Jane Pierson. When was the last time you spoke to Jane? Did she stay over or just drop by?"

"She was staying there. Mr. McGee doesn't do well in boarding. He doesn't like leaving the house. I don't know how long it's going to take before he settles down enough to eat now that the house's been blown up." She pursed her lips. "Of course, poor Jane. Who'd want to murder her? She is—was—a very dear girl. No one deserves to be killed, but really, Jane? She was such an innocent soul."

"Most innocent souls don't rack up seven counts of grand theft, ten counts of fraud, and five counts of racketeering." Dante looked up to find Pigeon's smile still plastered unwaveringly on her face. "I have her arrest record right here. Your friend Jane is fairly well known down in Vice."

"She had a few issues. Jane was hoping to break from that lifestyle. Which was why I hired her to care for Mr. McGee. She needed a place to stay for a few weeks, and since I was going to be in Chicago, it worked out for both of us."

"Until she got killed," Dante pointed out in a soft voice. "Was she fighting with someone? Perhaps her partner—the other Betty? They ran in pairs, didn't they? When they worked for you... or do they still work for you? Did you think Jane was in danger at any time? You made good time between arriving at LAX and getting home, even with that little walk you took."

"I took a walk because I needed time to think. Jane was troubled, but she was cleaning herself up. I don't know anyone who'd want to kill her. Even Madge—Jane's partner—should have been pissed off at her for leaving the business, but she understood. Sometimes it's just time to hang up the life and be *normal*." Pigeon's demeanor didn't change. Her smile remained plastered on her face and her shoulders were relaxed, but Dante caught a glimpse of steel in the woman's gaze as she cleared her throat. "Just like Rook did. To be as normal as any of us get."

"Rook...." Dante trailed off. "Explain."

"Detective, I know Rook sent you. He left me a message on my cell phone. Boy knew I wouldn't give you the time of day if you'd just shown up. I may have gone straight, but I didn't get stupid in the process." Pigeon picked up the water bottle, then cracked it open with a neat twist. "I went straight home from the airport because he said you'd wanted to speak to me. He's a good friend, and he promised you just wanted to talk. I owed him that much. Actually, I owe him more, but that's all he's ever asked of me."

"Let me clarify that for the record. You're referring to Rook Stevens, correct?"

"Yes, Stevens." She took a sip of water, then set the bottle down. "Beanie's boy. Tall, too pretty sometimes, and he's got those weird eyes. Just like his mother."

Dante tucked away that bit of information, then continued on. "How long have you known Mr. Stevens, and where did you meet him?"

"Rook? God, since he was about five." Pigeon eyed him. "Little bastard picked my wallet right out of my jacket pocket. He gave it right back to me. It was a game to him. He and his mom were at Rose's then. She was supposed to be a magician's assistant at the time, but all I think she did was play hide the rabbit with the guy and let her little boy run loose on the thoroughfare. He's a good kid, though. Smart."

"Who teaches a five-year-old kid to pick pockets?"

"Really, Detective?" Pigeon laughed. "You know that crowd. Word is you were up to your armpits in them for a couple of years. That boy was picking pockets before he was out of diapers. Probably the only reason that loser mother of his kept him around. Besides, that boy's got great hands. Best I've ever seen."

Dante tried not to think about Rook's hands and where they'd been on him, pushing forward with the interview. "You kept in touch with a five-year-old?"

"Hard not to know about the boy. His mother dragged him around the circuit. Hell, he's done more carnie time than most people I know. Think she started off with Hutchinson's, but I know he rode with Rose, then Bryar, and I think back to Hutchinson again when he was about sixteen. By then he'd… well, he'd gone on to bigger things."

"While you worked the Betties?"

"While I provided a dating service for women looking for security and love," Pigeon corrected quickly. "I've since left that business. Actually, Rook helped me. He went… well, he made a life change. Then I had a small… problem with a client. I contacted him to see if he could help me a bit. The boy's gone far beyond help. I have a bookstore and coffee shop opening soon. Good place for it in West Hollywood. He gave me backing."

"Out of the kindness of his heart?" The cynicism in his own voice was painful for Dante to hear, but he couldn't stop it from creeping in. "The Rook Stevens I know doesn't jibe with that image, somehow."

"That's 'cause you're a cop. He's been on the run from the likes of you since he was born. To the rest of us, he's someone you can count on unless you screw him over. Then you're dead to him. That was the mistake my sister made. It's like killing the goose that lays the golden egg." Pigeon's mouth turned down, and she dabbed a tissue at her eyes. "My sister and I had our differences. One of them was what she'd done to Rook."

"What exactly was that?" Dante leaned forward, his notes forgotten as Pigeon wiped at her eyes.

"She helped a cop try to frame him for something he didn't do." The tears were gone, replaced with a deep sniffle. "I told her not to. But she did it anyway. You know what happened then. Cops tried to nail Rook for a job, and they couldn't touch him. Timing really, because Dani's good at what she does... did. Any other time, he'd have been in trouble."

Dante's spine grew cold, and his stomach twisted in shock. "What cop? What did she do?"

"Some Italian guy. He was working a case against Rook and a couple of the others. We all knew about it. You can't help but notice when people get dragged in over and over but then let go. So she transferred Rook's prints onto a bracelet or something and gave it to this cop."

Dante tried to speak, but he stumbled, trying to wrap his head around Vince's duplicity and Rook's seemingly impossible good luck. "Why would she do that? If he helped you all out?"

"Because Dani was... jealous? Greedy? She'd already blown through everything she'd made on a job she'd done with Rook."

Pigeon looked up suddenly, and Dante knew he'd get nothing more on that subject than what she'd given him.

"Anyway, she wanted more... pay, but they'd all agreed on what was fair beforehand. For what she did, I think she got a lot more than she deserved, but Dani didn't think so. She wanted more, and she knew Rook still... well, he was holding on to his pay. Let's just call it that."

"So why was Dani in Rook's shop, then? Did she talk to you about that? Was there anyone who'd want to kill her that you know about?"

"She was probably in Rook's shop because she was going to rip him off," Pigeon stated baldly. "She had to have taken someone with her, because my sister sure as shit didn't have the skills to open a place up, not if Rook Stevens owned it." She nodded. "That boy is sneaky. He'd hide things in plain sight when the cops came over, but you still wouldn't be able to get your hands on it. I was serious when I said he's the best I've ever seen. Cunning. Thank God every time I talk to him that he wasn't made mean, or we'd be in a world of hurt."

"And Dani wanted… revenge?"

"To hear her, it was justice, but that's a lie. She just wanted what Rook has… or had. Last time I spoke to her, she said she was going to have a big job, one she could retire on." Pigeon sniffed again, her tears returning to bead on her pale lashes. "I just didn't know it was going to be Rook."

"One last question, then we can talk about the Betties. I'll need you to fill in as much as you can about Jane's partner," Dante said, scribbling as quickly as he could on the back of an old arrest record.

"Truthfully, I don't know much about Madge. She was Jane's friend, but, well, she's not one to listen to me." Pigeon sniffed. "I worked with Jane for setup on things. I don't think I even spoke to Madge more than three or four times. She was just teaming up with Jane as I was backing out."

"Okay, but really, anything you might remember will help." Dante added question marks next to Madge's name. "Getting back to the break-in at Rook's, the alarm system was turned off after being armed when Rook's assistant closed up the store. If what you say about your sister is true, and she couldn't have broken in by herself, did she bring the other two Betties in? Hank showed you their pictures, right?"

"Yes. They're Chris and Christine—those are the two you found in the bin. They didn't work with me. Copycats. Bad ones," Pigeon replied. "They'd have been able to help her shake the place down. They work… worked fast. They could strip a whole house in half an hour, or so I've heard. But getting through the door, no. They'd need a key. No patience for locks and alarms."

"So not even a whisper? Think, Pigeon." Dante pressed harder. "If she brought someone in besides the other two, then that's the person who probably killed her… killed them. I need a name. Or even someone who might know something."

"I *really* don't know. You don't… you just don't double-cross someone like Rook. Not that he'd retaliate, but he's done a hell of a lot for a bunch of people when they're hurting. You rip him off, and there'd be hell to pay. Most people who could do the job would never pull it off because it's Rook's place." Pigeon shook her head, sorrow chasing away her smile. "People respect Rook. He doesn't give anyone shit—well, more shit than usual—even when he does stupid things like take in that bubbleheaded blonde he's got working for him. That porny-looking one. Dumber than a bag of rocks, but he gives her a job and takes care of her. Just like he's done me. So if I knew anything, Detective Montoya, I'd have told you, or I'd have killed them myself, because I owe that boy everything. Every damned thing I own."

Sixteen

SHAKING MANNY had been easy, far easier than Rook would have liked to admit. An overheard phone call and a reluctant refusal to join friends at a dinner gave Rook the groundwork to lay Manny a path straight out of the hotel room door.

Five minutes later, Rook was out the door himself.

"I'm not lying. I'm staying put." Muttering to himself on the elevator got a few strange looks, especially from a silver-haired man dressed in a red tracksuit and cradling a small shivering dog of uncertain origins. He tucked himself deeper into the hoodie Dante'd left behind, covering most of the cut on his cheek. "I'm not leaving the hotel. Just that damned room. Not like I'm going to be up there wearing a metal bikini and waiting for sex."

The dog and his human bolted as soon as the elevator hit the main floor. Rook's last image of the pair was the canine's ears flapping up and down as it peered back at him, its pointy muzzle smearing drool across the man's shoulder.

"People," Rook grumbled, walking toward the lobby.

He hadn't been paying much attention to the hotel when they'd come in. Too tired to do anything more than lean against Dante and dig out the cards he had in his wallet, the only impression Rook had gotten of the main lobby was a huge space made up of glass, wood, and a hint of water. Seeing it again with a bit more of his senses about him, not much changed.

The hint of water turned out to be a three-story waterfall spilling down into a reflection pool, and he hadn't recalled the scatterings of couches and chairs set up as conversation nooks throughout the long space. Waist-high black river stone curves carved the floor into smaller sections, long stands of orchids and bright green grasses providing a colorful break to the honey wood and pearl-painted walls.

And in true Los Angeles ennui, no one said a damned thing about him walking around in oversized sweats and black Converse sneakers.

After snagging an apple and a bottle of fizzy water from the concierge's guest bar, he walked out of the hotel's front entrance and straight into a wall of meat.

It was a familiar wall and not one Rook particularly cared for.

Big didn't describe the man. Enormous came close, but Rook usually settled for gargantuan bordering on Godzilla.

And as usual, his temper was just as foul.

Standing a hair under seven feet, Stanley loomed over Rook, a bald block of suntanned muscle and snarl in sunglasses and a diamond earring winking from his right earlobe. As he reached for Rook, his hands blocked out what little Los Angeles sun could get around his mass. Then his fingers closed in on Rook's arms, digging into his stitched-up wound. He gasped when his fingers went numb, and the apple went flying, hitting the stone-paved driveway in a wet splat. A second later, the bottle he'd tucked under his arm followed, bursting on the edge of a curb.

"Mr. Martin wants to see you," the monster said, his voice pitched high, squeaking tone at odds with his bulk. One of the valets stepped toward them, then pedaled back when the man's snarl was turned on him. "You! Mind your own goddamn business."

"Fuck you, Lurch." A flash of teeth in the man's scowl was enough for Rook to bite down on a painful yelp, and despite knowing he wouldn't be able to break the man's viselike grip, he struggled anyway, then regretted twisting about when a hot shock wave pierced through his shoulder. "Swear to God, if you don't—"

"Let him go, Stanley," Archie called out from a black town car idling in the driveway. "You're hurting the boy."

"Rather rip his head off," Stanley muttered barely loud enough for Rook to hear, but he released Rook's arm, then gave him a slight shove toward the long sedan. "Get in. He wants to talk to you."

"Yeah, prepare to be disappointed." Rook shook his sleeve out, twisting his arm around to get the feeling back into his fingers. "'Cause I'm not getting into that car. And you, asshole, owe me an apple."

"Get into the car, Rook." His grandfather gestured at his bodyguard. "Give him the keys. He's afraid we'll drive off with him."

"It's not fear if you know what someone's going to do. It's called awareness." Rook caught the keys Stanley flung at his head. "Apples are inside to the right. And while you're in there, see if you can't find coffee for me and the old man."

Archibald waited until Rook got into the car, then grumbled, "He's going to kill you one day. It's like poking a bear."

"Yeah, as long as you're alive, he'll behave. Moment I get a call telling me you've keeled over, I'm buying a shotgun and a tank." He shivered, suddenly grateful for the car's warm interior, and unzipped the hoodie to get a look at his arm. Sinking down in the soft leather seat next to his grandfather, Rook pushed the fleece away from his shoulder and picked at his bandage. "Fuck, he's dead meat if I've popped these stitches open."

Blood speckled through the T-shirt he'd taken from Dante's gym bag, and Rook gently lifted up the edge of the bandage Manny'd insisted he put on. His skin looked like a bad makeup job from an old horror flick, but from what Rook could see, his stitches held.

"Are you all right?" Archie frowned, peering at the shadowed wound on Rook's arm. "If he hurt you—"

"You'll fire him? I'm fine, but shit, he could be less of an asshole." Rook snorted. "What am I saying? You like having a gorilla on tap. I'd have one too if it weren't so damned much to feed him."

"You've got your cop," his grandfather sneered. "He hid you well enough."

"I hid me, Archie," Rook corrected. Spotting a tissue box on the front seat, he leaned over to pull a few out. Dabbing at the blood on his wound, he glanced over at his grandfather. "That how you found me? You had someone tailing Dante?"

"Odd. You used to call him Montoya. A lot can change in a day, can't it?" Archibald shifted in his seat, running his fingers over the silver knob on his cane. "And no, nothing so old-fashioned as following him. I had my people tracking his credit card."

"I paid for the room. With burners. Okay, he gave them the card to use, but it was still mine."

"He bought a coffee and pastry at the lounge in the lobby this morning. Ah, here is the coffee." The elderly man leaned over to hit the window switch as Stanley approached the car with two coffee cups swallowed up in his massive hands. Archibald took the cups, then passed one over to Rook. "Thank you, Stanley. If you don't mind, Rook and I will sit here for a while and talk."

"Hotel's going to ask you to move this beast. You're in the drop-off area. And I didn't get my goddamned apple." Rook slid the cup into a space on the console between the seats. "Seriously, why are you here?"

"I was concerned after you left the hospital, and then I get a report you were struck by a car. What did you expect me to do? Wait for someone to call and tell me you were dead?" Archie looked away, staring at the passing traffic. "I'm not used to this... worrying. Your mother I wrote off years ago. But you... I'm trying here, boy."

They were *too* much alike. Rook knew it. He hated being controlled as much as his grandfather needed to control. Still, there was something darker than anger in Archibald's expression, and when Rook brushed his fingers over his grandfather's trembling hand, the old man blinked furiously at the dampness in his glittering eyes.

"I'll not cry over you, damn it," Archibald snapped. "If you're going to leave, then leave. Or stay. Just don't play cat-and-mouse games with me, boy. You'll lose every time. I can—"

"You should have stopped right after the game comment, Archie," Rook sighed. "Once you slide it into threats, it goes cattywampus, and you lose all your momentum. You've always got to take it a bit too far."

Silence reigned in the car for a minute, then another, punctuated only by Archie's noisy slurping. Rook broke the quiet first, rubbing at his injured arm as he spoke. "I was going to call you. I've been a bit out of it."

"The clinic report said you were dehydrated—"

"Really, Archie?" Rook rubbed at his face. "You and me, we've got to get something straightened out. Actually, a bunch of things. The first being, you've got to get your nose out of my shit."

"Why should I when you don't tell me what's going on?" Archie snarled back, any sign of the trembling old man wiped away. "I'm surprised you've lived as long as you have being alone. You're a disaster looking for a place to explode, boy."

Rook reached for the door handle. "I don't need your help to live, old man—"

"Sure as shit needed me when you asked for a lawyer now, didn't you?"

"And we're back to *fuck you*, Archie." He opened the door to slide out when Archie grabbed Rook's wrist.

"Don't. Just... *don't*." Archie tugged gently on Rook's arm. "I'm not... good at this. Goddamn it, I don't know what to do with you."

"You don't have to do anything with me, Archie," Rook replied, dropping back into the seat and closing the door. "You just have to let me go and trust that I'll come back. Because I'll always come back, Arch. You just have to let me decide when."

"And if you don't come back? Like your mother?"

"I'd like to think I'm a better person than Beanie," Rook quipped, getting a smile out of his grandfather's dour mouth. "Just... don't hold on so tight, Archie. I can't... breathe when you do."

"And your cop?" Archie tilted his head up, pursing his lips. "You ran to him when you needed someone. Instead of coming to me, your own flesh and blood. *He* hold you loose enough?"

"We'll see, old man. For right now, yeah." Patting his grandfather's leg, Rook sighed again. "But that's just for right now."

"WHAT DO you mean you left him there alone?" Dante struggled to keep his phone tucked in between his neck and shoulder as he dug a room key out of his pocket. "Manny, he's not—"

"I can't believe this film won one Oscar, much less two! The Academy were idiots."

The voice greeting Dante's entrance wasn't the husky charm of the man he'd picked up off a dive motel's floor the night before. And the matching pair of odd-hued eyes glancing at him before turning back to the television certainly wasn't what Dante expected to greet him after a long day of interviewing con artists and rescuing gray Persians.

Rook lay in a boneless sprawl across one end of the couch while his grandfather perched on the other side, his elbows sticking out on either side as he leaned on a cane. Half-empty bowls of popcorn and M&M's had replaced the delicate swirling fish statue on the room's coffee table, and the large screen television flickered with an old black-and-white movie Dante didn't recognize.

"I can't believe that woman was Glinda," Archie groused, digging out a handful of buttery popcorn. Chewing around a mouthful, he waved at the screen. "She looked better in color."

"That was filmed after this." Rook gave Dante a negligent wave. "Well, this one came before Oz. There are two sequels filmed after. Without Grant, but they spliced some shots of him into the second one."

"That all you do every day?" A tap of Archie's cane drew Rook's attention. "Watch movies?"

"Pays the bills," he replied. "And before you say that you'll pay my bills, remember the ticks you've got for grandchildren and how well *they* turned out."

"Alex isn't bad." Archie made a face, nearly identical to his grandson's, and Dante swallowed a chuckle.

"Alex also owns his own comic book store and doesn't trot over to you every time he stubs his toe," Rook pointed out. "Pretend I'm like Alex. Except much more of an asshole."

"Isn't that the truth. Montoya! In or out?" Archibald barked over the actors' banter. "We've already had someone call security because we were being too loud. Said they could hear us guffawing or something. Through the walls, supposedly. What kind of shit hotel do you bring my grandson to where people can hear through the walls?"

"Lies. The walls are soundproofed. You left the door open." Rook reached for a water bottle, and Dante saw him wince. "Fuck—"

"Turn it off. Kiss your grandfather good-bye, and time to get into a hot shower to loosen up those muscles, *cuervo*." Dante strolled across the room to stand in front of the television. Turning it off, he held his hands up to the moaning complaints coming from the couch.

"He calls you tequila?" Archie stood up, leaning heavily on his cane.

Dante stepped forward to help the older man up and caught a disgusted look from both men. Rook stood, then headed to the door, slapping Dante's ass as he went by.

"I'm old. Not dead. The day another man carries me, there'd better be a coffin around my body, boy."

"Sorry. Didn't mean to be courteous. I don't know what I was thinking." He stepped back, giving Archie room to get out. "And *cuervo*? It just means crow."

"Because his name is Rook?" Archie gave Dante the evil eye as he toddled by. "What's wrong with just calling him by his name? Something the matter with it?"

"Old man, stop stirring up crap." Rook opened the door for his grandfather. "Want me to walk you down?"

"Did you just miss the part where I don't need any help? Besides, you're banged up to shit. Goddamned cop can't even take care of you. Don't know why you even want him around." Archibald's cane slapped the door as he reached out to squeeze Rook's arm before he walked past.

"Because he's got a really nice dick and knows what to do with it. I plan on seeing what his ass is like next." Rook winked at Dante's exasperated groan. "What? It's not like he doesn't know I'm gay, Montoya. Not a big surprise."

"Jesus, the two of you—you deserve each other, I swear. Dear God." Dante gaped. The casual, caustic banter between Rook and his grandfather was a far cry from what he and Manny had between them. "I can't even imagine saying that to my grandpa."

"Well, we like things honest between us, Montoya," Archibald declared. "Call me later, brat. If I don't hear from you by tomorrow, I'm sending Stanley after you."

"I look forward to sending him back to you in a thousand little boxes," Rook shot back. "I might even pee on them first. Night, old man. Tell that naked mole rat you call a bodyguard to drive safe. I'm not ready to take over yet. Give me a few months. Then he can kill you."

Rook shut the door behind his grandfather, then turned to face Dante, a familiar cocky grin plastered on his handsome face. They stared at one another, and Dante studied the man he'd taken to bed the night before. As intimate as he'd been with Rook's lean body, he knew little about the man inside. A few tidbits and dribbles, but other than what he'd learned investigating Rook's crimes, Dante knew practically nothing.

And from what he could see, Rook rather liked it that way.

"Yeah, he stopped by once he found out you used your credit card downstairs," Rook tossed off casually, walking by Dante toward the couch. He tossed the candies and popcorn into a bowl, swishing them together, then put it on the kitchen counter. "He put a tracer on you. Asshole. Told him not to do it anymore—"

Rubbing his face, Dante mumbled, "Does *anyone* in your family follow the law? Or should we just build a prison around the old guy's house and call it a day?"

"Hey, I told him to cut it out." Rook grabbed the back of the couch. "Shit, okay. That hurt."

"Let's get you on the bed. You can shower later. Stretch out, and I'll bring you some meds. When was the last time you took something?" Dante slung his arm around Rook's waist, easing under to take his weight. "Hold on, do you want—"

"Just fucking get me to the bed, 'Toya." He hobbled forward, forcing Dante to keep up. "Sat too long. Lying down isn't a bad thing. Meds were hours ago. Right before I kicked Manny out to go play with his friends."

"He was supposed to stay with you." Dante eased Rook down onto the pillows. "Don't go anywhere—unlike the last ten times I told you that."

The pill count in the bottle was higher than Dante would have liked, even with Rook's distrust of a full dose. Talking to Rook was useless. Past experience told Dante he'd be in for a fight, and short of holding the man down to pill him like a cat, there wasn't any way for Dante to get more in him.

"Could crush it up in water...." Dante glanced over his shoulder at the man lying on the bed behind him. Rook had one arm over his eyes, but his toes were kneading the air. "Speaking of cats. What are you thinking? Drug him and that's it. He's gone."

Oddly enough, the thought of Rook walking out one final time left Dante unsettled. More than unsettled, disturbed. He came out of the bathroom and stared down at the mess of a man he'd fallen in with.

There was something to be said about lust. He'd slaked his thirst for men so rarely that when Rook crossed his path again, Dante was overwhelmed with the intensity of his want. Yet once wasn't enough to slake the simmering heat inside of him, not where Rook was concerned.

Rook's green eye peered out from under his arm, finding Dante in the room's growing shadows. "You're looming again."

"I tend to do that around you for some reason. Here, sit up and take these. There's some Tiger Balm I can put on you if you're sore. Might be better than a shower." Dante sat on the bed as Rook downed the pills. "So you kicked Manny out and got your grandfather here instead?"

"Nah, he was stalking me. I went outside for fresh air, and one of his goons grabbed me." Rook sat back against the headboard, rolling his shoulder. "Literally, the fucker grabbed me. Archie hires some real assholes. And before you get all pissy, I'm okay. Mostly scared the shit out of me."

"I don't get...." Talking to Rook about staying in didn't seem to be doing either of them any favors, but he was going to give it one more try. "*Cuervo*, someone is trying to *kill* you. You can't just go take a walk outside until we figure out who the hell is doing all of this."

"Once. Tried to kill me once. And hey, maybe they were aiming for you. You know, a vengeful admirer from afar who caught me staring at your ass." He tried to shrug the whole thing off, but Dante caught the worry in Rook's expression.

"I'd rather be doing other things to your body than picking up its pieces." Dante cupped Rook's chin, forcing him to look at his face. "Is it so hard to believe I don't want anything to happen to you?"

"It's kind of hard to believe someone wants me dead." Rook let himself get manhandled for a second longer, then pulled away. "Why now? I mean, I've done some shitty things in the past but nothing someone would want to kill me for."

"Dani? What did you do to her?" Dante angled closer to Rook. "Why would she be in your shop? You've never answered that. Not really."

"I don't have an answer." Rook's shrug was a study in minimalism, barely enough of a movement to be called a gesture. "Unless she was there to rip me off, but I don't keep the high-ticket items there."

"What are those?" He frowned, thinking back to what he'd seen at Potter's Field. "Some of the things you've got in that place ran to the high hundreds. I know you paid stupid money for that decoder ring, but that checked out to be worthless, charity on your part. How much higher can that shit go?"

"Dude, I've got a few Lugosi and Karloff one-sheets that if I dropped them onto the open market would go for over three hundred thousand each. That's just the tip of it." Rook chuckled when Dante huffed in astonishment. "The thing is to go find stuff that's worth something, buy as low as you can, and sell high. You'd be surprised at what people have in their attics."

"Jesus," Dante whispered. "What the hell can be worth that much? And who buys it?"

"Comics, cereal box toys they had to send away for… hell, even the right decoder ring can be worth thousands. My buyers are people with a lot of disposable money who like stuff from their childhood or even just a genre. Horror is big. So's sci-fi. Fantasy's making a comeback, though." Rook patted Dante's cheek. "See, I don't do nickel-and-dime shit, Montoya. The shop's so I can get rid of the piddly-ass crap and a nice place for me to live once I dumped a few dollars into walls and kitchen. But the good stuff's in a warehouse in WeHo, behind a shit ton of steel, locks, and under temperature control."

"What do you have that someone would want to kill for?" Dante got up to retrieve his notebook, needing to make notes. "Would Dani have known that? Or the Betties?"

"You talked to Pigeon, right?" Rook inched over to make room for Dante when he returned. "She'd know something about the Betties. I don't know about Dani. They weren't talking last I heard."

"She gave me some background. I've got to tell you something. About one of the Betties." Dante filled Rook in on the townhouse and the woman he'd found dead under the rubble. "She'd been killed at least two days before the place went up. That's the official guestimate. Pigeon was in Chicago."

"Jane. Who's the other one in that pair? Madge?" Rook frowned. "Charlene. They were Charlene's friends."

"Charlene, who has access to your inventory," Dante pointed out. "Would she have set you up?"

"Dude, Charlene can barely remember her bra size. She's not exactly a criminal mastermind," Rook snorted back. "She might have said something to one of them, but she doesn't have access to the warehouse. I don't think she even knows where it is. Or even if I own it."

"Someone else wouldn't know that. They'd think you had that kind of stuff at your store." The room phone rang, and Dante glanced worriedly at Rook. "Did you give anyone this number?"

"'Toya, it's probably the front desk kicking us out. Archie was an asshole to the room service guy when he came up with the popcorn. I had to give him a fifty-dollar tip on the room charge to keep him happy." Rook slid across the bed and grabbed the phone, groaning when he stretched. "God, this shit's getting old. Hello?"

The blood drained from Rook's face, and Dante caught the headset just as the phone tumbled from Rook's hand. Grabbing at Rook before he catapulted off the bed, Dante spoke into the phone. "Hello? Can I help you?"

"Let me go, Montoya." Rook struggled against Dante's arm. "Fucking let me go. It's Archie. Someone shot up his car close to the hotel. I've got to—"

"Sir?" A man's voice echoed over the line, coolly professional and curt. "You'd better hurry, Mr. Stevens. Your grandfather is asking for you."

Seventeen

ROOK WAS sick of the smell of blood.

Its cloying metallic odor haunted him, sticking to the inside of his nose and coating the back of his throat. Close by, someone was shouting, a screeching rise and fall of hysterical nonsense he humbly recognized as belonging to one of his mother's sisters, but he couldn't find enough energy inside of him to see who it was.

Especially since he was the reason she was losing her shit in the middle of Cedars-Sinai's emergency ward.

There were cops. There were always cops. This time they formed a wall between him and the rest of the Martin family who'd swooped down on the hospital's lobby. He'd gotten very fond of the blue-cotton fence cordoning him off, especially when one of his uncle's wives—a number three, if he remembered correctly—tried to fling a shoe at his head. The stiletto would have hurt if it'd landed, but apparently not as badly as the cuffs one of the baby-faced cops snapped around her wrist when she tried to knee Montoya in the nuts.

He didn't need their recriminations. Rook had his own to deal with. They clung to him, ghosts whispering of the pain and agony he'd brought down upon his grandfather. Sitting in the cold waiting area, Rook stared into the chaotic hall, riding the noise drowning him. If he'd only gotten into the car when Archie asked him to. If he'd not left the hospital that first night. There were too many ifs for Rook to wrap his head around and nothing loud enough to suppress the guilty echoes bouncing around in his brain.

The cold seeped into him, reaching down into places already iced over in his guts, and Rook looked blindly about, searching for something to anchor to.

And finding it in a tall, strong-jawed cop who'd cradled him in his sleep the night before.

Dante stood talking to one of the other officers, another faceless blue uniform in a sea of navy cotton. He wore his serious detective demeanor, attentive and focused, with a stern expression Rook figured they taught in an academy somewhere in the hills. The idea of Dante Montoya standing in front of a mirror practicing a variety of cop-centric faces made him smile despite the dread pressing up from his belly, and in that moment, Dante glanced his way and Rook felt something in his chest... hitch.

He was caught in the molasses of Dante's gaze, a delectable heat Rook halfway wished he'd let consume him. The cops finished their conversation, and Dante drifted over, sliding in between the islands of Rook's relatives, his shoulders firm and taut as he withstood their rapid-fire assault of questions.

"For all we know, he's the one who did this," his aunt sniped. It was a classic juvenile ploy, speaking loud enough in a childish singsong, daring Rook to call her out. "He probably arranged for someone to kill Daddy, and now—"

"How are you doing?" Dante crouched down in front of Rook, his fluid roll of accented English masking the rest of the conversation. "Do you need anything, *cuervo*?"

"Nah, I'm... fuck, 'Toya. This is... it's crazy." He leaned forward, leeching off the man's warmth. "Why the hell would someone do this? What happened? *Why* did this happen?"

They'd come downstairs to a sea of sirens, lights, and ambulances. The black sedan Rook'd shared with Archie not more than a B-movie before sat with blown-out tires and shattered windows, its sides pierced through with bullets. Blood smeared the sidewalk and cement driveway, run through with tires and footprints. A pool of vomit lay next to the valet's station, and Rook remembered stepping around it, as if tracking the remains of someone's late lunch through his grandfather's blood would be something Archie would not tolerate.

It'd been the sight of a paramedic struggling to pump life into a young man wearing a hotel uniform that drove him to his knees.

It'd been the man crouched in front of him who lifted him back up again.

A scrub-clad man paced down the hallway and stopped short at the horde of Martins. They descended, a murderous screeching flock pecking ruthlessly at the slender bald man, stabbing him with questions and accusations until he beat them back with an officious sniff.

Clearing his throat, he said, "Which one of you is Rook Stevens? Mr. Martin is asking for you."

Standing up was the hardest thing Rook'd ever done in his life. Worse than the day he'd pulled his first job and forgot to take his haul and harder than when his mother first climbed onto the back of a motorcycle to go get a pack of smokes, only to vanish for nearly six months. He'd been alone and adrift most of his life, anchored to no one but himself, and there in the linoleum hell of sanitized air and squeaky-voiced blondes, Rook was afraid.

Deathly and deeply afraid to take a step, then another to stare down something he'd not imagined he'd ever face—the death of someone he'd just begun to love.

"Fucking old man," Rook muttered under his breath, pushing past Dante with a brush of his shoulder. "He... better be okay."

Their hands met, fingers brushing for a long instant, and Rook nearly pulled back, needing to bury himself in Dante's chest. There was the promise of warmth and safety there, such an alien need Rook was caught between the want of Dante's arms and the fear of needing the man so much it crippled him.

The rub of Dante's fingertips on his palm would have to be enough.

"Do you want me to go in there with you?" Dante edged Rook in, holding him in place. His breath ruffled Rook's hair, a hint of coffee and mint folded into a sweet whisper.

"No, you hold them back." The air was poisonous, filled with mutters and accusations. "And as much as I hate guns, I don't mind if you wing them or something. Because fuck, they're just—"

"Shitty?" He gave Rook a little push toward the hallway entrance where the nurse stood waiting. "Go on. I'll be here. When you're done, the cops will want to talk to him if he's up to it. Well, if the vultures here leave anything."

"Can you see about his goon?" Rook walked backward a step. "Guy's an asshole, but...."

"Just because he's an asshole doesn't mean you want him dead." Dante's crooked smile did silly things to Rook's stomach. "I'm on it."

The room was stark, colder than the frigid confines of the waiting area where he'd left his relatives. In the sea of beige walls and steel rails, a flotsam of machines floated around a single bed, its occupant nearly buried under thick blankets and tubes. Archie lay against the white sheets, parchment gray and stiff, his lean face gaunt and drawn. As Rook approached, the old man's eyes fluttered open, and they floated over

Rook's face before snapping into focus. Struggling to sit up, Archie lightly cursed the tight cocoon of blankets pinning him to the mattress, and Rook strode over, the weight in his belly lightened at the sound of his grandfather muttering fuck under his breath in a hot, angry stream.

"Do they think I'm going to fucking break loose like King Kong?" Archie feebly kicked at the end of the blankets, trying to loosen them from under the mattress. "Help me out here, boy. Give me some room to breathe under this."

"They probably think you're going to do a runner." Rook couldn't stop a silly grin from stretching over his face. "The other hospital probably gave them a heads-up about me so you'd be trapped."

"Probably." Archie pulled a sour face. "Leeches. If you've got money, they want to keep you in as long as they can to bleed you dry, but if you're poor and really need help, you're out the door before you've swallowed those fifty-dollar aspirins they give you."

"Do they even give out aspirin?" Tugging the blankets out from under the mattress, Rook fluffed them up so his grandfather could move about. "How's that?"

"Better. Now find me a hot nurse, and I'll be great." He took a breath. "Never mind. You'd go out there and bring me back something with a dick. I'll get Stanley… shit, Stanley—"

"Dante's checking on him," Rook said as he pulled a chair close to the bed. "Doctor said he took a bullet to the lung and thigh, so he'll be in surgery. You and I—now we've got matching scars on our arms, which pisses the family off to no fucking end, because you know, they're assholes. Your concussion's bigger than mine, which is kind of impressive, old man, because you know, I was hit by a fucking car."

"You're younger. You bounce better. When you're a sack of bones like I am, we just rattle about like dice in a cup." Archie squeezed Rook's hand once, then clutched at the blanket. "Thought you'd gotten rid of me?"

"Right, you and roaches are going to be the only things left after the apocalypse. Tooling around. Driving old lady Buicks and eating Twinkies." Studying his grandfather, Rook noted the bandages along his neck and jaw, frowning at the speckles of blood coming up through the gauze. Nodding at the immobilizing cast on Archie's left hand, he asked, "Broken or shot?"

"Broken finger. Busted the damned thing trying to grab the door handle when Stanley swerved the car. Didn't think he'd gotten enough speed in, but we nearly went through that driveway rail, and I'll bet you the car's a total loss. Damn thing was only a few months old. I'd just worn in the backseat so it fit my scrawny ass."

"You're rich enough. You can hire an ass double and have him squirm around a car seat so it's ready for you." Rook snorted when his grandfather struggled to flip him off. "Want me to hold your fingers down for you, old man?"

"Shut it. I'm left-handed. I'll have to practice." Archie glared at a shadow skulking across the hallway near his room door. "Doctor or one of my stupid children?"

"Orderly. Well, someone holding a piss pan," he said, craning to get a look. "And Alex's mom isn't too bad. Quiet."

"She's like a Milk Dud. Chewy and sticks to your teeth. Not bad, but let's face it, in a box of chocolates, that's not what you're going to be reaching for first." He shifted, groaning, then pushing Rook's hand away when he reached for the call button. "Don't call anyone. I'm just trying to get comfortable. Answer me this, are *you* doing okay? You're not hurt or anything, right?"

"Yeah, I'm fine." Rook grabbed the call button anyway, keeping it out of his grandfather's grasp. "I wasn't in the car with you, remember?"

"Idiot! I know you weren't in the car with me. I'm asking because, after we got hit, I kept hearing some asshole open the door and say, *He's not here. Stevens isn't here.*" Archie's voice wavered. He closed his fingers over Rook's wrist, painfully digging his nails into the tender flesh below. "Who is after you, boy? And what do I have to do to stop them?"

THE TIME went well past late and was into early dawn by Rook's third cup of bitter diner coffee. The hours spent with Archie tore him down, and as a milky sun rose on Hollywood Boulevard, Rook sat staring out at the buzz of traffic inching across the soupy morning. He'd lost track of the trucks he'd counted ambling past the diner's enormous windows, the panes speckled by dirt and insect splatter.

Perched on a busy corner near the shopping monstrosity erected to anchor Hollywood's growing obsession with its own sycophants, the diner normally gave Rook a good place to sit and watch the area's unique blend of tourists, locals, and the bottom-feeders desperate for anything coming their way.

In the too-early-for-food hours, however, pickings were mighty slim.

A sunbaked woman in a pink boa and star-spangled bikini stood on the median between the street's lanes, her impossibly orange curls teased up into a crowning mess over her teak-hued wrinkled face. Her body shimmied with loose skin over her thighs and gut, flapping as she waved a sign announcing to passersby she was available as a tour guide to the stars. The veins in her arms were a black tangle thick enough they were visible from across two lanes of traffic, and Rook's chest ached in sympathy when he caught her looking over her shoulder periodically to watch for cops.

Dante slid into the booth across of him, his legs jostling Rook's as he got comfortable. A waitress sidled up to the table, a pot of hot coffee at the ready to top off their cups, and Rook half heard Dante thank the woman as she rattled back his order to him. Rook shook her off when she asked if he wanted something other than coffee, going back to stare at the older woman who could have been the server's twin if they'd taken similar paths.

"You doing okay, *cuervo*?" Dante's hand came down over Rook's, pressing their fingers together. Their fingernails rubbed, a pearl on pearl sensation Rook realized he'd never really felt before. Something on his face must have piqued Dante's curiosity, because the cop tilted his chin up and asked, "What? What're you thinking?"

"It's weird. How much you touch me. I never would have thought you'd be... so touchy." His mind wasn't firing right, and words he should have known were slipping away under the fugue swamping Rook's thoughts, but he fought to find what he needed to say in his mind's stew. "You're out."

"Yes...?" Dante drew the word out, confusion clouding his face. "And?"

"I mean, like, you're really out," Rook murmured, sliding his fingertips over Dante's outstretched palm. "It's weird. Because you... stroke and do things, like when we walk, you touch the small of my back. Like when we were in the hospital and I started to go down the wrong hall, then you caressed me there. In front of those cops. In front of everyone."

"I'm not ashamed to touch you." Reaching for the packets of sugar at the end of the table, Dante shrugged. "I'm gay. We've been... together, and even if it's been a little bit crazy—you're a little bit crazy—I like you. And I'm also half Mexican, so you're going to see me eating burritos once in a while. There's going to be a lot of really normal things you're going to catch me doing. Just so you know."

"See, gay? Not a thing to advertise when I was growing up." Rook pressed his lips together. "I got used to hiding it. Okay, just not really talking about it. Think it's why my mom left. You know?"

"You really think that?" Dante shook a creamer out into his coffee, stirring as he looked up at Rook. "You think she left you there with those people because she thought you were gay? You were what? Seven? Eight?"

"I told her I liked boys like she did. I thought she was going to vomit." He shrugged, refusing to let the image of his mother's disgusted look surface up from his memories. "She split the next morning with some guy she'd just met. Hard not to make that connection, you know?"

"So when Archie...." The cop exhaled hard, clicking his tongue against his teeth. "You figured your grandfather would be the same way."

"I came at him, you know? Because he was this thing to be conquered, not an actual person." Rook leaned on his elbows, jostling the table. "Archie was like the bogeyman. He was why Beanie—my mom— left home. And then she left me."

"How did he get a hold of you, then? Call? Sent someone?"

"He didn't know about me. Beanie never contacted them, and I'd... well, when you and your partner came around to fuck up my life, she figured I might need a lawyer or something. She gave me Archie's name and where everyone lived." It'd been an odd night, cradling his drunken mother as she railed against her father's machinations while pushing Rook to give her money. "I don't know if she called someone or... anyway, he found me out... and there we were. Shit, I can't even think here, Dante. Tonight... yesterday. So much has fucking happened. I just know today when I thought—when I saw him there in that damned bed, he looked so fucking small, and it... *killed* me. Inside."

"Archie loves you. He was glad to see you were okay." Dante snorted at Rook's incredulous smirk. The waitress returned, filling their cups and dropping off Dante's plate of bacon, scrambled eggs, and toast. Pushing the plate between them, Dante tapped the fork at Rook's elbow and said, "You eat and I'll talk. Or I listen and you eat and talk. But either way, you eat."

The fried pork crumbled on Rook's tongue, nearly cardboard tasteless under the ashen worry he'd heaped on himself. Chewing, he swallowed, catching a hard glare from Dante when he tried to put the bacon back onto the plate. Another bite and his stomach rebelled, but he continued chewing, chasing the bite down with a gulp of scalding sweet coffee.

Rook's words bubbled up from inside of him, percolating until he couldn't breathe, and the emotion they carried tightened his throat. He had to speak, had to get out the one thing he couldn't take back down, because it would burn into his soul and he'd carry the scar of its swallowing for the rest of his life.

He sounded small when he spoke, so far away from the man he thought he'd become. Instead, Rook found the broken child inside of him—a child he thought he'd buried years ago when his mother faded into the distance behind a roar of engine noise and blue smoke.

"I was so fucking scared, Dante," he whispered, looking back out at the woman standing in the street, hoping to feed on someone else's dreams of touching the stars. "Just so damned fucking scared."

The bacon fell away, disappearing somewhere. Rook didn't know or care because his world was suddenly filled with Dante, the cop's—his cop's thick arms wrapping around him, pressing him into a broad muscled chest where a heart beat in strong strokes in time with Rook's own fluttering pulses. Everything around them faded, sliding away from the walls Dante erected around them.

Rook heard nothing. Felt nothing other than the man who'd come around the table to embrace him, to hold him steady as his world fell apart and he had nothing to stand on. The edge of a cliff suddenly appeared beneath Rook's feet, and he stared down into the blackness of loss, mourning a grandfather he thought he'd lost and possibly would never ever truly be loved by. A step forward, and Rook knew he'd tumble down, shattered on rocks he'd sharpened with his own acidic tongue... only to be saved by Dante's touch.

"I almost lost him, 'Toya," Rook mumbled into a crease in Dante's shirt. The man smelled of coffee, soap, and tired male, a familiar comfort he'd grown too used to. He'd have to let go soon, too soon, but for now, for then, Rook allowed himself to hold on as tightly as he could, unwilling to be flung back in the maelstrom he'd been thrown into. "God fucking damn it, I'm not... I can't do this. I can't *care*."

"You already care, *cuervo*. No stopping that once it happens." Dante's fingers were in his hair, stroking away the prickles across his scalp. "I'll have the waitress pack this up, and we can eat it back at the—"

"Fuck the hotel," Rook grumbled, pulling away from Dante to rub at his eyes. "I want to go and lie in my own goddamned bed, on my sheets, and let you hold me. For however long you can be there, but fuck it, I'm sick of running away—from me… from the psycho that's out there… even from Archie. I'm tired of it, 'Toya. I just want to go… *home*. And I don't even have a goddamned home. Can you do that for me, Dante? Will you just take me home and… stay there with me? For a little bit?"

"I can do that, *cuervo*." Dante caught the waitress's attention, motioning her over. "And babe, I'll hold you for however long you want me to. And even then, I *might* not let you go."

Eighteen

IT WAS quiet in the middle of Hollywood.

The morning had turned dewy and gray by the time Dante got Rook up into his loft above Potter's Field. Within seconds of the elevator doors closing behind them, the skies were a threatening black, crackling with the promise of lightning and fury. Pouring a senseless Rook into bed was less trouble than Dante thought it would be, especially after a judicious application of a pain pill, ibuprofen, and tooth-brushing. With the loft's blackout curtains drawn, the rooms were plunged into a thick darkness, and Dante stumbled a bit as he left Rook sleeping off his trauma to get his head around the murders.

Spartan was one word Dante had in mind about Rook's place. Its dearth of furniture was sad in a way, as if Rook never planned on having more than one person in the apartment—himself. While comfortable, the couch was kept company by pieces of lawn furniture, but Rook's coffeemaker definitely was geared to a heavy user. Brewing up a strong carafe of Italian roast, Dante contemplated the deaths he'd been assigned, then retired to the living room space to construct and file reports on his laptop. He spent nearly two hours doing paperwork, serenaded by Rook's soft snuffling and melodic murmurs before turning his attention back to the murder board in his notebook.

A ping from his e-mail turned out to be an information dump from a detective working Vice in West Hollywood, and Dante read through the initial message, then shot off a promise of beer, eternal gratitude, and future favors. Running briefly through the notes was dizzying, but he quickly picked out familiar names among the stacks of references in the other detective's reports.

"Rook's got to be the center of it," he mused, sipping at the rich black coffee. Scribbling down the key people gave him a laundry list of names whose sole connection was a nebulous dotted line to his irascible lover. Drawing a large square in the middle of a blank page, Dante sat staring at the empty block until his cell phone burbled a cheery tune. Shaking his head at the number, he answered the call. "Yeah, Camden?"

"Montoya!" Hank blasted through the speaker, and Dante pulled the phone away from his ear. "Just wanted to touch base. I'm still out for a couple of days. Doc won't sign my release form yet."

"Yeah, I don't think I want to share a car with a ginger howler monkey. Tone it down a bit. I don't know what's louder—you or the explosion," Dante teased. "Can you hear me?"

"Oh, I can hear you. I've got speakers on this thing. Wife made me go into the bathroom and close the door. Says I'm breaking her eardrums." His partner's voice dropped a notch. "Better? I'm working on volume controls. Are you back at work? Or did the captain pass our stuff off to someone else for right now?"

"Well, my ears aren't bleeding, and no, he gave me a day, but shit's happened." After filling Hank in, Dante paused long enough to take a sip of his cooling coffee. "So what do you think?"

"It'd be easier if we could run this down together, but it'd be a tossup who'd kill me first, the captain or the wife." Hank grumbled under his breath. "The Pigeon didn't seem too broken up about her sister. Are we sure she's out of the game?"

"Pretty sure. She's been clear of Vice for a while now, and everything seems to check out. Our victim in the townhouse definitely was on track to go clean. She was known to Winters, one of the detectives down in WeHo. Apparently he was working with her to get information on current players, which included her former partner. Pigeon wasn't on the negotiation table there, but the sister, Dani, was."

"Strong-arm on Pigeon's part or loyalty on our vic's?"

"I'm going with loyalty. Pigeon's the one who suggested Jane go talk with WeHo. From what he'd gotten from the vic, there's stuff that might have even rolled over to the feds." Dante called up an e-mail he'd gotten from the other detective. "Winters said Pigeon's involvement was cloudy, so he didn't think he'd get anything solid on her, but our vic had some good stuff against the ex-partner, Madge, and a few others who were running some dangerous cons. Jobs that included our original victim, Dani Anderson."

"He give you any details?" Hank asked. "Any known associates between Dani and Madge?"

"Cast of thousands, or at least hundreds." Dante scrolled through electronic reports. "Madge Stalgetti with a hell of a lot of AKAs. He didn't specifically target a connection between Madge and Dani, so other than Jane mentioning they knew each other and were working on something together, that's all Winters's got. Apparently our girl Madge is quite the go-getter. Jane told Winters her ex-partner had about five cons going, including a long con big enough for them to never work again."

"Isn't that what they all say?" his partner shouted into the phone. "Did our vic say what it was exactly?"

"No, only that it was something she wanted no part of." Dante skimmed a paragraph. "It's what turned Jane completely off of the partnership. Winters states Jane knew the intended victim and didn't want to cross him. She and Madge fought over it. Ugly fighting. Seems Madge and her partner or partners were very serious about doing this job, no matter what the cost. Whatever was said, Jane believed Madge was willing to kill to pull this off, and that wasn't a line she was going to cross."

"So, two questions," Hank drawled. "The *him* in this case? Think that's your boy, Stevens? And was Madge's new partner our first victim, Dani?"

"Yes and probably," he answered. "Remember, Pigeon said people don't want to fuck him over. He's someone you go to when you're up against the wall, so screwing him would bring down murder and mayhem on your head if it got out. Apparently, he's likeable."

"So not the Stevens *we* know and love." Camden laughed. "Well, me. You've probably already known and loved him a lot by now."

"Focus, Hank." Dante glanced at the corner of the bed he could see around a bank of bookcases. "And as for Dani being Madge's partner, if you *were* going to fuck over Stevens, she'd be the one who'd do it. They parted badly. Good reason to hook up with someone if it let her get back at him."

"And the other two Betties ended up being collateral damage?"

"Stands to reason. They were known for cleaning a place out quickly. With all the stuff at Rook's shop, they'd be a good addition. Madge would have known them and could have brought them in," Dante pointed out. "Something went sideways, and Dani was killed. Could be Madge's cleaning up loose ends."

"But what was the reason for it?"

"Could be Dani had another agenda, and Madge decided to permanently end the partnership. Leaving the body there was a good idea on her part. My guess is Madge wants Rook Stevens out of the way.

Pinning a murder on him is a good place to start, but she didn't count on him having a flush of high-price lawyers in his back pocket." Dante scribbled Rook's name in the empty box in the middle of the page. "They were looking for something. He said all of his expensive stuff's over at a warehouse off-site, but nothing so rare it's life changing."

"We've already established he lies, Montoya. Or have you forgotten that?" Hank asked. "For all you know, he's got the goddamned Maltese Falcon over there."

"He probably does, but nothing that's a disappear-to-a-tropical-island hit." Dante chuckled. "He's inventoried everything out. I'll get a price list when he wakes up, but the stuff he runs is pretty unique. Dumping it would send up red flags like crazy. So it makes no sense on that end."

"So they were probably after something that's in that building, and you're over there having a slumber party." His partner sighed. "Great, I'm going to have to break in a new partner because my last one got his dick dipped and his head shot."

"No one can see in, and he's beat. He had more things hit him yesterday than the Egyptians had plagues," Dante replied. "We're fine. It's daylight, and the angles are off for a hit from the street. I checked. Besides, they've already taken a shot at him here. Chances are good if Madge is going to go at him, it'll be from another angle. I just don't know what or where."

"Okay so *Rook* says he doesn't have the golden goose over there, and the ones he *does* have wouldn't be enough to kill for. Thing is, Montoya, people have killed for less. Shit, you and I've picked up the pieces of a kid shot up because he had a cool backpack. A pencil that changes colors is a life-changing hit to some people." Hank grunted. "Hey, you ever think that maybe *you're* another angle? Against Stevens, I mean?"

"No one but you and the captain knows… okay, his family. Pigeon. Manny." Dante counted off the people he'd come into contact with. "Yeah, half of Los Angeles. Fuck. I'll be careful. As soon as he gets up, I'll move him out, but I can't promise he'll stay moved. They invented the word stubborn with him in mind."

"Oh good, so happy the two of *you* have found each other. That's all the world needed."

"Nice. I think our next move should be to find Madge," he suggested. "Pigeon doesn't know where she is. She left off fucking with people before Jane did and kind of fell out of the loop."

"I'm with you on Madge. Pump Rook… for information." Hank burst into a peal of loud, hearty laughs when Dante groaned in protest. "This is never going to get old. Seriously, maybe he knows someone who knows someone."

"I've got a couple of contact names from Winters. If they'd cleared you for work I'd have taken you with me, but I guess I'll go at it solo."

"Not going to happen. Any place you go, I go. Fuck the doctor's orders. And well, I won't say anything to the wife. Just don't get me blown up this time."

"We'll see." The tired Dante held off with coffee and work finally snuck up on him and he yawned, his jaw popping. "I'll keep you caught up as I go. But for right now, I'm crawling into bed."

"Yeah, you do that, Montoya," Hank shot back. "Most of all, keep your head down. And while you're there, keep Stevens's head down too. Last thing I need is for you two to end up like Dani Anderson, 'cause I don't want to break in a new partner."

THE BED dipped with Dante's weight, and Rook swayed on the mattress as Dante settled on top of him. Naked and warm, he fit into the dips of Rook's body, his cock thickening as it nestled into the part between Rook's cheeks. Stretching out over him, Dante drowned the world out with the taste of Rook on his tongue when his lips found the soft burr of Rook's nape.

At some point, Rook'd kicked the blankets off, and he'd sprawled across the bed, stretching out his limbs as far as they could go. As Dante cuddled into him, he pulled himself in, squirming under Dante's weight as he shivered in the shared heat of their bodies.

"You awake?" Dante chuckled when he got a sharp elbow to the ribs. "Guess so."

"Talking to yourself out there, or did someone call up to ask you about aluminum siding?" Rook mumbled softly. "Heard you muttering, then my brain said fuck it and went back down."

"Hank. He's as deaf as a post still. Talking to Camden is like having an air raid siren pressed up against my ear." Dante's teeth nipped down Rook's spine, stopping for a larger nibble when he got close to a shoulder blade. "Just going over the case. We agreed Madge is our probable in this whole thing. We just need to find her. Any clues about where she'd be tucked away? Secret underground bunker you all know about?"

"Nothing about Madge," he sighed into the pillow. "A few clues about you, though."

"Those aren't clues. Those are dirty thoughts." He wiggled his hips. "Really interesting dirty thoughts."

"Same thing. Both lead to bigger and better things." Rook shifted under Dante, and he slid to the side to let Rook turn over. "Shit, this stuff is just crazy. I didn't even know the Betties, haven't seen Dani in years, and now it's like *Lord of the Flies* around me."

The room was full of milky shadows, the day held back by thick blackout curtains, but a soft LED sconce from the bathroom brushed enough of the darkness away to pull the grays to gentle hues. Rook turned his shoulders and propped his head up on a pillow, bringing his face into the light. Dante stretched up, tasting Rook's lips with a quick kiss. When he pulled away, Rook growled, then wrapped his fingers into Dante's hair, giving a short tug to show his annoyance.

"Get me started, then back away. You, Montoya, are a cock tease." Rook tugged again, then let go.

He enjoyed exploring Rook. There were stretches of skin on the small of the man's back where Rook could barely stand to be touched without laughing, and Dante'd discovered a kiss on the inside of his lover's thighs could turn his bright blue and green eyes to storm and foamy ocean with lust. He didn't need the light to know Rook's shoulders ran to blush when stroked or that he bit his lower lip at least three times before finally gasping soft erotic mewls as he became aroused.

"I wanted to talk to you a bit. Don't make that face. I like talking to you." Trailing his fingers down Rook's stomach, Dante skimmed over Rook's belly, watching his muscles jump when touched. "I've got a list of people Jane pinged as trouble. Mind if you take a look at it later? See if any of them pop?"

"You trying to seduce me into doing what you want, 'Toya?" Rook groused. "'Cause I'm kind of liking this police interrogation method you've got going. You don't have to stroke me off just to get me to do what you want."

"Sad to say, I'd be doing this no matter what." His lips were back on Rook's skin, this time teasing Rook's nipple. "Just take a look and see if you know anyone."

"I probably know a lot of people. The Betties just weren't some of them, but yeah, I'll go look. We didn't run in the same… circles. Fuck, Dante. I can't think when you do that. You're turning off my brain."

"Like brain off and sleepy?" He'd never teased anyone awake before. Hell, Dante couldn't remember the last time he'd woken up to a guy and hadn't wanted to slide off the bed toward the door. Sex with Rook was easy and playful, with a hint of surprising tenderness amid the aggressive lust. It was something Dante could get used to… provided he could keep Rook close by. "Or are you up for a little bit? Pun's intended, *cuervo*."

Rook cocked his head, and something in his expression gave Dante pause. Distrustful to the bone, the skepticism in Rook's tone dug something up from deep inside of the lanky thief. Dante didn't want to read too much into Rook's hesitation, but there was a glimmer of hurt and trepidation hidden in the man's brash sneer.

"What's going through that busy head of yours, Stevens?" Dante propped himself up on an elbow.

"Guess I'm wondering what's going to happen once you catch Madge… or whoever's doing this." Rook's husky rasp came off strong, but there was a thread of something desperate there. "I go back to hunting down old cereal box toys, and you… put your cape back on and leap tall buildings in a single bound? And what? We see each other for coffee and a fuck? How does this work?"

"More than coffee," Dante admitted slowly. "Definitely more than fucking. I'm not going to put words in your mouth. *Chingado*, I can barely put them in mine, but you and me, we're… how did you put it? Tangled?"

"You fucking anyone besides me?" Rook fell back into the shadows with a slide of his shoulders and ducking his head. "Because I don't want to screw up something you've got going already."

Comprehension dawned on Dante, a slow sunrise of emotions caught in the clouds of Rook's distrust. Shaking his head, he replied in a gentle voice, "Rook… *cuervo*… I'm going to be very honest with you, and I want you to listen to me. Really listen to me, okay?"

"Sure, whatevers. Talk," he tossed back. "Say what you've got to."

The apprehension was back. Dante felt it rolling off Rook's skin, and he put a hand on Rook's stomach, spreading his fingers over his lover's hard belly.

"I'm not with anyone else. I don't plan to be. Just you." Dante felt Rook's sharp intake of breath reverberate across his palm, and he pressed down, anchoring the man lightly to the bed. "You say you suck at relationships. Well, I've never had one. Not really. I've dated a few guys, and well, being a cop is hard for some people to deal with. I've also never liked anyone enough to try. Really try to make it work. Not until now. Not until you."

"Manny said you hated me. Before. With the whole shit about your partner and—"

"More honesty? Yeah, Vince left me with some serious anger," Dante cut in. "Did I hate you? I hated the thought of you. Took me a while to figure that out, *cuervo*. I'm with you because you get under my skin, and I kind of like you there. Thing is, are you here with me? Are you willing to trust me not to hurt you?"

"I don't get hurt, 'Toya. Shit like that...." Rook trailed off when Dante brushed his thumb over Rook's lower lip. "Dude, I'm not...."

"You lie to yourself, babe. More than you lie to me, and that's saying something," he whispered. "I'm not asking you to be honest with me about how you feel. That's going to take a hell of a long time. I know it. I know you. But today in the diner, it was the first time I felt like I was hearing the real you. Nothing fronted. Nothing to work the system. Just you. It was nice. And it made me feel... like you needed me."

"You're a dick, you know," Rook grumbled, looking away. "Today was... fucking hell. It was too much, Dante. I felt like I was drowning, and... fuck. I *hate* needing people. I hate needing *you*."

"You've spent your whole life making sure you don't need anyone, Rook. Because you couldn't trust the people who should have taken care of you. Your mother. Shit, even the people she dumped you with." Nudging up against Rook's long body, Dante leaned into him, touching skin to skin. "I know you push people away because you're scared. Hell, I do the same thing. I didn't want to fall in love. I didn't want complications. Shit, I barely wanted to know who I'm having sex with, but then... there's you. And now I want... different. I want you. With me. However that is. Can you do that? Can you try to trust *me* enough not to push me away?"

There was an eternity folded in between the moment Rook's eyes shuttered and when he parted his lips and said, "Yeah, Dante. I can do that. I trust you. All the way."

Nineteen

IT WAS different this time. Gentler. Tender. With a softness Rook didn't know if he could stand without breaking apart under Dante's hands. It was as if Dante's touch tore him open, peeling back layers of filth and disgust until Rook lay open for him to delve into, the very deepest parts of his soul bared for Dante's pleasure.

As well as Rook's darkest fears.

Their coming together had none of the roughness they'd had before. Lying naked against one another, Rook had time to explore Dante's body, to see what life had left on the skin under his fingertips. He found a few old scars, bleached white from time on Dante's golden skin. His lover murmured soft encouragements when Rook kissed a tiny starburst mark he found on Dante's ribs, a reminder of a long-ago fishing trip where Dante'd thought he'd pretend to be fly-fishing with a bamboo pole.

"You're lucky you didn't catch a hook in the eye," Rook tsked. "Could have blinded you."

"That's what my mother said. Right as she was screaming at one of my uncles for not watching me." Dante gasped when Rook bit the spot.

"Manny said you were… that they kicked you out." Flat on his belly and stretched out beside Dante, Rook lifted his head and stared up Dante's muscled chest. The man was all planes and strength, a fierce, powerful predator cloaked in golden skin and gentled voice. Rook couldn't imagine anyone… any family… rejecting a son like Dante, not when he was everything Rook was not.

"I talk to my mother. She calls me. I don't call the house," Dante explained. "I made a choice. I either lived how they expected me to, or I became my own man. The price of that was my family. But they made me pay it. I didn't want to. I didn't have to."

"And you have Manny," Rook pointed out.

"And I have Manny," he agreed. "You talk at the worst times, you know that?"

"You're the one who brought his mother into the room."

Dante twisted quickly, grabbing Rook, then flipping him over onto his back. Gulping in surprise, Rook flailed, nearly slamming his elbow into the side of Dante's head.

"Dude! Warn a guy."

"Hey, Rook." Dante licked Rook's left nipple, blowing on it to tighten the bud. "I'm now going to fuck you. Just a warning."

"Good to know," he shot back. "I'll try not to fall asleep while you're doing it."

Rook'd already dug out the condoms and lube he'd stashed in the chest of drawers, tossing the handful of packets onto the bed where they glittered a sleek gold on the sheets. Dante reached for one, and Rook's insides clenched in anticipation. On his back, Rook had a full view of Dante's thick erection, and even in the dim wash of shadows, its florid length stood out sharp against the pale latex sheath Dante rolled over it.

"Just putting it on, *cuervo*." Dante glanced down, his hands busy as he kneeled on the bed between Rook's parted legs. "I want to spend some time with you first. Right now, it's all about you."

It felt weird to lie back and let Dante have his way. His skin itched, and there were whispers in Rook's mind telling him to move, to take control, to do *something* other than spread out and allow another man—Dante—to take what he wanted.

A moment later, the voices were quieted, dulled and muted as Rook finally realized Dante wasn't taking. He was giving.

The press of Dante's thumbs along the long muscle of his thighs warmed his skin, then the muscles beneath when his lover worked his fingers over the taut balls of stress living in his legs. Still bruised from the car and aching where he'd been shot, Rook briefly fought the seductive promise of relief from the pain. Dante's touch seemed like another form of pill, something else to get hooked on and then mewl for after it was jerked away.

There was too much of his mother in that moment—addicted to chemicals to make her heart race or slow down—and of all the times when he called out for her in the middle of the night and found only the cold emptiness of her abandonment.

His bones began to sing, the core of his body tightening with want when Dante's dark hair brushed over his chest. The tip of Dante's tongue touched the center of his chest and began a trail down to his belly button, stopping only long enough to rim its curve before heading back up to his nipples. Tiny nips from Dante's sharp teeth released sparks along Rook's cock, its sheath peeling back and pulling down from its head.

He couldn't hold back a gasp when Dante slid a fingernail around his cock's ridge, barely scoring a line around its plum-shaped head. The slight burn set his dick on fire, and when Dante gripped his shaft, Rook couldn't help rocking his hips up to feel the glide of Dante's callused palm over his cock.

There was no sense of time passing, and Rook fell into a fold of sensual joy he could barely think in, much less escape. The play seemed to last forever and still, not long enough. Dante played with him, running his pinky under Rook's foreskin, then following up with a lap of his tongue.

"Dante... fucking hell," Rook whimpered. Dante *breathed* on his damp cock head, a pucker of lips and a whispery gust barely strong enough to ruffle the hair on Rook's belly, but his body reacted as if he'd been caught in a thunderstorm.

Then Dante wrapped his mouth around the tip of Rook's cock, and Rook lost his mind.

It seemed as if his lover's hands were everywhere. Rubbing at his nipples while his mouth sucked Rook's seed up from his balls. He dug his fingers into Dante's hair, more to have the man under his touch than to guide him down his shaft. A sloppy wet sound echoed from Dante's lips when he pulled back off Rook's cock, a soft pop, then another long lick of Dante's tongue down to Rook's balls. He nuzzled them, rolling the sac in his hand, then suckled at the velvety pouch, slickening Rook's crease with a thin sheen of spit.

Rook kneaded Dante's shoulder, his arms stretched out to an ache as he tried to keep hold of the man working his way across Rook's senses. Dante's hair was silk in Rook's fingers, sleek and soft on his belly when Dante lowered his mouth to the hollowed dip of Rook's hip. He left kisses along the way, brushes of affection wet with promise, and then Dante broke through the lulled peace Rook floated on with a casual brush of a thumb over Rook's leaking cock head, startling his too sensitive nerves to an almost painful, tart ache.

The smell of vanilla oil reached his nose as Dante pressed his fingers against the edge of his hole. Rook swallowed, unable to do anything other than ride the pleasures of Dante's mouth working his cock and the shallow burn of his body being opened up by Dante's touch. His shoulders seized up, anticipating the push in, and when it came, Rook cried out, fighting the urge to close his knees and force Dante back.

"Lift up for me, *cuervo*," Dante murmured, cupping the back of Rook's thighs in his powerful hands. "Put your legs up so I can be inside of you. Please?"

It would have been easy enough to whisper *no*. To show Dante he would stop what they were doing at a moment's notice, just to say he could. Just to *show* he could.

And that he trusted Dante enough to *actually* stop.

Not like the others before. Not *ever* like any time before.

"Please back, Montoya," Rook teased, resting his calves on Dante's rolled shoulders. In the soft light, Dante's features were both wicked and peaceful, a rush of softness in his sloe-eyed gaze while his mouth offered the darkest of sins.

Then Dante was in, and Rook broke apart once again.

ROOK STRETCHED around him, clenching down hard on Dante's cock as if he never wanted to let go. Dante tried not to laugh at the thought... tried not to imagine Rook never letting go. He'd spent his life working toward a normal he'd known as a child. A nice house in a good neighborhood, having family near him, and eventually finding someone he'd love.

Certainly not a foul-mouthed con artist with a penchant for lying and shoving people away. The face of Dante's imaginary lover was much like his own, and there he was, balls-deep in a funky-eyed pretty man who'd stolen a hell of a lot more than his heart.

"Fuck," he muttered, falling into Spanish. "I don't want him to let me go."

They burst through the awkwardness of finding a rhythm nearly as soon as Dante struck Rook's core. Their bodies were seamlessly joined together, moving in slow, long drives until Dante felt as if he would peel apart from the inside out. Rook's heat closed in over him, milking his dick with each pass, and when he angled his hips up, he brought Rook up off the mattress, striking at the spot inside of him hot enough to send shudders under Rook's skin.

Their bodies grew wet, moist from sweat and sticky along their stomachs where Rook's cock smeared cum in the tight space between them. He took his time, rolling his hips slowly when it seemed as if his lover was about to lose control, then speeding up as Rook dug his fingers into Dante's hips.

Each dip in was another lash of possession, and Dante shifted his knees, parting Rook's legs farther so he could deepen his plunging strokes. He wasn't sure who was possessing whom. Not when Rook clamped down on his dick hard enough for Dante to ease his thrusts.

"Is this good, *cuervo?*" Bending down, Dante captured Rook's mouth, whispering hotly over his tongue. He played inside his lover's mouth, sucking and pulling on Rook's lips until they were as pink as his hole. Rook's body pulled at him, tantalizing Dante with its heat. "Do you like it like this? Or do you want me to go deeper."

"You talk too much, Montoya," Rook growled, digging his nails into Dante's arms. A rock of Dante's hips made Rook hiss, and he arched his back, driving down on Dante's length. "Yeah, 'Toya. Just... damn, *there.*"

Resting his weight on his knees, Dante grabbed Rook's legs, angling them up against him. Rook's ass parted, welcoming him in, and Dante eased in farther, loving the stretch of Rook's body around him. Splayed out on the bed, Rook's body lay underneath him, clenched tight and marbled in the dim LED light. Shadows danced across Rook's face as he moved, his lower lip dimpled from bite marks, and his fingers were nearly white as his hands clenched the bedsheets, waiting for Dante to move again.

"Dante—shit, I can't take it," Rook pleaded. "Just... go. Fuck me."

He heard the roughness in Rook break. Beneath the snarling and the sneer, there was a man Dante wanted to reach. He'd touched that man before, hearing laughter bursting like starlight from Rook's mouth when he'd teased for a sleepy kiss in the middle of the night.

Needing to hold his lover, Dante slowed his thrusts and leaned in, wrapping his arms around Rook's shoulders, then pulling him in tight. He rocked into Rook's clench, barely moving his hips, but the motion was enough to slide Rook over him, sending them closer to the edge. A spot of wetness dampened Dante's shoulder when Rook ducked his head down, tucking his face into the curve of Dante's neck.

"I've got you, *cuervo*," Dante whispered. "Just let go. I'll be here to catch you."

Watching Rook lose himself in pleasure took Dante's breath away. His lover's face softened, layers of hardness falling away before Dante's eyes as he stroked Rook's face, urging him to let himself be loved. Lust-riddled and glutted, Rook's eyes lost focus, and his lashes swept down over his glittering gaze to hold back a storm of tears threatening to break. A vulnerability crept over Rook's mouth, his lips parting to take Dante's as his sibilant cries heated their kiss.

Dante felt the first splash of hot seed on his belly long before he saw Rook's face contort in climax. Stiffening around Dante, Rook's ass pulled Dante in, the muscles of his long body seizing up, then giving over as he rode another spurting orgasm. Holding Rook to his chest, Dante fell into the cresting tide, his balls riding up into his body as his cock rippled with gushing spasms. Caught between the sear of Rook's hold on his dick and the musky scent of Rook's spill on their skin, Dante gripped Rook's shoulders, riding out the waves of his peak, drifting along the ridge of pleasure as every inch of his body went numb from the shock running through him.

They lay gasping, small tremors ratcheting through them, and Rook stirred beneath him, moaning softly when Dante's softening cock slipped free from Rook's inviting warmth. He sighed, wishing he could stay nested in Rook for the rest of the day, but a creaking moan escaped Rook's bitten mouth, so he slid to the side, lifting his weight from Rook's torso. The light from the bathroom played out over the bed, and Dante was reminded of the ocean of bruises riding Rook's skin when he turned over, his rib cage heaving hard to recapture his breath. The dappling was sharper than the day before, darker as the marbling worked its way up to the surface.

"You make me lose my mind. You make me forget the crap that's happened to you." He lightly kissed a triangular purpled mark on Rook's side, then whispered, "Do you want me to get you something? Do you hurt? Shit, *cuervo*, if I've hurt you…."

"You should shut up, Montoya. You're exactly what I needed now." Rook's grumble was back, full force and deep. "Just hold me so we can get some sleep. And if you don't snore too loudly, I might even let you fuck me again once we wake up."

DANTE'S LIST was a who's-who of people Rook either worked with or avoided like the plague. Scanning the names, he used a pencil to cross off people he knew were in prison or dead. Sadly, the list didn't seem to get significantly smaller, no matter how much graphite he used.

A cup of coffee showed up at his elbow, positioned carefully on a slatboard bookcase he'd picked up at a ninety-nine cent store a few blocks down. It wobbled with the extra weight, barely strong enough to hold itself up, much less a mug filled with hot liquid. Dante must have had the same thought because he picked up the cup and moved it over to the table he'd commandeered as his workspace, making room amid a laptop, small printer, and a forest of paper files he'd retrieved from his car.

"This is crazy. You've got practically all of Los Angeles on this list." He took a sip of the coffee, peeling his lips back from his teeth at its bitter strength. "Fuck, what is this? Battery acid? I thought cops not being able to make coffee was a myth."

"Do I need to put more sugar into it for you, Your Highness?" Dante smirked at Rook's upraised middle finger. "You said black."

"I said blech when you asked if I liked it black," he muttered, handing the cup back to his lover. "See if you can strain out the copper wire you put into it while you're adding some of that sugar."

"I could just kiss you and sweeten that damned mouth of yours." Dante hoisted himself off the couch to head back toward the kitchen area. "Could be the coffeemaker. You've got about twelve of the damned things in here. What are you doing? Opening up a Starbucks?"

"People kept giving them to me. Like housewarming presents. That and towels." Rook shook his head. "It's like fucking suburbia threw up in my bathroom closet."

"Did you call Archie?" Dante called out from the counter. "I had a couple of follow-up questions to ask him if he's up to it."

"Yeah, he said his pet goon was doing well too." He frowned, trying to recall if he was remembering the right Brian Johnson from the list. "You know, I was kind of weirded out by something he said yesterday. About when the guy who shot the car up opened the door. He said something about me not being in the car with Archie. Why would he think I was there?"

"Might have been behind the hedge. Think about the front of the hotel and that block-long evergreen stand they've got going there." Dante returned with Rook's coffee, placing it carefully on the table. "Could have also thought the driver was you."

"Stanley's like eight and a half feet tall. We don't even look alike," he pointed out. "Makes me wonder if maybe the guy didn't see Stanley bring Archie's car from the parking structure. Like maybe he was dropped off?"

"Hotel's got cameras. We've got things lined up to look at the videos. I'll ask the lab to make sure they look at the street-facing ones first. Could be worth something." Dante tapped at the paper in Rook's hand. "More importantly, I need you to focus."

"What exactly am I focusing on? Someone I know who's hooked in with Madge?" He ruffled the sheet beneath Dante's nose. "I keep telling you, I don't know Madge. Shit, other than Pigeon, I don't even really know a lot of people copping to those kinds of cons. It's a crappy thing to do to people."

"And stealing stuff is okay?" Dante's eyebrows lifted, and Rook snorted at the judging look on his lover's face.

"Better than jacking them over personally. Lifting things... they're just things. What the Betties do is fuck with your life. Hell, Dani was good for that too. Or she used to be." He shrugged. "Problem with those kinds of cons is that people fall in love... and then you're fucking them over. With me, it was just business. They had. I wanted. Simple as that."

"Who'd someone like Madge go to if she wanted to switch what she did? Because that's kind of what she's doing now."

"If it's Madge," Rook murmured. "I don't know. You said she was stripping the place with the other Betties, but they're dead. So maybe she was done with them and didn't want to split whatever they thought they'd get three... four ways? But she'd need someone to crack open the locks."

"Which you've changed," Dante replied. "Suppose she's not interested in lock picking. The shooting yesterday tells me she's lost patience with the whole thing. She's moved straight into killing. Her partners. And probably you if she can do it."

"That's nuts." The thought of someone he didn't really know trying to kill him seemed outrageous. Especially for a score they didn't even know for certain would be there. "Why would she kill them? Jane, that one I get. Ex-partner who's going to the cops right before Madge gets her big hit. Not something I'd do, but I understand it. The others don't fit unless they got impatient, and she was done with their shit. But she'd still need another partner. Someone she really trusts."

"Why do you think that?" Dante looped his arm over the back of the couch. "We've got Pigeon saying Madge and Dani were talking about a job they could retire on. Maybe Madge is losing her cool, taking everyone around her out so she won't have to share the profits."

"Madge's in long cons. You don't pull those kind of tricks unless you can wait shit out, and usually there's someone to help you out of jams." Pulling his legs up, Rook stared off at the wall across from him. "*Someone's* getting itchy. Maybe it is Madge. We're looking at this wrong. I've got to think about this like if I were running the job."

"Okay, what would you do, then?" Pursing his lips, Dante looked across the room. "Besides stare at a bunch of bricks."

"Shut up. It helps me think," Rook muttered, slapping at Dante's fingers as they wandered over his thigh. "*If* I were going to run a job up against a thief, I'd want to make sure they were holding, had something really good stashed. But if I didn't know where it was exactly, I'd need help getting the mark out so I could look."

"Problem is, you say you don't." Dante grinned when Rook glared at him. "Hey, you lie. I accept that about you. I'm just saying that if you *do* have something you'd want to confess to, it can't be to me."

"I've stolen things. Let's just leave it at that." There were secrets he had. Deep and long secrets he knew he couldn't share with the man sitting next to him. The trust in Dante's eyes *hurt*, and not for the first time since he'd tumbled in with the cop, Rook wondered if Dante would stick around long enough for him to finally shed the last of his old life.

"Get back to this alleged second person. The now impatient one. Why would they want to hurry things along?" Speculation flitted over Dante's face. "Because they can't find this mythical big score, and you're in the way, but they don't know for how long."

"How the fuck do you get that from all of this?"

"You said it yourself. When you were standing over there talking to Charlene, you told her you weren't going to run anymore. That you were going to fight for the life you'd made. Suppose they don't believe you. Suppose they know how you operated in the past and are scared you're about to run. If you did, you wouldn't leave this big score behind. You'd take it with you."

"Solid reasoning. Mostly," Rook muttered. He let Dante's hand skim over his thigh, then wrapped his fingers through Dante's, playing with a gold ring his lover had on his pinky finger. "What the hell am I missing? Shooter? That's easy. Cheap, and they do what they're told. But where the hell would she get the idea I've got something for her to steal?"

A week ago, he'd have thought he was crazy for wanting a cop—this cop—touching him. It wasn't so long ago when his world was so black and white, he couldn't see anything other than pain and sorrow where people were concerned, and now, in his own home, he was holding hands with the one man who'd sworn to take him down.

"Shit, Montoya. It's you. It's not me running that they're scared of." Rook's heart stalled, twisting at the thought of what he'd brought down on himself by allowing Dante in. "*You're* what's different. It's because I'm with you. They—Madge and whoever else—they know I'm with you. I bet you that's it. They're scared I'm going to dump whatever it is they think I have and go full legit. Well, not like I'm not now."

"You keep saying that." Dante patted his knee. "But do they believe it? You said it yourself, you're not in the game anymore. You don't know what's going on. You've broken from that life."

"I like that you didn't say allegedly there. Makes my heart go all soft and warm." Rook snorted.

"Even Pigeon didn't have much. I heard firsthand how information dries up once it looks like you're no longer on that side of the line. Hell, we need you to give me one name at least... someone Madge might run with just so we can find her, and you don't know anyone."

"No, but I know people who might. Out but still kind of in touch. Might know something at least. Why the hell didn't I think of this before." Rook skimmed the list, looking for names he'd crossed off nearly as soon as he read them. "Here, JoJa. That's who'd know something about Madge."

Confused, Dante took the paper from Rook, crinkling it between his fingers. "Who the hell is JoJa? He? She?"

"They." Rook grinned at his lover. "You want information, they'll have it. But it'll cost you. Or more importantly, it'll cost me. Let me take a shower, and we can head down there."

"You're sure as hell not coming with me," Dante protested, snagging Rook's belt loop before he launched off the couch.

"They're not going to talk to you. You're a cop." He worked himself loose from his lover's grasp. "What they want to be paid in, you don't got, 'Toya. You need me in this. And 'sides, the fucking bitch tried to kill my grandfather. I owe her for that."

Twenty

"THIS IS a bad idea," Dante said again. "I just want you to know that. You shouldn't be out here. Docs haven't cleared you."

"Yeah, I know," Hank replied loudly. "I heard you the first twenty times you said it. I'm not that deaf. Besides, you needed backup to do this. You think I'm going to let you walk into... whatever this is... by yourself, you're fucking crazy, Montoya."

On a rainy late afternoon, West Hollywood became a landscape of bokeh and sharp lines. With its quilt-patterned streets and patchwork architecture, the neighborhood spooled out from under Los Angeles's hills, clutching tightly to Santa Monica Boulevard as it stretched its way out to the coast. Organic food chains battled to edge in beside entrenched tiny businesses, slyly packaging their expansive presence to fit into the area's eclectic blend of brash hues and Old World styling.

Dante drove past a corner café, marveling at the fire-eater performing near its entrance in defiance of the rain spitting down on the slow-moving sidewalk traffic. A few feet away, a woman waited at the crosswalk for the light to change, holding back a pack of dogs on rainbow leashes as she chatted to a tall black man in red platform boots. One of her dogs, a small wire-haired terrier, bounced about, its tiny body clearing the shoulder of a placid-faced mastiff standing patiently next to it.

"Gay neighborhood, right?" Hank's eyes followed the man in heels as he crossed the street.

"Little bit. Yes." Dante eyed his partner. "Why?"

"My wife's kid brother is coming to live with us. Kid's fourteen and came out last weekend in full glitter, glory, and rainbows. Her parents aren't... well, I think it's going to come down to him or them." He shrugged off Dante's frown. "It's a nonissue. We've already chosen him. Fuck them."

"Every day, you surprise me, Camden." He shouldn't have been shocked. Hank, for all his bluster, was solid, a good man to have at his back. After Vince, Hank was a damned good partner and someone Dante'd finally been willing to trust.

"Hey, I like the kid. A hell of a lot more than I like her parents. Just wondering if we shouldn't see if he can go to school around here, maybe. Not far from our house. As the crow flies." His partner scowled slightly. "What I don't like seeing is all the bars. How many fucking bars do you all need?"

"And again, just as I begin to respect you, you go and tear down the pedestal I was building. You all?" Traffic picked up, clogging the broad street. "You don't go to bars?"

"I'm married, remember?" He flashed the ring on his finger. "I haven't seen a bar since this thing came on. And I don't intend to have a long walk to a volcano to get rid of it. Hey, turn right. That's our street coming up. Let's hope your boy hasn't steered us wrong."

"He wants this over with as much as anyone else." Dante eased the unmarked onto a side street. "Cocky when it was just him. I think them coming after his grandfather shook him up. There it is. JoJa's Curiosities. Just need to find a place to park."

It'd been a battle with Rook. One common sense appeared to have won, but Dante wasn't certain. They'd gone at it, angling around each other until the air was hot enough to scald milk, and still Rook hadn't been willing to give in. At wit's end, Dante played the one card he knew Rook couldn't fight—a few handcuffs and the bed's metal frame.

"How long do you think it took him to get out of those?" Hank leaned over the front seat to retrieve the brown-paper-wrapped flat Rook'd set aside before Dante manacled him to the bed they'd shared.

"Probably five minutes. If that. I also zip tied the door from the outside." He shrugged at Hank's mocking, outraged gasp. "I told him I called his assistant to let him out. Charlene said she'd be there within the hour. And he'd already called JoJa's to tell them I was coming. He might be pissed off at me, but Rook won't jack this up."

"What do you give another guy after you've fucked him over?" Hank unfolded himself from the car, hefting the large package under his arm. "Me? I know flowers and chocolates are good. If it's really bad, then it's a really big gift card from a shoe place in the mall. Never jewelry. Apparently that means I've cheated on her, and she'll carve off my dick when I'm asleep."

"And you stay married to this woman?" Dante chuckled.

"Laugh now, Montoya. After what you pulled today, I'd be wearing metal boxers if I were you." Hank scanned the busy street. "What is this place? Some kind of pawn shop?"

"Collectibles. Froufrou. Rook said they deal with specialty items." Dante began to cross, hopping quickly onto the median. "Two owners, JoJo and Janet. Apparently they were fences at one time."

"And let me guess. Now they've gone clean like your lover and the woman with the cat." Hank snorted. "I'm calling bullshit. How many people go clean after years of ripping people off?"

"Four so far. I'm not holding my breath they're all legit," Dante replied, shielding his face from the spray kicked up by a passing delivery truck. "Come on. I don't want to get whatever that is wet. Rook said it's a pay to play deal with these two. And from what I understand, you're holding about seven grand under your arm that he's coughing up as a bribe, so don't drop it."

The rain began to turn icy, and Dante sprinted across a broad cement sidewalk scribbled with a pastel hopscotch game. A few feet away, two teenaged girls sat giggling at a coffee shop table, cowering beneath a narrow awning as they tried to wash chalk daubs from their hands. Hank was close on Dante's heels, shaking himself off like a soaked golden retriever once he reached the overhang stretched along the curio shop's front. Taking the package out from under his jacket, Hank inspected the paper, showing Dante the outer wrapping was dry.

"We're all good." He shivered. "Shit, it's cold."

"Probably warmer inside." Dante opened the door, striking a tiny bell dangling above the jamb.

"You sure Stevens didn't call ahead and kill the deal?" Hank paused at the threshold. "Right now, this is our only lead. Nothing else is panning out."

"Yeah, pretty sure." He dug through his pocket, found what he'd taken off Rook before he left Potter's Field, then held it up for Hank to see. "I took his phone too."

"FUCKER!" ROOK spit at his own front door. "Son of a fucking bitch!"

There had to be a level past anger. Some point beyond boiling rage and straight through magma fury. Either way, Rook knew he'd reached it. A pair of handcuffs dangled from his left wrist, and another remained fastened to the headboard frame Dante'd bound him to. Too pissed off to remove the other bracelet, it jangled and sang as Rook pounded at the heavy door Dante'd somehow wedged from the outer hall.

"That's what you get for trusting a cop, asshole," he raged at himself, pacing off a few feet before returning to pound at the door. "Son of a...."

Cursing wasn't going to get him very far. It felt good, but other than leaving him dead tired, it wasn't good for much. A part of him wanted to call JoJa's and tell the women not to talk to Dante, anything to set the cops back a few steps, but the memory of Archie's gaunt, pale body lying in a cold hospital bed stopped him in his tracks.

He also apparently didn't have a phone. And his laptop was probably keeping his cell phone company.

"I can't believe he did that to me. Fucking... cop," Rook growled. "Okay, screw him. I'm leaving. I'm not waiting for Charlene to get me out. She'll laugh her fucking weave off."

Getting out was... complicated. Scaling the side of the sheer-faced building was out. His harness and ropes were stored away in the warehouse not far from where Dante and Hank were shaking JoJo and Janet for information. Not to mention the damned storm hammering the outside walls. Rappelling in the rain sucked. He'd done it before but in full equipment.

And he hadn't had the threat of someone picking him off the wall like a clay pigeon at the time either.

"Tear the place apart just to get the fuck out of here?" The chill rooms were metal boxes laid into the brick wall without room for him to squeeze through to get to the hallway outside of his front door. In ensuring there was no direct access to the loft from the elevator or stairwell, he'd effectively imprisoned himself with his paranoia. "Pride isn't worth breaking anything, Rook. How hard is it to just fucking wait? Sit down. Charlene's going to be here soon."

A few minutes later, he'd shed the other handcuff and was already climbing the walls.

"Screw this. The door can come fucking down for all I care. *Shit*. Dude. God, Rook, you are *so* fucking stupid." Taking a deep breath, Rook stalked over to the island separating the loft's kitchen from its living space. A quick rifle through a catchall drawer provided him with what he needed, and Rook went around to the front of the island, armed with a screwdriver and a sharpened temper. "Okay, Dante. *Now* I'm aimin' to misbehave."

He'd debated long and hard over a bottle of tequila and regrets the first night he'd opened up the loft after its initial renovations. The chill rooms were empty narrow coffins of cold air and maybes, and the only furniture in the whole space was the king-sized mattress, box spring, and frame he'd spent way too much money on. Standing in the empty expanse, Rook'd wondered where he was going to put the remains of his past life.

Because he'd had no intention of ever going back to it. None whatsoever.

But the thought of tossing away nearly a decade and a half of hard work and cheap thrills seemed... sacrilegious. Especially since he wasn't quite sure he'd be cut out for a normal life.

"You're getting the shit shot out of you, and you're related to a man Genghis Khan would be terrified of," Rook reminded himself sharply. "How the fuck is this a normal life?"

Because now, he had a cop. A cop who thought nothing of clicking a pair of bracelets on his wrist and ankle just to keep him safe... or contained. Rook hadn't quite decided which, but he was more than willing to hear Dante's stumbling excuses about why he'd done it.

"So going to fucking do the same thing to him one day. Just when he least expects it. Going to take those damned handcuffs and...." The thought of Dante's muscular body stretched out on his bed made Rook hard. It was difficult enough to think. He didn't need the image of golden skin, wicked smiles, and a dick stiff enough to hammer nails with in his mind as he worked. "Okay, handcuffs later. Breaking shit open happens now."

The island was a solid build. He'd made sure of it. Now it was time to crack it open.

"Next time, just put a door. What the hell were you thinking?" Rook felt along the panel's edge, looking for the slight depressions he knew were there. His fingertips were less sensitive than they'd been in the past. Years out of the trade meant he'd lost a bit of his touch and instincts, but Rook closed his eyes and let his intuition guide him back to where he needed to be.

He'd been good—damned good—at what he'd done. There wasn't a house or building he couldn't get into. He just hadn't realized one day, he'd have to actually break himself out. Letting his mind wander, he dove down into the nothingness he kept in his mind, skimming the surface of his thoughts until nothing remained but the sound of the rain pounding at the glass and the feel of fine wood beneath his fingers.

"There you are." Keeping his finger on the spot, Rook guided the edge of the screwdriver under the hidden tab, then popped it out. After finding the remaining three, he sat back on his haunches and took a deep breath. "Just open it, stupid. Not like you're going to be cracking safes or anything. You're just going to get the hell out of your own house."

Twisting the locking screws open, Rook heard a click, and the hidden door he'd installed on the back of the island swung open.

His hands shook a little—he wasn't too proud to admit that. When he reached for the pouches he'd left rolled up on the narrow spacers built in behind the island's drawers, he had to shake his hands out before he touched the waterproofed fabric. Placing the bundled-up rolls onto the counter, he took a second before untying them, steeling himself for the rush he knew would hit his blood as soon as he saw his old tools.

He shouldn't have waited. Or perhaps waited longer, because the adrenaline hit him, and it felt nearly as good as Dante making him come.

Everyone's kit was different. Some preferred a brutal smash and grab, but Rook learned quickly that it was a dirty way to go. He might as well call the cops himself if he'd done that. Instead, he'd gone with finesse, sets of picks and electronic sniffers, trinkets he'd known better than he'd known his own soul. Sadly, none of them would help him now. Instead, Rook grabbed the long tube set diagonally into the space, popped its lid, then shook out the telescoping baton he'd hacked into years ago.

"Ah, I think *you'll* work." It was a piece he'd used only once or twice before. A pair of snips, a hollowed-out baton, and cables attached to a squeezing clamp on the fat end of the stick made for an ugly tool, but when he'd needed something a bit more flexible to ease around a heavy door to cut open a chain, it'd worked. A large compact mirror fixed to a long stem would give him an idea of where he needed to go, and the roll of duct tape from the junk drawer would help him get there.

The segments jiggled as he approached the door. Once he had them through the tiny slit he could make by leaning on the door, he'd tighten the cables to give himself enough tension to cut through whatever Dante used to string the lock closed. Angling the mirrored tool first, Rook found the view he needed, then duct-taped the stem into place.

"Really? A zip tie?" Rook shook his head as he worked the segments out through the crack. Guessing at the length he needed, the articulated baton would barely reach, and he once again questioned his wisdom in using the space's original wide, heavy door. "'Course, this was a damned dance studio. What the hell was that teacher trying to keep out? Zombies on a ballerina-only diet?"

A twist of his shoulder, and he brought the snips into contact with the zip tie, then pulled on the cables to snap the baton into its rigid form. The shears closed down on the ties, their sharp edges easily slicing through the thick plastic, and the door gave way, sliding quickly out on its greased rails and into the hallway beyond.

"Great, fucker turned off the elevator from downstairs. Stairs it is." Taking the dimly lit stairwell down meant meandering through the maze of corridors below, but without a landline in the loft, Rook didn't have a choice. He got to the bottom quickly, hoping to use the shop's phone to call one of Archie's pet gorillas to come get him, then grinned when struck by a sinister plan. "Shit no. I'll call Manny. Bring his uncle over. That'll teach him."

There didn't have to be much spin on the story. The handcuffs, combined with the whole Dante fucked him over and left him, would be enough to score sympathy with the tenderhearted ex-drag queen. Stalking through the back of the shop on his bare feet, Rook quietly rehearsed what he was going to say, looking for the right tone to lay down to work Manny over.

A light was on. From the corona leaking out into the narrow corridor, it looked like one of the overhead lights in the main sales room was shining at full sunburst. Grumbling, Rook headed to the front, realizing too late he should have put shoes on before walking across the shot-up storefront. A sliver of something caught his toe, and he had to stop to yank it out. Hopping around on one foot, he reached out to balance himself on one of the few tall display cases left intact after the decimating firefights prone to erupt in his shop. He'd just gotten the speck of metal out when Rook heard heavy footsteps stomping across the store's main floor.

"Dante, that better be you. I swear to God, if you're turning this into some fucking horror flick and try to scare the shit out of me, I'm going to be pissed," Rook grumbled, watching his step as he headed to the phone. Emerging from the back corridor, Rook passed the elevator, then turned the corner. "Because *really*? Do you see me as the damned plucky cheerleader?"

And right into the one person he least wanted to run into—Dante's missing Betty.

STANDING SIDE by side, JoJo and Janet were as different as salt and pepper. Both were sweet faced and dressed in clothes Manny would call midcentury retro, but where JoJo was a brightly hued mod-inspired peacock of a woman, Janet was more subdued Woodstock fertility goddess, a study in earth tones and gravitas. Built generously, they sat as Rhyme and Reason personified behind the counter of their shop, majestically curious at the pair of detectives wandering about.

"You know, we don't do...." Janet began to speak, then looked at her younger partner. "Rook *did* tell you we don't take in stolen goods anymore."

"He mentioned it," Dante murmured softly.

"Dante. That's a neat name." JoJo cocked her head and smiled, her green-shot ponytails bobbing about her ears.

"My mother teaches literature. She named me after Alighieri." He picked up a crystal pyramid from the counter, his heart skipping a beat when he saw the price tag on its bottom. Carefully putting it back down, he said, "JoJo's interesting. I box at a gym called JoJo's."

"It's a cool name. I kind of want to get a goldfish or something and call it MoJo." The woman fussed with a quiver of quill pens sticking up from a mug bearing the shop's name. "It'd be better if it was a monkey, but that's a hell of a commitment."

A full set of armor stood proudly next to what looked like a wooden chainsaw on a handle, shark teeth rimming the edge of the blade section. Posters lined some of the open wall space, antique broadsheets announcing mysteries and magical entertainments from old burlesque shows. A few feet away, a glass case held a branch with a multitude of butterflies pinned to its surface, their colorful wings so numerous Dante could barely see the bark underneath.

There didn't appear to be any sense to its organization, and Dante wondered if JoJa's average patron was meant to wander in its labyrinth of odd items for hours on end, trapped without a skein of twisted wool to lead them back out.

Dante stopped, entranced by a metallic helm with wires and prongs bristling out of the top of it. "What is this?"

Like all of the shop's items, the piece seemed to be a solitary display, standing alone on a sleek black plastic mannequin head. While not cluttered, the curio store was packed with niches and alcoves, each space lit up to highlight a certain article for sale.

"That there is a hair curler." JoJo bounced out of her chair, joining Hank and Dante on the floor. "Well, it was supposed to be. This one allegedly electrocuted two of its owners before the line was declared too dangerous to use."

"What the hell do you two *sell* in this place?" Hank was brought up short by a narrow display cabinet set in front of the foyer. Tall glass bottles sealed tight with cork stoppers and metal bands were arranged in a delicate display of varying heights to show off their floating contents. "Are those... *eyeballs*? Those are *fucking* eyeballs!"

"Some of them are, yes. Those in the small one on top purportedly belonged to a dodo, but we seriously doubt its provenance. The glass is too finely made for the period. Although there was some lovely glasswork back in the thirties." Janet emerged from behind the counter to peer at the cabinet. "That one is a baby two-headed shark. The globes there on the lower shelf are actually dyed jellyfish suspended in a glycerin compound. Wonderful man down on Venice Beach makes them. He won't share what he mixes together to hold them in place, but they sell really well. They're hard to keep in stock at Christmas."

"And to answer your question, Detective," JoJo piped up. "We sell the curious and the macabre. Didn't you see that on the sign outside? The very best in death, decay, and delightful."

"But people... really buy this stuff?" Dante studied what looked like a toothy pair of silver tongs in a glass case, reading off the placard set on the blue velvet in front of it. JoJo's round spectacles flashed purple starbursts as they caught the light. "I mean, who doesn't need a... Victorian testicle massager? With knobby teeth to gently stimulate blood flow?"

Hank held his hand up above his head. "Me. Don't need it. I'm good."

"No one uses...." Janet laughed, adjusting a string of beads she used to leash her eyeglasses around her neck. "Okay, some people might use that. But most of the things we carry are decorative only. For instance, we have a prototype of an electric chair, but a salesman's sample, so no wiring. A conversation piece only."

"Or something a kid would use to fry his sister's Barbie doll," Hank muttered, walked away from the display case, then lay the wrapped flat on the counter. "Not to cut this Addams family attic tour short, ladies, but we've a case to move on."

"Of course," Janet acquiesced, moving to stand in front of the antique cash register taking up one corner of the sales area. "Let's see what you've brought us."

"Rook always has such nice things." JoJo's silvery laughter jingled as bright as the bell over the shop's door. "Every once in a while he runs into something he thinks we'll like and gives us first bid."

"So he keeps you in dead baby sharks?" Hank muttered, giving Dante a piercing glance. "Good to know that's what you're in bed with."

"Let's just crack this open and let the ladies take a look at what he gave us. I was busy with... other things when he brought this up from downstairs. I didn't see what it was." Dante cut the package's string, then peeled back the waxy paper wrapping. Two thick cardboard flats lay beneath, sealed at the corners with metal clips. He popped them open, lifted the top board, then stepped back, letting the two collectors take a look at what was inside.

"Ooooh, a Houdini playbill from the Argyle." JoJo's whisper was steeped in an awe Dante usually only heard when little girls saw a rock star for the first time. "Oh, Janet, look at this."

"Gloves," Janet admonished.

Pairs of white gloves suddenly appeared on the counter, and Dante waited as they were donned, then the poster inspected carefully. Janet's cunning gaze shot out over the edge of her glasses, pinning Dante with a fierce challenge.

"And he's just letting us have this?"

"Someone's trying to kill him. Rook thinks you might know how we can find her. Consider it a preemptive thank you on his part." Dante briefly sketched out what they'd gathered, then took out a set of mug shots they'd gathered on Madge. "Do you know this woman? Have you seen her lately? Do you know where she might be?"

It was a risk interviewing the women. Either could be friends with their suspect, and despite Rook's assurances they would never betray him, Dante'd seen people turn on one another at the smallest slight. He and Hank were going to have to take what JoJo and Janet said at face value, hoping a lead would bring them to Madge's front door. Too much was riding on trust, and he didn't have enough evidence of anything other than Rook's promises and intuition.

"Ah, that's Madge... oh, what the hell was her last name? I can't remember." Janet took her glasses off, then chewed absently at an earpiece. "She used to work for Deb. In that twin scheme she ran. She quit that. Deb, I mean."

"A long time ago, I think now," her partner piped up. "At least two years? She hooked up with Jane to run the Betty scheme. But Madge's had a few partners. Not for long, though. She's not a very nice person."

"Most of the Betties aren't, dear," Janet tsked. "Difficult to be a nice person if you're busy scamming people. I heard from Rook about the two they found all cut up in the bin."

Hank took out the tightly focused shots of the three people murdered and left at Potter's Field. "We suspect Madge had a hand in killing Dani Anderson, our first victim. And we're guessing she somehow got the other two to work with her. Then she killed them too."

"Or at least that's what we speculate." Dante stepped in. "Can you name any other Betties? Maybe Madge contacted them."

The names JoJo rattled off meant nothing to him, but Dante recorded them in his notebook, nodding when JoJo spelled one out.

"You say she's trying to kill Rook? That seems kind of weird," Janet murmured, closing the playbill back up in its wrapper. "I mean, considering...."

"Considering what?" Dante leaned on the counter.

"That Madge's mother *works* for Rook," JoJo replied. "Has for a bit now."

"We went over Rook's employees. They're all part-time, and none have access to...."

Dante and Hank exchanged weighted looks. They'd been careful, tracking down as much background information as they could on the people surrounding Rook. Only one seemed to defy tracing, and Dante'd put that down to the transient nature of the lives she and Rook led.

"Fuck. No. Not... shit, she's been under our noses the whole damned time."

"I am completely lost," Hank grumbled. "Who the hell are we talking about?"

"Charlene Canada." JoJo gently patted Hank's hand, as if to console him. "*She's* Madge what's-her-name's mother."

Twenty-One

"FUCKING HELL," Rook spat, ducking down to the floor.

He'd been seen. No doubt about that. Madge—or at least he thought it was Madge—flashed a gun in her hand, and he fell right back into old habits. Survival at any cost. Running his hand along the edge of the shattered glass cabinet, he cupped what he found, then tossed it at the woman's face. In the nova-brightness of the front room's overhead lights, the broken glass and metal fragments sparkled and glittered as they flew into Madge's face, a rainbow spray of edge and pain.

Rook didn't stick around to see if he hurt her. Turning on his heel, he was off, heading for the docking bay door set into the right corner of the building. It was hard going. His feet were being sliced up by the damage left on the shop's floor, and his toes were growing sticky with blood. Madge's screams chased him, her swearing peppery and profane amid his panicked gasps for air. A gunshot went off, and a corner of a cinder-block column he'd just ducked past exploded into a hail of dust and cement fragments.

The seemingly practical design of back rooms and showcases had somehow become a deadly maze, one where placing his left hand on the walls would only lead him further into trouble. There were too many cut-throughs, ones he'd chosen to make it easier to move large collectibles into but now were blocked by crates and boxes filled with what used to stock the front room so repairs could begin.

"Too damned efficient. Fucking movers. Why didn't you leave me a way out?" Rook muttered, having to backtrack again. He and Dante'd gone straight up to the loft or he'd have seen the mess.

The back room was a disaster, and he couldn't find a clear path to the bay. He needed to get something on his feet. If the sound of his panting didn't draw Madge to him, the trail of bloody footprints he was leaving behind were as plain as a dotted line in an old Family Circus cartoon.

He missed the soft beeps and whirs of toys and collectibles, mostly because the low sheet of noise would have masked his movements. Only the air-conditioning units on the cold displays rattled about, barely a whisper of buzzing to keep him company while he hunted for something to put on his feet.

Most of the common things he kept in the storeroom were things he could place in the Potter's Field display cases up front to catch a tourist's eye. Rook didn't need flashy and pretty. He needed solid and serviceable. He found a pair of gold-sequined moccasins worn in an old Flash Gordon movie, much too small to get his toes into even if the bells dangling from the shoe's laces weren't bad enough.

There were even less practical things, mostly feminine in nature, and for the first time in his life, Rook wished he hadn't said no to the pair of platform boots someone tried to pass off as wardrobe from a bad '70s rock star movie.

"Okay, what do I have in here?" Keeping an ear out for Madge, he slowly pulled out a box on one of the bottom shelves. His feet were beginning to ache, and panic was making Rook's pulse race, but he took a breath. "Get a hold of yourself, Stevens. Just like a job. This is *just* like a job. Focus. Oh, fucking bless you, Charlene, for your label machine fetish."

Rook found a pair of black leather hi-top Converses tucked into a box marked *robot movie shoes*. A half size too big for him, they were roomy on Rook's feet, but he tied them up tightly, wrapping the excess laces around his ankles. He squished about in the soles as he took his first step, but there was no pain.

"Got everything out, then," he murmured. "And for fuck's sakes, stop talking to yourself."

It was a bad habit, one he'd picked up when he'd done his first job. Keeping up a constant monologue helped push his fears back when he'd been dangling forty feet in the air off the edge of a balcony after the owners of the mansion he'd just robbed came home. Talking to himself made him feel less alone then.

Now it would only get him killed.

A shadow moved through the subdued blue tinge of the back storerooms. If he could get around to the front and around the right corner, it was a long sprint to the rear entrance. To the left, the stairwell was closer, and the loft was defensible, with its thick, heavy door and locks, but he'd be trapped, unable to get out or contact anyone.

"Not like they can smoke me out. So going to kill Dante for taking my phone and laptop." Rook crouched, seeing another long shadow join the first. There was a tinge of voices, lost under the hum of a nearby compressor. "Shit, I can open a goddamn window and shout at someone down on the sidewalk if I've got to. Up it is."

He didn't have much in the way of weapons. Everything heavy and substantial was crated up and in the warehouse miles away. A hockey stick from a cancelled wizard's show was the best Rook could do, but its length would make wielding it among the tight spaces too difficult. He got three steps out into the corridor when someone came out of the stairwell, swinging the door wide. Caught between diving back into the storeroom or attacking, Rook grabbed the first heavy thing he could find, a tiny bat from a ballpark giveaway.

"Fuck it. Attack, then run up." He steeled himself for the sprint. Then his world exploded into a confetti of crazy and noise.

There were shouts behind him as the shadows became people. Madge's screams for him to stop were joined by a deeper, unfamiliar bark. Booms followed his exit, and Rook winced at the sound of breaking glass and more swearing. Raising the bat above his head, he launched at the person coming out from behind the stairwell door, hoping to catch them off guard.

Her blonde high ponytail was Rook's first hint he'd made a mistake, and then he caught a glimpse of Charlene's look of horrified surprise as he brought the bat down. Turning, Rook tried to angle it away from the woman, but the wetness in the loose Converses twisted him about and he stumbled, slamming into the corridor's brick wall. Pain shocked down his arm, the crenulated surface digging through his thin shirt and into his stitched skin. Something gave, tearing apart, and Rook dropped the bat, his fingers too numb to hold on to the handle.

"Shit, Char. Come on! Get upstairs!" Another shot rang out, this time the bullet slamming into a wall near his head. "Fuck... go!"

"God, Rook." Her expression turned cruel, then pitying. "You are so stupid. So very stupid."

"DISPATCH SAYS there's a pileup on the Sunset ramp off of the 101. She doesn't know if there's anyone getting through," Hank screamed at Dante. "Do you have the sirens on?"

"Lights and noise. Both on," Dante shouted back. "You can't go in with me. Can't risk it."

"Montoya, you can just fuck—"

"I'm serious, Camden. You can't hear a fucking thing, and if there's shit going down in there, I don't want you to get in the line of fire." He cut through the traffic, pushing cars aside in a stream of churning lights and hailing noise. "I can't fucking believe I did this. *Canicas*, what the hell was I thinking taking his damned phone?"

"Watch out for the bus! The *bus*, Dante! Watch the fucking bus!"

Hank gripped the dashboard, bracing himself against the car door as Dante slid the sedan's tires up over the curb to avoid a bus swerving into their lane. The car careened off the cement buffer, slamming hard back onto the asphalt, and drifted to the left, hydroplaning on a shallow pond pooling over a blocked drainage grate.

"God, you're going to get us killed."

"Hold on," Dante warned his partner. The unmarked car screeched around a corner, and Dante was forced to slow down as he passed through a red light, modulating the siren to warn oncoming traffic. "We're a block out. Just... I need you to get someone here, Hank."

"We're going to look like assholes if he's up there chewing his nails."

Hank's grumble was nearly as loud as his shouting. Dante risked giving his partner a stern look.

"Shit, I'm just saying, he might be okay. You go in without backup, and *if* someone's there, the captain's going to string you up by your balls, Montoya."

"I *called* Charlene to let him out." Something gurgled in Dante's insides, and fear crinkled his throat. "*Fuck*."

"Just drive, Montoya," Hank ordered as he tapped back into the car's data connection. "I'm going to tear Dispatch a new asshole."

"FIVE-MINUTE MONOLOGUE, or am I just supposed to stand here while you beat the shit out of me for something I don't know about?" Rook edged against the wall, clutching his injured shoulder. "'Cause for the life of me, I've got no fucking clue what you're looking for here."

Charlene's betrayal settled wrong in him. Worse than wrong. It gouged out a part of his soul. He should have known... should have suspected something, especially since he'd found her tit-deep in his chilled closet looking for a damned costume, of all things, but instead, he'd bitten at one of the oldest tropes in the book—the dumb blonde.

With the rear entrance door at his back, and for all intents and purposes, about a mile away, Rook only had one thing going for him— his mouth. What he couldn't do was let the blockheaded mountain walking behind Madge get a hold of him. So far it looked like none of them could hit worth a damn unless it was to shoot an old man in a slow-moving town car, but he'd make a pretty steady target sprinting down the hall. Unless he could get something between him and them, Rook knew he was shit out of luck.

"So, nice long con?" Rook calculated the time he'd known Charlene, actually known her, as he took a step back to distance himself from the loft's stairs. "*Years.* Did you play the brainless tit-and-wiggle for everyone, Char? Or just me? Because I've got to hand it to you, I figured you were about as smart as a dog-chewed stick."

It was still closer, but there was no way he could shove Charlene out of the way and get the stairwell door shut behind him. The lack of a lock was also a deterrent. He'd have nothing to bolt it down so he could make it up the stairs and shut the loft door.

The back entrance was still his only hope.

Another step back, and Charlene danced with him, taking a step forward. Madge and her scowling shadow fell in around the corner, tightening the space up. Rook eyed the thug, gauging his quickness. Sometimes the big ones could fool you. He'd known a Samoan fire dancer who once crossed the speedway in less than ten seconds when one of the balloon girls screamed for help. Of course, Rook recalled, it'd also taken the enraged man less than five seconds to nearly rip the guy's arm off, so there was that to look forward to if he didn't make it in time.

Madge was worrisome because of the gun. She waved it about, her fingers trembling and squeezing down on the trigger as she glanced at Charlene. Something was off between the two women, something Rook couldn't quite place until Charlene's head dipped into a shadow and the resemblance between them became clear.

"Fuck, you're sisters?" Rook guessed offhandedly. They'd be closer to mother-daughter or aunt-niece from the wear and tear on Charlene's face, but even if she'd faked a low intelligence, vanity and ego weren't something people sublimated well. She bit a little, smoothing her forehead with her fingers. "Should have seen it, but... I didn't really get a good look at Madge. The name, though. Really? Madge? Or did you hork that up just for the cons you ran with Pigeon?"

"Rook honey." Charlene crooked her finger at him. "You and I need to talk about the stash you kept from before you quit doing jobs."

"Babe, I've got nothing. Everything I had went into this place." He faked a grimace, clutching his arm tighter. He didn't have to put too much of a spin on it. He'd definitely torn his arm open. Blood was gushing from the wound, and his fingers seemed to be doing a piss-poor job of keeping his fluids inside where they needed to be.

"No, see, that's where you're lying," Charlene hissed back. "I know better. *Dani* knew better."

The pinup-girl image she'd so carefully cultivated turned ugly, more a caricature of a woman chasing a moose and squirrel than the sexpot Rook knew her as. The smear of red on her lips looked more like the blood running down the length of his arm, and the clicks of her heels on the cement floor were as loud as gunshots with every step she took toward him.

"Dani was fucking crazy, Char," Rook pointed out. "Delusional. She was also the crackpot who'd thought I somehow smuggled forty gold bars out of that last house we did. Do you know how goddamn heavy those things are? *Over twenty-five pounds each*! And I tossed forty of them into my backpack and whistled my way down the outside wall?"

"Not the gold." She dismissed his claim with a shrug. "The gems. She kept track of those. Even had a fake primed to give to that cop, but he went off all half-cocked and wanted something else. Something bigger. See, it never came up on the market. That big piece of ice. She *knew* you still had it."

"So she brought a fake with her for what?" He shook his head and apparently went a step too far, because the bald mountain behind Madge shifted and was suddenly much too close for Rook's comfort. Working his arm up, Rook shook his hand, sending more drops onto the floor. "Look, you three can walk out of here still. No one knows you're here—"

"That cop does." Madge spoke up. "He called Mom, remember? I say we kill him, toss the place one last time, and you be here acting like you found him dead. Cop's already fucked him. He won't be back for a while, right?"

"God, I feel sorry for your sex life, Madge," Rook muttered. "Especially if guys fuck you once and they're out the door."

The gun came up, and this time it was steady, pointing straight at Rook's chest. Sneering much like her mother, Madge snarled, "Keep talking, asshole. There's nothing I'd like better than to shove this up your ass and empty it. I've been wanting to kill you since we started this whole goddamn mess, but Mom didn't want to."

"It's a simple question, Rook," Charlene interjected. "You've got a few million dollars' worth of jewelry hidden here. Where is it?"

"*If* I had it, like I'll tell you, and after you get Gojira there to pack it up, you guys waltz out of here and let me live?" He was beginning to shake, getting colder with each inch he crept back. The wall somehow wavered in, and Rook ducked, not wanting to hit his head on it. "I'm not as stupid as your kid looks, Char. Even if I *had*, telling you would only get me a bullet in the back of my head. Madge is all primed for it."

"Not the back," Madge snorted. "In your mouth. Just so I can say I'm the one who finally shut you the fuck up."

"Morris is here to help you remember, Rook." Charlene laughed at the grimace Rook gave her. "Look, I've been taking this place apart bit by bit. I've found most of your empty cubbyholes, but you're a sneaky asshole, kid. You always have been. A sneaky, slimy asshole no one likes and no one trusts. Hell, even your own mom didn't want to be around you. Madge might not be as smart as you, but at least I can stand her. Can't say that about you."

"Nice, and to think I gave you those burner cards." The ground in front of him should have been coated with drops of his blood, but Rook couldn't risk looking down to check. Hoping he'd shaken off enough to wet the tiled area between the stairs and the rear door, he chanced leaning against the wall, needing its support. For once his procrastination about painting the floor with a layer of grit would pay off, despite all the times he'd nearly killed himself walking on the slick spot after a light rain.

"Those cards paid for Morris here. How's it feel to know you paid to get your own grandfather killed?" Madge waved the gun again. "This is taking too long. Morris, just grab him. You can't miss this time. He's the only big-nosed skinny guy around."

"I do not have a *big* nose." It was now or never. Morris's bulk took up much of the slender corridor, and it was all the opening Rook needed.

He got a few feet down the corridor, or at least so he thought. The world folded in on him suddenly, and everything either slowed down or sped up. Rook wasn't quite sure. He felt Morris's hands in his hair, then the pain of being jerked back just as the narrow hallway exploded with sound. It felt as if firecrackers were popping down the side of his cheek, and a rush of cold air somehow got into his marrow, stiffening his entire body. He was leaking out too much blood, or too quickly. Either way, Rook knew he was losing hold on his consciousness. He just had to make it to the door.

A slat of light opened up at the end of the corridor, and Rook blinked against the stain it left on his eyes. Morris twisted, screaming in Rook's ear. Then the ground slid out from under him. Under Morris's dead weight, Rook tumbled down. All he could feel was wet and ice, a glacial chill moving across his skin. Then his head slammed into the floor, leaving him drowning and helpless in a sea of fading stars.

THE DOOR kicked in easily, flying into the far wall, and Dante stepped in, the muzzle of his gun aimed at the ground as he worked his back against the wall. Dante saw the flash of a firearm at the end of the hallway and Rook fold to the floor, a large, hulking man landing on top of him. The smell of gunpowder and blood hung in a rank curtain across the hall, and at the other end, Charlene and Madge stood partially silhouetted in a corona of light.

"Behind you, Montoya," Hank called out, and Dante almost turned, ready to shout at his partner to go back to the car as Madge drew a bead on them.

"Police! Drop your weapon!" He pulled his gun up, aiming for the shorter of the women. Madge turned her head, looking at her mother, her face caught in an angry grimace. "Last warning, Madge. Put the gun down now before—"

It was Charlene who began the gunfight. Pulling the automatic out of her daughter's hands, she squeezed the trigger, popping a round off. Dante dove down, praying Hank sought cover behind him. Rolling to the side, he angled his Glock up to fire, but Charlene was gone.

"Hank, check on Rook. And cover them." Dante forced himself to run past his lover, his legs growing heavier with each step he took away from Rook's prone body. "Shoot her if she gives you shit."

He swore he saw Rook breathing, focused on the faint pull of his rib cage Dante'd seen beneath his bloodied shirt. Madge cowered as he went by, and Hank swore something fierce. His own footing faltered when he hit the odd tile space near the stairs, and Dante grabbed at the far wall to keep his balance, smearing a trail of blood behind him as he stepped onto the cement floor.

"*Cuervo's* going to be okay. Looked like his arm again. Not a lot. Just a little bit," he consoled himself while he ducked around a pillar in the dark confines behind the main room.

He'd not paid much attention to the warren Rook had laid out behind his store's front area, and now Dante regretted not intimately memorizing the floor plan when he had the chance. Charlene had the advantage, spending months in the building, going over every inch of the place as she looked for what JoJo and Janet described as a silly rumor. It seemed fantastical that Rook would have held on to the biggest haul of his thieving career, stashing it away somewhere in a building where anyone could run across it.

"If what you were looking for was actually here, Charlene, don't you think you'd have found it by now?" Dante called out. He banged his knees against a pile of heavy boxes, and he bit down on his lip, listening for the woman's reply. "How long did you look? Months? A year? Two years? How many people have you and your daughter killed for nothing more than a story?"

"You don't know him, asshole!" Charlene's voice echoed from somewhere in the front room. "You think just because you've fucked him, you know him? Do you know how many guys have had his ass? Shit, most of the carnies dipped into that piece of shit before he was even fifteen, and *none* of them could tell you if he was lying or not."

A rattle followed, chains and metal on something solid. Dante tried to remember if the front door had been blocked off from the outside or if it'd just been locked up. Nothing came to mind but the splatter of blood on Rook's side and the pale moon of his face nearly hidden beneath his tangled brown hair.

"I will not shoot her." Dante pushed down the fury Charlene's words pulled out of him. "*Dios en el cielo*, please help me not shoot her."

Something broke, shattering loud enough for Dante's nerves to crawl to the surface. He could hear sirens finally, hearty wailing creeping through the open back door. Sending a quick prayer that one of the wails belonged to an ambulance, he stepped into the main room, shielding himself behind a pillar.

Charlene was there, waiting. She stood in an uneven stance, a heel stem missing from one of her high fuck-me shoes. Her hands were steady, primed to take the shot, but the barrel of her gun shimmied, a tight circle of nerves from too hard of a grip.

"You shoot me now, Charlene, and there's no going back for you," Dante warned, ducking back behind the pillar. A single pane of glass remained intact on a display case near the entrance, and with the lights on full, he could see Charlene's reflection. Her hands were wavering, the gun beginning to drop down. "A lot of people have died already for this. Do you want to add a cop to that list?"

"It was just supposed to be him… and Dani. Finally got that bitch dead, and then the cops showed up." Charlene lost her balance, and Dante almost slid out from behind the column, but she caught herself before he could get clear. "But Jane—fucking Jane—she brought the cops down on us. Ran out on Madge and called the police before Rook could get what he fucking deserved."

"So you planned to kill Dani, then? What about the other Betties?" Dante spotted a bank of light switches on the column next to him, each labeled carefully with locations. Dousing his area in darkness would help cover him long enough to take a good shot at Charlene, but he couldn't chance her firing as he ducked out. Keeping her reflection in view, he called out, "And why kill Rook? After all he's done for you."

"Done for me? Please! No one does anything for anyone," Charlene scoffed. "The other two Betties, God, they were a joke. Madge didn't even know I killed them. They wanted more than their share—like they spent hours tearing this place apart and schlepping shit back and forth for that asshole. So I said, fuck it. It was just going to be me and Madge."

"Doesn't explain why you wanted Rook dead." Dante heard boots in the corridor, a concentrated stamp of shuffling whispers of leather on cement. Twisting his shoulder, he caught sight of a SWAT-vested cop slowly coming out of the back room, a combat assault rifle up at the ready. Dante moved his jacket aside, showing his badge, then nodded to the front room where Charlene ranted on.

"If we let Rook walk away from this, he'd have been after us like white on rice. Once he gets his teeth into something, he doesn't let go," she called out. "And if I've fucked this up, at least I'm going to take you with me."

Charlene got one shot off, and Dante stepped out from behind the column, firing straight into her. A second later, the incoming SWAT team joined in, the first responder at the back room piercing Charlene's jerking body with a burst of rounds. It was the longest three seconds of Dante's life, seemingly endless noise and screams as Charlene tried to empty her gun into the men killing her. Dante felt something hot hit his vest and then a punch of pain before the air rushed out of his lungs, but he stood firm, needing to see Charlene drop.

She fell hard, a broken aging fashion doll with popped-out legs and arms. He moved forward, covering her with his weapon, but a milky film was already filling her lifeless eyes by the time Dante reached her side. Puddles of blood were beginning to form beneath her still twitching body, running hot into large pools under her punctured torso. A moment later, her body gave up its fight, collapsing in on itself as her chest gave up its final breath.

A hand on his shoulder startled Dante, and he whirled about, nearly clocking Hank in the face. Breathing hard, he got a grip on himself as the SWAT team poured into the front room around him.

"Ironic," Hank croaked loudly.

"What?" Dante quickly stepped back to avoid the blood sluggishly leaking from Charlene's already cooling body.

"That's pretty much where we found Dani," his partner tsked. "Guess you really do reap what you sow."

Twenty-Two

A WEEK, more stitches, and a hospital stay later, Rook found himself opening the door to his West Hollywood warehouse, then pushing his cousin Alex in. One of the few Martins he could stand—the second, counting their grandfather—Alex reluctantly agreed to Rook's request of a no-questions-asked, no-stories-told favor. His cousin shared his lanky body and face, but there the resemblance ended. A blond-haired, sparkly eyed nerd and raised in the fold of old money with loving parents, Alex was everything Rook wasn't… and then some.

He was also a genuinely nice guy who'd fallen in love with a cop—right after a dead body fell through the roof of his comic book store.

"There is nothing in here that you can—" Alex's voice dropped, a reverent whisper Rook had only heard from people outside of old cathedrals. "Oh. My. God. Rook…."

The squat warehouse held the crème de la crème of his collectibles. Kept at a chilly temperature to preserve the delicate pieces, lit glass display cases ran in rows down the middle and around the warehouse floor. Below many cases were thin drawers where he'd stashed vintage papers and posters. Most of the cases held one or two items, many from movies and television shows, but a few, like the one he led Alex to, contained books.

"Here's what I have for you, cousin," he explained, opening the case. "A first edition, second issue *Alice in Wonderland* with full gilt cover, Appleton cancel title page, and notated by its illustrator, Tenniel. Say something, Alex. You're turning blue."

"Fuck me," his cousin whispered, pushing his glasses up the bridge of his nose.

"Can't. First cousin. I think that's illegal here in California." He intercepted Alex's sharp glance with a smirk. "Look, I'm guessing. I've never had a cousin before you, and well, those sheep. I wouldn't touch them with a ten-foot pole. You… I'd consider it."

"What do you want for it? The book?" Alex's glasses gleamed, casting reflections of the book's red and gold cover. "No favor can be this much."

"Just your help. And your silence." Reaching into the case, he folded the book up in the soft microfiber cloth it lay on. "This is a two-person job, and you're the only other person I can trust."

"What about... Dante? You don't trust him?"

"*He's* why I'm doing this. And no, if I brought him in on this, it would... fuck everything up. Fuck *us* up." He handed Alex the bundled-up book. "Will you believe me if I tell you I'm doing the right thing here? Finally?"

"No, because you're bribing me to help you."

"No, I'm bribing you to keep your mouth shut," Rook corrected. "Is it working?"

"God, yes," Alex sighed and put the book back down in its open case. "Okay, what do you want me to do?"

The wooden crate was where he'd left it, buried among others stacked up against the warehouse's far wall. Shoving aside a small box, Rook wedged himself behind the crate and pushed it out onto the floor. Startled, Alex stepped in, moving his still injured cousin out of the way, then forced the heavy box farther out.

"You're hurt, remember?" he scolded. "Get out of the way."

"Just a couple more feet. I'll go get a crowbar and hammer from the toolbox." Rook grumbled under his breath as he walked away, "You're as much of a fussy asshole as Archie."

"Heard that." Grunting, Alex gave another shove.

"Good!" Shouting back at his cousin, Rook came back with the tools. "Don't get too crazy over there, Bruce Banner. I just want to open the damned thing, not move it cross-country."

"Is this good?" Alex panted, his shoulder up against the waist-high wooden box. "Or do you need more clearance?"

"It's fine. Get out of the—" Rook wrestled with his cousin as Alex took the crowbar from him. "Dude, I can do this."

"Shoulder. Remember?" He hefted the bar, wedging it under the crate's top. "Besides, this way I'm armed for when the zombies leap out of this thing and attack me."

"You are a sick, twisted puppy, cuz." Rook grinned. "Probably why I like you best."

"You like me best because I'm the only one who's nice to you. Well, me and my parents." Alex wrenched the top up an inch. "Stand back in case it flies off. I don't want to have to explain how I broke your nose."

"Just get the top up. The sides unhook." Rook grabbed the edge of the lid after Alex got it off the rest of the way. He slid it out of the way, then undid the metal hooks holding the sides up. Stepping back, he let the crate's sides fall outward and waited for the dust to settle.

Nested into curled wood chips, the box inside gleamed gold and red where the light was able to reach it through its packing. It was an elaborate piece of movie construction, topped with two winged angels facing one another and embossed with intricate, archaic symbols. Resting high on upside-down finials, the box stood nearly as tall and wide as the crate it'd been in, its two broken-down rods, used to slide into the oarlock-style rings set below the box's lid, lay beneath it.

"Rook, that's the—ark," Alex whispered, awestruck. "Like from—is it really?"

"One of them. But with a bit of modification," Rook admitted, drawing an Allen wrench from his pocket. "Now comes the hard part."

It was easy enough to find the locks he'd hidden along the underside of the ark's lid, but with each turn of the wrench, a small piece of his old life died inside of him. It took him nearly five minutes to work the interlocking mechanism, cranking the tumblers until he couldn't turn them any more. When he was finished, Rook straightened up and sighed heavily at the shooting pain running down his arm.

"Time to lift the lid up. Watch your fingers. It's going to be heavier than it looks," Rook warned. "There's a casing inside. We're going to have to pull it up and then move it aside. Okay?"

It was slow going. When he'd planned the cubbyhole, Rook knew he would only be opening it again under the direst of circumstances. Purposely created to require two people, the mechanism and process forced him to ask someone else for help—something he wouldn't dream of doing in a million years. Yet there he stood, grunting and moaning while his cousin Alex swore about doing inventive things with Rook's balls when they were done. The inside casing finally cleared the ark's sides, and they maneuvered it carefully to the floor. Alex stood first, peeking over the ark's lip, and Rook heard him gasp in alarmed surprise.

"Fuck, Rook. Those are... diamonds? And... holy crap. Just... it's all jewelry." His cousin grabbed the edge of the prop and stared down at the interior of the box. "How much do you have in here? What are you going to do with them?"

"I'm going to drop it all off with the cops. Okay, they won't know it was me, but that's where it's all going. Here, I've got to put gloves on and get them into bags. They're wiped totally clean, so don't touch any." Rook pulled a pair of latex gloves from his jeans pocket. "If you don't handle them, you're not a part of this. It's all on me."

"So they're stolen? You stole this? Are you crazy?" Alex suddenly let go of the ark, hastily wiping at its edge with his shirt. Catching Rook's mocking smirk, he smiled ruefully. "I'm being silly, aren't I?"

"Yeah, a bit." Rook grabbed the pristine velvet bag he'd left under the pile of stones, then carefully began to scoop the loose gems into its opening. "This won't take long. You can head out if you want. Just don't forget to take your book."

"No, I'll stay and help you put this back together," Alex promised. "Why are you doing this? Now, I mean?"

"Because Dante needs me to be... better than who I am. Who I was." Rook blinked furiously, refusing to let his emotions get to him. "And this is the only way I can do it. Be that. So yeah, it all goes."

"He means that much to you?" his cousin asked gently.

If anyone in the family would know what it was like to be with a cop, it was Alex. His boyfriend, James, worked Homicide and lurked on the edges of family gatherings, as if daring someone to say something foul to Alex so he could shoot them.

"Dante? Yeah. See, he makes me feel... safe, Alex. And until I met him, I'd never felt safe before," Rook admitted softly. "So all of this shit? It's nothing to me. Not compared to that. Not compared to... *him*."

CONSTRUCTION ON Potter's Field was in full swing when Dante showed up with takeout from a Cantonese restaurant down the street. Stepping around a pile of beams, he maneuvered past a man spot-welding a wall frame around the elevator shaft, then made his way into the store's sales room.

Where he found Rook and Manny chatting over what looked like blueprints for the store's resurrection.

Rook looked a little tired and worn, but the pale grayness he had following Charlene's death appeared to be gone. He was still moving a bit tenderly, favoring the arm the ER had to stitch back up. But he still looked *damned* good.

It'd taken Dante a good deal of emotional manipulation to get Rook to stay overnight. Loss of blood and trauma apparently didn't faze him as much as having Archie worry about him. Having both Rook and his grandfather on the same floor seemed to appease them. Others in the family, however, had other ideas.

Dante quickly learned it was best to ignore the argumentative Martins and shut the hospital room door in their faces after he'd wheeled Archie into Rook's room so they could visit. Apparently in Rook's family, life was much simpler behind closed doors.

"Hi." He treaded carefully, not sure he liked seeing his uncle and lover with their heads together and cackling over something. As casually as he could, Dante ventured in, "What are you doing here, Manny?"

"You're looking at the new manager of Potter's Field." Manny beamed, clapping Rook on the shoulder. "We were just talking about the renovations. I was agreeing with Rook it was a good idea to make a separate entrance to the loft's elevator from the outside. It's healthier to keep work space and home space apart."

"I'll still be able to get into the shop from the lift," Rook explained. "There'll be a door connecting that part of the building to the front, but I'll be the only one with the key. Manny's talking about how to add windows back there, but I'm not going to punch more holes into the side of the building just yet."

"You… um… have a business, Manny," Dante reminded his uncle. "You do… stuff in the back cottage. Remember? Hair. Makeup. That kind of thing? And no offense, but what do you know about movies?"

"Dante, I love you, but really, how many drag queens need me to do their faces and hair on a daily basis?" Manny poked him in the chest. "And please, I was in entertainment for years."

"Knows a shit ton more about musicals than I ever will." Rook leaned on the counter. "And hey, this will free me up to go estate picking. I just want to find stuff, not boss people around."

"I happen to like bossing people around. Keep your mouth shut there, Dante. Now, I'll look through the applications. We'll get a full staff in by the time we reopen." Manny gathered up a pile of papers from the counter. "I'm going to guess you're not coming home tonight, *mijo*."

"You've got *lotería* night tonight, right?" Dante jiggled the bags of takeout. "I think Rook and I will pass. I can miss the whole shouting, screaming, and drunken singing."

"I'm going to have to get a dog or something to keep me company." Manny kissed Rook's cheek. "I barely see him… or you. You two have to come spend more time at the house."

"How about if we just hook you up with someone hot and call it a day?" Rook asked, barely wincing when Manny struck his tender arm, and Dante leaned over to accept his clueless uncle's buss.

"Yes, that idea I like." Manny headed to the back door, taking a second to glance at one of the worker's rears. "I will see you two later."

"So you hired my uncle?" Dante put the bags of food on the dusty sales counter. "Really?"

"Really. I trust him. And well, after…." Rook's expression turned stony. "Fuck, it still hurts, you know? Charlene. *Bitch*."

"Yeah, I know, hon." He did know. Or at least understood.

They'd spent hours talking about Charlene and Vince, each picking their way through a field of pain and broken hearts. For him, it was hard to see his former partner tumble down the last few inches of the pedestal Dante'd put him on, but Rook's pain was deeper. Charlene had been Rook's first step into a new life, not knowing she was bringing a hell of a lot of his old life with her.

"It'll be good. He won't be tearing this place apart looking for God knows what." Rook's attempt at a smile was feeble but better than he'd had all week. "And hey, we've already agreed that if we break up, I get to keep him in the divorce. So, there's that."

"Charming," Dante drawled. "Speaking of God knows what, you have any idea about a satchel of stolen jewelry dropped off at the main station today?"

Rook's face was a flawless mask of curiosity and innocence. "Nope. Not a clue. Why?"

"Because one of the stones was an exact match for the fake Dani had in her pocket. Huge stone. Couldn't miss it 'cause it's an odd cut, so the evidence people recognized it as soon as they opened it up." He leaned over, placing his hands on either side of Rook's hips, trapping him against the counter. "Funny, huh? That someone would have a change of heart and return it. After all these years."

"Yeah, funny," Rook replied, his expression unchanged. "Huh. Well, I don't know about you, but every time you and I are in here together, someone shoots this place up. So, do you want to go upstairs, fuck, and then eat cold Chinese food while we watch a movie? Doesn't have to be in that order."

"You're going to be the death of me, *cuervo*." Laughing, Dante captured Rook's mouth in a deep kiss, then whispered, "You know you can trust me. With... whatever. With anything. You know that, right?"

"Sometimes it's better if some things are left unsaid, Montoya. It's hard, you know? Habits? Dying hard? All of that shit." Rook bit Dante's lip hard, then let go when he yelped. "Maybe. Almost. Yes. You're too... I don't want to break this. And I know that's stupid, or you think that it's stupid, but not to me. So, just a little bit of... time, okay?"

There were whispered fears in Rook's voice and shadows clinging to his luminous eyes. A lifetime of doubt lay beneath the surface of his skin, his soul burdened by abandonment and loss. He was asking a lot of the former thief, and with the thick lie strung between them, Dante could see Rook fighting the urge to flee, his first instinct always to run.

Instead he stood firm, cradled between Dante's thighs, his mouth warmed from their kiss.

"As you wish, *cuervo*." Dante pushed into Rook until they were pressed in tight, their bodies growing hot with the contact. "As you wish."

RHYS FORD admits to sharing the house with three cats of varying degrees of black fur and a ginger cairn terrorist. Rhys is also enslaved to the upkeep of a 1979 Pontiac Firebird, a Toshiba laptop, and an overworked red coffee maker.

Rhys can be found at the following locations:
Blog: www.rhysford.com
Facebook: https://www.facebook.com/rhys.ford.author
Twitter: @Rhys_Ford

Clockwork Tangerine

By Rhys Ford

The British Empire reigns supreme, and its young Queen Victoria has expanded her realm to St. Francisco, a bustling city of English lords and Chinese ghettos. St. Francisco is a jewel in the Empire's crown and as deeply embroiled in the conflict between the Arcane and Science as its sister city, London—a very dark and dangerous battle.

Marcus Stenhill, Viscount of Westwood, stumbles upon that darkness when he encounters a pack of young bloods beating a man senseless. Westwood's duty and honor demand he save the man, but he's taken aback to discover the man is Robin Harris, a handsome young inventor indirectly responsible for the death of Marcus's father.

Living in the shadows following a failed coup, Robin devotes his life to easing others' pain, even though his creations are considered mechanical abominations of magicks and science. Branded a deviant and a murderer, Robin expects the viscount to run as far as he can—and is amazed when Marcus reaches for him instead.

http://www.dreamspinnerpress.com

Creature Feature 2

By Rhys Ford & Poppy Dennison

Two Men. One Apocalypse.

Rise of the Revenants

Vampyres are on the loose in Detroit, and novice hunter Taz Cohen is on the job. The mission seems simple: stop the vamps. But Taz knows nothing about the mythical creatures, so he's in for the fight of his life. Then he meets insanely attractive construction worker Darren Foster, who jumps into the battle with both feet. Sparks and bullets fly as they struggle against the vampyre horde and their attraction to each other. Avoiding gruesome death from the undead might be easier than shielding their hearts from each other.

Legacy of Blood and Death

For Javi Navarro, Detroit will become another blood-splattered city in his rearview mirror after he puts its dead back into the ground. Expecting an easy hunting job, Javi instead finds a kiss of ancient vampyres on the hunt for a descendant of their long-dead creator.

Reclusive Ciarnan Mac Gerailt abandoned his family legacy of blood and death magic after it nearly destroyed him. Unfortunately for Ciarnan, the Motor City can only be saved if he resumes his dark arts and joins forces with Javi Navarro, the hunter who brought the vampyre apocalypse—and hope for the future—straight to Ciarnan's front door.

http://www.dreamspinnerpress.com

Dirty Kiss

A Cole McGinnis Mystery

By Rhys Ford

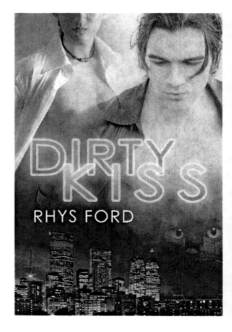

Cole Kenjiro McGinnis, ex-cop and PI, is trying to get over the shooting death of his lover when a supposedly routine investigation lands in his lap. Investigating the apparent suicide of a prominent Korean businessman's son proves to be anything but ordinary, especially when it introduces Cole to the dead man's handsome cousin, Kim Jae-Min.

Jae-Min's cousin had a dirty little secret, the kind that Cole has been familiar with all his life and that Jae-Min is still hiding from his family. The investigation leads Cole from tasteful mansions to seedy lover's trysts to Dirty Kiss, the place where the rich and discreet go to indulge in desires their traditional-minded families would rather know nothing about.

It also leads Cole McGinnis into Jae-Min's arms, and that could be a problem. Jae-Min's cousin's death is looking less and less like a suicide, and Jae-Min is looking more and more like a target. Cole has already lost one lover to violence—he's not about to lose Jae-Min too.

http://www.dreamspinnerpress.com

Dirty Secret

A Cole McGinnis Mystery

By Rhys Ford

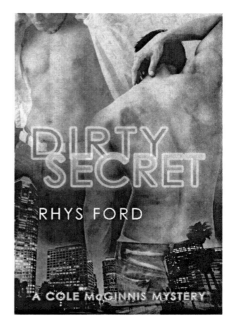

Loving Kim Jae-Min isn't always easy: Jae is gun-shy about being openly homosexual. Ex-cop turned private investigator Cole McGinnis doesn't know any other way to be. Still, he understands where Jae is coming from. Traditional Korean men aren't gay—at least not usually where people can see them.

But Cole can't spend too much time unraveling his boyfriend's issues. He has a job to do. When a singer named Scarlet asks him to help find Park Dae-Hoon, a gay Korean man who disappeared nearly two decades ago, Cole finds himself submerged in the tangled world of rich Korean families, where obligation and politics mean sacrificing happiness to preserve corporate empires. Soon the bodies start piling up without rhyme or reason. With every step Cole takes toward locating Park Dae-Hoon, another person meets their demise—and someone Cole loves could be next on the murderer's list.

http://www.dreamspinnerpress.com

Dirty Laundry

A Cole McGinnis Mystery

By Rhys Ford

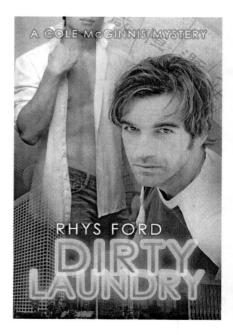

For ex-cop turned private investigator Cole McGinnis, each day brings a new challenge. Too bad most of them involve pain and death. Claudia, his office manager and surrogate mother, is still recovering from a gunshot, and Cole's closeted boyfriend, Kim Jae-Min, suddenly finds his teenaged sister dumped in his lap. Meanwhile, Cole has his own sibling problems— most notably, a mysterious half brother from Japan whom his older brother, Mike, is determined they welcome with open arms.

As if his own personal dramas weren't enough, Cole is approached by Madame Sun, a fortune-teller whose clients have been dying at an alarming rate. Convinced someone is after her customers, she wants the matter investigated, but the police think she's imagining things. Hoping to put Sun's mind at ease, Cole takes the case and finds himself plunged into a Gordian knot of lies and betrayal where no one is who they are supposed to be and Death seems to be the only card in Madame Sun's deck.

http://www.dreamspinnerpress.com

Dirty Deeds

A Cole McGinnis Mystery

By Rhys Ford

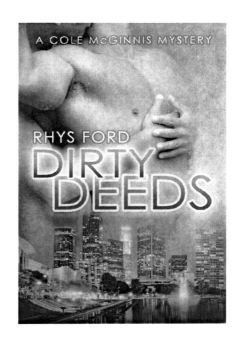

Sheila Pinelli needed to be taken out.

Former cop turned private investigator Cole McGinnis never considered committing murder. But six months ago, when Jae-Min's blood filled his hands and death came knocking at his lover's door, killing Sheila Pinelli became a definite possibility.

While Sheila lurks in some hidden corner of Los Angeles, Jae and Cole share a bed, a home, and most of all, happiness. They'd survived Jae's traditional Korean family disowning him and plan on building a new life—preferably one without the threat of Sheila's return hanging over them.

Thanks to the Santa Monica police mistakenly releasing Sheila following a loitering arrest, Cole finally gets a lead on Sheila's whereabouts. That is, until the trail goes crazy and he's thrown into a tangle of drugs, exotic women, and more death. Regardless of the case going sideways, Cole is determined to find the woman he once loved as a sister and get her out of their lives once and for all.

http://www.dreamspinnerpress.com

Down and Dirty

A Cole McGinnis Mystery

By Rhys Ford

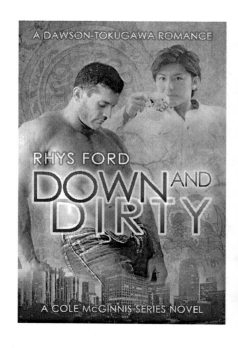

From the moment former LAPD detective Bobby Dawson spots Ichiro Tokugawa, he knows the man is trouble. And not just because the much younger Japanese inker is hot, complicated, and pushes every one of Bobby's buttons. No, Ichi is trouble because he's Cole McGinnis's younger brother and off-limits in every possible way. And Bobby knows that even before Cole threatens to kill him for looking Ichi's way. But despite his gut telling him Ichi is bad news, Bobby can't stop looking… or wanting.

Ichi was never one to play by the rules. Growing up in Japan as his father's heir, he'd been bound by every rule imaginable until he had enough and walked away from everything to become his own man. Los Angeles was supposed to be a brief pitstop before he moved on, but after connecting with his American half-brothers, it looks like a good city to call home for a while—if it weren't for Bobby Dawson.

Bobby is definitely a love-them-and-leave-them type, a philosophy Ichi whole-heartedly agrees with. Family was as much of a relationship as Ichi was looking for, but something about the gruff and handsome Bobby Dawson makes Ichi want more.

http://www.dreamspinnerpress.com

Fish and Ghosts

Hellsinger: Book One

By Rhys Ford

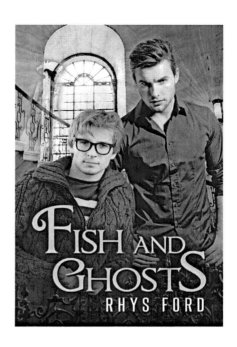

When his Uncle Mortimer died and left him Hoxne Grange, the family's Gilded Age mansion, Tristan Pryce became the second generation of Pryces to serve as a caretaker for the estate, a way station for spirits on their final steps to the afterlife. Tristan is prepared for challenges, though not necessarily from the ghosts he's seen since childhood. Determined to establish Tristan's insanity and gain access to his trust fund, his loving relatives hire Dr. Wolf Kincaid and his paranormal researchers, Hellsinger Investigations, to prove the Grange is not haunted.

Skeptic Wolf Kincaid has made it his life's work to debunk the supernatural. After years of cons and fakes, he can't wait to reveal the Grange's ghostly activity is just badly leveled floorboards and a drafty old house. More than a few surprises await him at the Grange, including its prickly, reclusive owner. Tristan Pryce is much less insane and much more attractive than Wolf wants to admit, and when his team releases a ghostly serial killer on the Grange, Wolf is torn between his skepticism and protecting the man he's been sent to discredit.

http://www.dreamspinnerpress.com

Duck Duck Ghost

Hellsinger: Book Two

By Rhys Ford

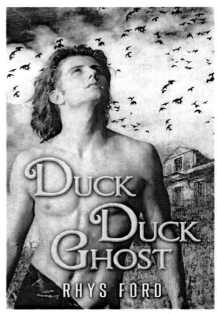

Paranormal investigator Wolf Kincaid knows what his foot tastes like.

Mostly because he stuck it firmly in his mouth when his lover, Tristan Pryce, accidentally drugged him with a batch of psychotropic baklava. Needing to patch things up between them, Wolf drags Tristan to San Luis Obispo, hoping Tristan's medium ability can help evict a troublesome spirit haunting an old farmhouse.

With Wolf's sister handling Hoxne Grange's spectral visitors, Tristan finds himself in the unique position of being able to leave home for the first time in forever, but Wolf's roughshod treatment is the least of his worries. Tristan's ad-hoc portal for passing spirits seems to be getting fewer and fewer guests, and despite his concern he's broken his home, Tristan agrees to help Wolf's cousin, Sey, kick her poltergeist to the proverbial curb.

San Luis Obispo brings its own bushel of troubles. Tristan's ghost whispering skill is challenged not only by a terrorizing haunting but also by Wolf's skeptical older cousin, Cin. Bookended by a pair of aggressive Kincaids, Tristan soon finds himself in a spectral battle that threatens not only his sanity but also his relationship with Wolf, the first man he's ever loved.

http://www.dreamspinnerpress.com

Sinner's Gin

Sinners Series: Book One

By Rhys Ford

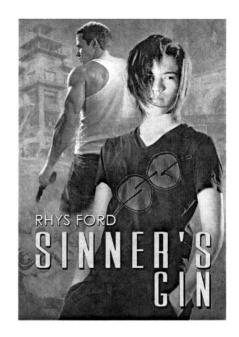

There's a dead man in Miki St. John's vintage Pontiac GTO, and he has no idea how it got there.

After Miki survives the tragic accident that killed his best friend and the other members of their band, Sinner's Gin, all he wants is to hide from the world in the refurbished warehouse he bought before their last tour. But when the man who sexually abused him as a boy is killed and his remains are dumped in Miki's car, Miki fears Death isn't done with him yet.

Kane Morgan, the SFPD inspector renting space in the art co-op next door, initially suspects Miki had a hand in the man's murder, but Kane soon realizes Miki is as much a victim as the man splattered inside the GTO. As the murderer's body count rises, the attraction between Miki and Kane heats up. Neither man knows if they can make a relationship work, but despite Miki's emotional damage, Kane is determined to teach him how to love and be loved — provided, of course, Kane can catch the killer before Miki becomes the murderer's final victim.

http://www.dreamspinnerpress.com

Whiskey and Wry

Sinners Series: Book Two

By Rhys Ford

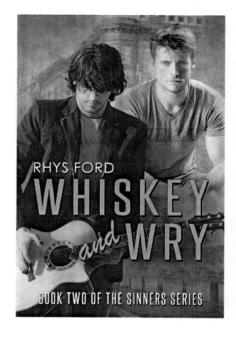

He was dead. And it was murder most foul. If erasing a man's existence could even be called murder.

When Damien Mitchell wakes, he finds himself without a life or a name. The Montana asylum's doctors tell him he's delusional and his memories are all lies: he's really Stephen Thompson, and he'd gone over the edge, obsessing about a rock star who died in a fiery crash. His chance to escape back to his own life comes when his prison burns, but a gunman is waiting for him, determined that neither Stephen Thompson nor Damien Mitchell will escape.

With the assassin on his tail, Damien flees to the City by the Bay, but keeping a low profile is the only way he'll survive as he searches San Francisco for his best friend, Miki St. John. Falling back on what kept him fed before he made it big, Damien sings for his supper outside Finnegan's, an Irish pub on the pier, and he soon falls in with the owner, Sionn Murphy. Damien doesn't need a complication like Sionn, and to make matters worse, the gunman—who doesn't mind going through Sionn or anyone else if that's what it takes to kill Damien—shows up to finish what he started.

http://www.dreamspinnerpress.com

The Devil's Brew

Sinners Series: Book 2.5

By Rhys Ford

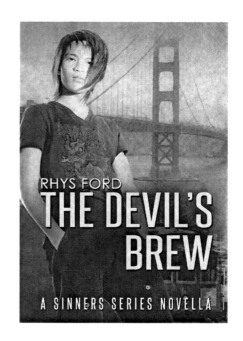

Miki St. John's life has been turned upside down, but it's the best thing that's ever happened to him.

His best friend, Damien Mitchell, is back from the dead. He has a dog named Dude. And more importantly, he and his lover, SFPD Inspector Kane Morgan, now share Miki's converted warehouse.

For the first time ever, Miki's living a happy and normal-ish life, but when Valentine's Day rolls around, Miki realizes he knows next to nothing about being domestic or domesticated. Nothing about the traditional lover's holiday makes sense to him, but Miki wants to give Kane a Valentine's Day the man will never forget.

Can he pull off a day of wine and roses? Or will his screwed-up childhood come back and bite Miki in the ass?

Again.

http://www.dreamspinnerpress.com

Tequila Mockingbird

Sinners Series: Book Three

By Rhys Ford

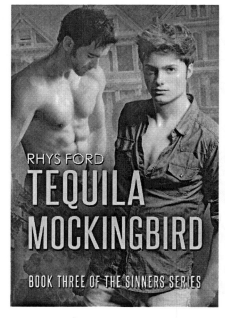

Lieutenant Connor Morgan of SFPD's SWAT division wasn't looking for love. Especially not in a man. His life plan didn't include one Forest Ackerman, a brown-eyed, blond drummer who's as sexy as he is trouble. His family depends on him to be like his father, a solid pillar of strength who'll one day lead the Morgan clan.

No, Connor has everything worked out—a career in law enforcement, a nice house, and a family. Instead, he finds a murdered man while on a drug raid and loses his heart comforting the man's adopted son. It wasn't like he'd never thought about men — it's just loving one doesn't fit into his plans.

Forest Ackerman certainly doesn't need to be lusting after a straight cop, even if Connor Morgan is everywhere he looks, especially after Frank's death. He's just talked himself out of lusting for the brawny cop when his coffee shop becomes a war zone and Connor Morgan steps in to save him.

Whoever killed his father seems intent on Forest joining him in the afterlife. As the killer moves closer to achieving his goal, Forest tangles with Connor Morgan and is left wondering what he'll lose first—his life or his heart.

http://www.dreamspinnerpress.com

http://www.dreamspinnerpress.com

DIRK GREYSON
DAY AND KNIGHT

http://www.dreamspinnerpress.com

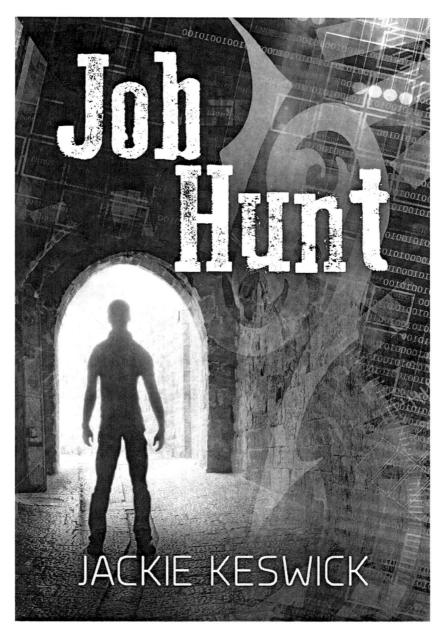

http://www.dreamspinnerpress.com

CPSIA information can be obtained at www.ICGtesting.com
Printed in the USA
LVOW10s1959301015

460458LV00019B/523/P